BOOKS BY
ALEXANDER McCALL SMITH

FROM A FAR AND LOVELY COUNTRY

FROM A FAR AND
LOVELY COUNTRY

ALEXANDER McCALL SMITH

Alfred A. Knopf Canada

PUBLISHED BY ALFRED A. KNOPF CANADA

Copyright © 2023 Alexander McCall Smith

www.penguinrandomhouse.ca

Knopf Canada and colophon are registered trademarks.

Library and Archives Canada Cataloguing in Publication

Title: From a far and lovely country / Alexander McCall Smith.
Names: McCall Smith, Alexander, 1948- author.
Series: McCall Smith, Alexander, 1948- No. 1 Ladies Detective Agency series ; 24.
Description: Series statement: No. 1 Ladies' Detective Agency ; 24
Identifiers: Canadiana (print) 20230197795 | Canadiana (ebook) 20230197809 | ISBN
9781039004412 (hardcover) | ISBN 9781039004429 (EPUB)
Classification: LCC PR6063.C326 F76 2023 | DDC 823/.914—dc23

Jacket illustration by Iain McIntosh

Printed in the United States of America

10 9 8 7 6 5 4 3 2 1

This book is for Mandy and Ashok Ferrey.

FROM A FAR AND LOVELY COUNTRY

CHAPTER ONE

CARBOLIC SOAP AND BIRTHDAY CAKE

PRECIOUS RAMOTSWE, daughter of the late Obed Ramotswe of Mochudi, near Gaborone, in Botswana, near Heaven, wife of Mr. J.L.B. Matekoni, *garagiste;* friend to so many, but particularly to Mma Silvia Potokwane, and of course Grace Makutsi, formerly of Bobonong, who was, in turn, wife of Mr. Phuti Radiphuti and a graduate of the Botswana Secretarial College—with ninety-seven per cent in the final examinations; *that* Precious Ramotswe lay in her bed, opening first one eye, then the other, and subsequently, after only a few short seconds, closing both once more.

Waking up in the morning, as she had now done, was never too difficult; the hard part, she always thought, was what happened afterwards. To begin with, you had to remind yourself where you were. Those first few seconds of consciousness could be quite detached from everything else. You knew *who* you were, of course, and you knew you were in your bed, but you did not necessarily remember where you had just been: there might still be drifting around a few fragments of a dream, the remnants of some curious and unreal events in which the sleeping you had just been participating, and you had to put those out of your mind as the real day began. The mind was good at that—it remembered not to remember, so to speak, because it knew that dreams could not be allowed to clog up memory, which had far more important things to do. And so, the strange conversations of the night, the odd transports back to childhood, the unlikely dramas and surprises—all these were swept away as the light of day signalled the beginning of your real life, as yourself, facing another day of being you.

Now, on that particular morning, Mma Ramotswe was fully awake, and conscious of the fact that she was alone in her bed, and that her husband was no longer there. You could always tell when there was somebody else in bed with you, and, equally, when there was not. There was the silence, of course—there was the absence of the breathing noises that husbands tended to make—and then there was something about the way the mattress sloped when there was nobody to counteract the weight on one's own side. And then, if you turned in your bed, as she now did, you saw that there was nobody there, and you began to listen for sounds from deeper within the house. For the sound of your husband in the kitchen, for example, preparing breakfast in bed for you as a treat, because today, you suddenly remembered, was a somewhat special day, being your birthday, when breakfast in bed—or even a simple cup of red bush tea placed steaming on the bedside table—would be so welcome. Not that you expected it as your right, but it would still be a nice touch.

She listened hard, holding her breath for a few moments so as to hear better, but there was no sound coming from the direction of the kitchen. And there was nothing to be heard from the other two bedrooms, because it was that odd, quiet time of the year, the school holidays, when the children were away for three weeks. They were staying in Lobatse with the families of schoolfriends, helping with the planting and the cattle, and learning to love the land, which is something we all should learn to do when we are young. No, the house was quite silent, and that meant that Mr. J.L.B. Matekoni had already gone off to the garage, as he sometimes did when there was a lot to do and rather too many cars waiting for attention, like a line of patients nursing their complaints in a hospital waiting room.

Mma Ramotswe sighed. You should not begin your birthday with a sigh, though, and she quickly turned the sigh into a deep breath, the sort of breath you take when you are deciding to be positive about the day ahead. She then put on her housecoat and slippers, and made her way into the kitchen to fill the kettle. As she entered the room, her eye fell on a note displayed prominently on the table, and she smiled. That would be the message he had left for her, saying something like, *Happy birthday, my dearest wife— I am so sorry that I have had to go to work early on this special day, but I'll make up for it later. Your loving husband, Mr. J.L.B. Matekoni.* Something like that.

She picked up the note and read it. *Gone to work,* it said, rather tersely. *See you at tea time. Don't forget to buy soap for the garage, please.* The please was underlined—not out of politeness, but to emphasise the importance of the request. And that was all. There was nothing about her birthday—just that reminder about the soap that he needed for the washbasin in the garage so that he and his assistant, Fanwell, could get the grease off their hands after attending to engines and before handling the upholstered steering wheels of the cars in their care. Soap was important, she thought, but so were birthdays—and if one had to rank the two things in order of importance, she would say that from the point of view of the person whose birthday it was, birthdays outranked soap.

She made a conscious effort not to feel upset. Mr. J.L.B. Matekoni stood out for his politeness, even in a country like Botswana, where people were naturally courteous towards one another. He was not one to use cross words, nor did he ever forget the traditional decencies—the formal greetings and enquiries about whether you have slept well, and whether your family have slept well, that sort of thing, which had always been observed in Botswana but were under threat, as such things were under threat everywhere, throughout the world. And there was another thing: he never raised his voice and not once had she heard him swear. Nowadays people swore with very little provocation, using language that, when she had been at school in Mochudi, would have brought the wrath of the authorities down upon one's head. She vividly remembered the day when a boy in her class at school—a boy of eleven or twelve, who had a reputation for being short-tempered—had used bad language within the hearing of one of the teachers. He had imagined that nobody could hear him, or at least no adult, but he had been wrong, and he had been picked up by the scruff of his neck and taken to the boys' washroom, where his mouth had been washed out with Lifebuoy red carbolic soap. He had howled in protest, as that soap was known for its sting, but he had not sworn again, in the schoolyard, at least.

She had told Mma Makutsi about that incident, and Mma Makutsi had nodded and said, "Quite right, Mma. That's the way to do these things."

Mma Ramotswe had expressed reservations. "That was the way they *used* to do things, Mma. I'm not sure you can do that sort of thing these days."

Mma Makutsi looked at her incredulously. "That's ridiculous, Mma. Why not?"

"I think it's to do with rights," Mma Ramotswe explained. "People have more rights these days, Mma."

Mma Makutsi's look of incredulity turned to one of dismissal. "Rights, Mma? Even children? Even boys like that foul-mouthed boy you mentioned?"

"I think everybody has rights now," said Mma Ramotswe.

Mma Makutsi shook her head. "Children need to be told what to do, Mma. You cannot let them run round without being told what they can do and what they can't do."

"Oh, that's true, Mma," Mma Ramotswe conceded. "Children have to be disciplined."

"Well then," snorted Mma Makutsi. "How do you discipline a child who's using rude language? You tell me, Mma. You tell me. How do you discipline a boy like that? You wash his mouth out with carbolic soap—that's what you do. And if he starts shouting about his rights, you say, 'And we have a right not to listen to you speaking like that, young man!' That's what you say."

Mma Ramotswe said nothing. She thought that Mma Makutsi had probably not taken her point about how the climate of opinion had changed, and the old ways of punishing children for their transgressions had been discredited. You were not meant to slap children these days, and you certainly weren't meant to beat them in the way in which children used to be beaten, even in living memory. You spoke to them sharply; you told them of the consequences of their actions for others; you reasoned with them. And she was pleased with these changes, because violence merely begat violence, as everybody knew now—or should know, even if they had yet to learn that.

But Mma Makutsi, who, in spite of her more modern clothes, was still rather more old-fashioned than Mma Ramotswe in these matters, now had more to say on the subject.

"In fact, Mma Ramotswe," she continued, "I can think of quite a few people who would benefit from having their mouths washed out with carbolic soap. Adults, this time—people who use very bad language in front of other people. They don't seem to care. They use these words as if they don't mean anything." She paused. "That man who works in the supermarket—you know the one? He's always shouting at his staff and using very rude language. They're too frightened of him to tell him not to shout so much—or to call them the names he calls them, which he certainly should not do. They should do that—they should stand up to him—but they don't. That's one man who would benefit from a bit of carbolic soap, Mma."

Mma Ramotswe inclined her head. She knew the man Mma Makutsi was referring to, and she smiled as she thought of how outraged he would look if somebody were to manage to wash his mouth out with soap. It was a lovely thought—a bully dealt with by the very people he had bullied, which was always something nice to contemplate. And, Mma Makutsi was right about the carelessness of some people, about the lack of respect for the feelings of others, and for decency, but once again she did not imagine that a programme of washing people's mouths out with soap would help very much. And so, she said nothing, and Mma Makutsi, feeling that she had won the argument—if it had been an argument—looked satisfied, as people who have made their point forcibly may look.

Now, standing in her house in Zebra Drive, Mma Ramotswe thought of Mr. J.L.B. Matekoni's mildness and how he would never intentionally upset anybody, particularly her. He loved her with all his heart—he had once told her as much, in a rare moment of self-reference—and she, of course, reciprocated. He was proud of her—she knew that because Mma Potokwane had once told her about what he had said about his good fortune at being married to her. So, if now he appeared to be ignoring her birthday and had written a note that seemed a bit curt, that was probably because he had a lot on his mind.

She was in no doubt that he had simply forgotten her birthday. Now that she cast her mind back over the previous few days, she realised that she herself seemed to have forgotten that her birthday was coming up. She had not thought about it at all earlier on in the week, and it was only yesterday that she had reminded herself that the following day was the day in question. Had she said something to Mr. J.L.B. Matekoni at that point, then he would undoubtedly have remembered—but she had not, and this was the result. So, she could hardly blame him for the omission: forgetting to do something did not involve any intention to harm—it was something that happened to you, rather than something you decided to do. And there was a difference between those two things, she thought.

And there was something else to bear in mind: Mr. J.L.B. Matekoni was a man, and men, by and large, did not remember birthdays as well as women did. That was not to run men down unfairly—Mma Ramotswe would never do that—but you had to admit that men had their drawbacks, just as women did, and one of the failings of men was a lack of inclination to remember birthdays. Women, by contrast, remembered the birthdays of their friends, and often of their friends' parents or children. Mma Ramotswe remembered Mma Potokwane's birthday, because it was the day after the birthday of the late Seretse Khama. But she also remembered the birthdays of at least two of the housemothers at the Orphan Farm, and those had no important dates attached to them.

The first of July, 1921: that had been when Sir Seretse Goitse-beng Maphiri Khama had been born—a day of the utmost importance for Botswana. He was the grandson of Khama III the Good, and had become, in his time, the Paramount Chief of the Bamangwato people; and then, on that windy night in 1966, when the Bechua-naland Protectorate was laid to rest, first president of a brand-new country. Mma Ramotswe's father, Obed Ramotswe, had admired him greatly, and had even met him once—something of which he had been so proud. And she, in turn, was so proud of her father, so proud; and not a day went past that she didn't think of him and of

what he had stood for. And her mother, too, who had died when
she was so young, but who must have been a fine woman, because
that was how her father described his wife, and he was never wrong
about that sort of thing. Mma Ramotswe was proud of her, too,
and wished that she had known her. Not to know your mother left
a big hole in your life, but then . . . She stopped herself. Everybody had holes of one sort or another in their lives, and you should
not spend too much time thinking about what you lacked. You
should think, rather, of what you had, and she had so much—this
house, this wonderful, if occasionally forgetful, husband; these kind
friends, even if Mma Makutsi could occasionally be a bit sharp and
Mma Potokwane was sometimes a bit pushy; the children, whom
they had fostered, but who were like their own children now; her
business; her country, that great beautiful stretch of Africa—there
was so much to be grateful for.

She made herself a cup of red bush tea, extra strong, because it
was her birthday, and prepared herself two pieces of toast that she
spread thickly with butter and jam, and then made a third piece,
once again because it was her birthday, and if you can't eat three
slices of thickly buttered toast on your birthday, then when can you
treat yourself to such a thing? Then, her breakfast finished, and
feeling in a rather better mood, she dressed in one of the brightest,
most positive dresses in her wardrobe, and set off in her van for
the office. She would park under her usual acacia tree and resist
any temptation to call in at Tlokweng Road Speedy Motors next
door. She would see Mr. J.L.B. Matekoni when he and his assistant, Fanwell, came to join her and Mma Makutsi for morning tea
at ten—unless, of course, he remembered her birthday before then,
and, dropping his tools, came running through to the office to beg
her forgiveness. But that, she thought, was improbable, and she put
it out of her mind. It was far more likely that she would have to say

something like, "You haven't forgotten what day it is today, Rra?" And he would hit his forehead with the palm of his hand and say, "Oh, my goodness, Precious, how could I possibly forget?" That was possible, she supposed, just possible; but, as Mma Makutsi would say, nobody should hold their breath.

She parked the van and made her way to the front door of the office. Looking up, she saw the sign that they had erected, a few years ago now, that announced in large letters, *The No. 1 Ladies' Detective Agency,* with, underneath it, in much smaller lettering, *Under personal management.* Mma Ramotswe had put that in on the suggestion of the signwriter, who had said that, in his experience, wording like that reassured clients and was, in general, good for business.

"Your sign is your mission statement," he said. "Your sign not only says what sort of business you have, but what sort of person you are."

Mma Ramotswe looked doubtful. "I don't see how it can do that, Rra. Just a few words outside a building—how can they say very much about the people inside?"

The signwriter smiled—a knowing smile, from one who had painted signs for many of those who had yet to learn how important signs were.

"A sign says many things, Mma. Forgive me for pointing it out, but people do not always understand signs. You read what a sign says—you take that in—and then you read what it *doesn't* say. That can be important."

He looked at her for confirmation that she was following his line of argument. Then he continued, "Let me give you an example, Mma. There are many signs that say 'So-and-so and Sons, Butchers', or whatever. What does that sign tell us?"

"That it's a butchery?" offered Mma Ramotswe.

The signwriter raised an admonitory finger. "Yes, Mma, but . . . but . . . What about the sons, Mma? What does that tell you?" He smiled. "You're the No. 1 detective lady, I think, Mma. What would a No. 1 detective say about that?"

"That he has sons?"

"Ah!" said the signwriter. "You are very observant, Mma. And you are not only observant; you are right, too. The butcher has sons, and these boys are in the business. So that means he is thinking long term, Mma. That is the important thing. People who think long term, about who is going to take over the business when they are late—and we all become late, Mma, sooner or later; there's no denying that, I think—those people are going to be careful about their reputation. They are not going to go after the quick profit; they are going to think of long-term relationships with their clients. And that leads to a different style of business, you see."

It was a long speech for a signwriter, or indeed anybody, to make, and now that it was finished Mma Ramotswe felt she had nothing to add. So, she simply said, "Thank you, Rra. That is very interesting."

"So, with these words *Under personal management*," he continued, "you are sending a very powerful message, Mma. You are saying, 'If you come to this business, you will get personal attention.'"

Mma Ramotswe said that she thought that was important. She did not like the anonymity of the telephone, when you could not see the person you were talking to, and indeed you might even be talking to a machine. That was an appalling thought—that you would go to all the trouble of saying good day to a machine and asking it whether it had slept well, and the machine would simply say, in that strange voice that machines have, "Please press 1 to make your enquiry," or something like that. How could you possibly say to a machine, "Have you had much rain up at your place?"

or "How are your cattle doing?" There were things we needed to say to one another, but that did not interest machines in the slightest.

"Personal attention is very important," said the signwriter. "As is the fact that a business has been going for some time. You can say something like 'Established . . .' and then you put the date, which should be at least ten or twenty years ago. That is very good for business. It means that you know what you're doing."

"Or that people have yet to catch up with you," joked Mma Ramotswe.

The signwriter smiled weakly. "But it is not very funny, Mma. There are some people who should not be in business at all. They start a business and then, one month later, where is that business? It has gone, Mma, because these people are no-good people, that is why." He waved a hand vaguely in an easterly direction. "There are many no-good people out there. Too many."

Mma Ramotswe's gaze followed the direction in which he was pointing. It was towards the scrub bush beyond her tiny white van and its sheltering acacia tree. Were they there, these no-good people to whom he was alluding? Were they skulking among the stunted thorn trees and the dusty shrubs, waiting for the opportunity to set up a shaky business somewhere and then close it down a month or so later? She saw a movement in the bush, but it was only a goat, standing on its hind legs to nibble at a scrap of low foliage; it was not a no-good person at all.

And now she stood beneath that sign, looking up at the lettering, where the paint of the word *personal* had begun to peel away—eroded, perhaps, by the dry winds that could spring up from the Kalahari; or blistered by the unforgiving sun of a succession of hot seasons. Fanwell could get up on a ladder and renew it, she thought; he had some artistic ability, and had once painted a water-colour portrait of Mma Makutsi. Grace had not approved of it, and although she had accepted it with congeniality, she had been dismayed at the prominence that Fanwell had given to her large round glasses. Mma Ramotswe had sensed this, and had overheard her muttering sniffily, after Fanwell had left, "Artists should not try to fix cars, and mechanics should not paint pictures of other people, I think."

Fanwell was rather better at touching up scratches on cars, using the small pots of special paint he kept for the purpose. That paint would do for the rejuvenation of the sign if a suitable colour match could be found. She would have to make that match, though, because men were often a little bit colour blind and could not always be relied upon to get colour co-ordination right. In fact, most men would not even be able to say what colour co-ordination was—apart from Phuti Radiphuti, of course, who, being in the furniture trade, was used to selecting covers for sofas and chairs.

She let herself into the office. It was stuffy, and she opened a window to allow air to circulate. She had a desk-top fan, a new acquisition, perilously placed on an old telephone directory, and she switched this on. Paper ruffled in the current of air, and she felt immediately cooler. They were going through a spell of hot weather, but there was rain in the offing, and that would lower the temperature when it came. It would settle the dust too, and bring immediate relief to the parched earth.

The electric kettle was filled with water, and she now switched this on. Mma Makutsi would arrive shortly, she imagined, and they would have a cup of tea together before they started work. At least Mma Makutsi would have remembered her birthday and would probably even have a present for her. The previous year, she had bought her a box of lace handkerchiefs and a tin of Turkish delight. And Mma Ramotswe, in turn, had bought Mma Makutsi a cookery

book and an apron with a pizza motif for her birthday—both had
been well received.

The kettle had barely had time to boil before Mma Ramotswe
heard Mma Makutsi drive up outside. Phuti had bought her a small
red car, and now she often drove this in to work, sometimes taking
Mma Ramotswe's parking place under the acacia tree. Mma Ramotswe never said anything about that, although she was sure that
Mma Makutsi knew that it was her place. The problem with things
like that was that one could not really reserve them. Theoretically,
anybody was allowed to park there, as the ground belonged to the
government and not to any individual proprietor, but that was not
the point. A parking place under an acacia tree was a moral as
opposed to a legal issue. Those who had parked there for years—as
Mma Ramotswe had—had a right that sprang from long usage, and
other people should take account of that, but they did not always do
so. At least today, on my birthday, thought Mma Ramotswe, my van
is in its time-honoured place.

The door opened, and Mma Makutsi appeared.

"It's going to be hot again today," she said as she crossed the
room to her desk. "I said that to Phuti when we got up this morning.
I said, 'It's going to be hot, Phuti,' and he agreed with me. He said it
might even be hotter than yesterday, unless it rains, which he didn't
think it would. And I think that—"

She stopped. She had hardly glanced at Mma Ramotswe, but
now she had noticed her dress.

"Well, Mma," she continued, "that is a very attractive dress, that
one. It looks very good on you, I must say."

Mma Ramotswe inclined her head. "You are very kind, Mma. It
is one of my favourites. I don't wear it very often."

Mma Makutsi sat down at her desk. "Very wise. Perhaps you
should keep it for special occasions—and only wear it then."

Like my birthday, thought Mma Ramotswe. Like today.

"But even when it isn't a special day," Mma Makutsi went on, "it may be nice to dress up a bit. Wearing something nice—like that dress—makes you feel a bit better, I always say."

She busied herself with a letter that had been lying on her desk. As she opened the envelope, she frowned. "These people, you know, Mma—these people who were worried because their staff were stealing from them. Remember that case? They had that out-fitters' shop and they said that their sales assistants were stealing the clothes . . ."

"And you discovered how they were doing it, Mma. Yes, I remember that case, Mma Makutsi."

As Mma Makutsi continued to read the letter, her frown deep-ened. She continued to speak about the case, if in a slightly dis-tracted way. "Yes . . . yes. And they were going into the shop in their old clothes and then changing into some of the shops' clothes during the tea break, and throwing their old clothes out of the win-dow. It was very cunning . . ." She drifted off before she exclaimed, "Really, Mma, they are the end! Those people are the end."

"The people stealing the clothes?"

"No, the owners of the store. That very tall man and his extremely short wife. Them. What does she see in him, I wonder. Maybe she doesn't even see him at all, because he's up in the clouds and she's down there on the floor. Silly people. They're the end, Mma."

Mma Ramotswe smiled at the image. "People see different things in others," she pointed out. "You never can tell when people are going to be suitable for one another."

Mma Makutsi did not consider this. Now she tossed the letter aside in a gesture of contempt. "They're refusing to pay our bill."

This was unusual, but it was an issue that every business faced. Mma Ramotswe asked why the clients were disputing their fee.

"They said that we didn't arrest the staff members who were doing this. They're saying that we should have arrested them."

Mma Ramotswe burst out laughing. "But who do they think we are? Police? Is that what they think?"

Mma Makutsi shook her head in disbelief. "There are some people who don't understand what a *private* detective is."

"We shall have to send another bill," said Mma Ramotswe. "We can explain it to them tactfully."

"I shall write them a letter," Mma Makutsi said. "I shall write them a letter and tell them that if they don't pay the bill, I shall arrest *them*."

They both laughed, although, in Mma Ramotswe's case, it was with some effort. My birthday, she thought. My birthday.

Mma Makutsi now got up to make the tea, and as she did so, the telephone rang. It was Mma Potokwane.

Mma Ramotswe responded to her friend's greeting, and then waited. She imagined that the phone call would be made to convey birthday wishes, and that as she acknowledged these, Mma Makutsi would realise her omission and make suitable amends. But no such sentiments came through from the other end of the line; Mma Potokwane had called to see whether Mma Ramotswe would care to come out to the Orphan Farm that morning.

"There is something I'd like to discuss with you, Mma," the matron said. "It's easier to do some things in person, I find."

Mma Ramotswe felt her spirits lift. Such as wish somebody a happy birthday, she thought. Such as give them a birthday present.

"Of course, Mma," she said. "I think so too."

She hoped that Mma Potokwane might say something more, but she did not, and so Mma Ramotswe offered to make the short journey out to the Orphan Farm later that morning.

"And we can have lunch," offered Mma Potokwane.

Mma Ramotswe smiled knowingly. A birthday lunch would make up for a lot of the morning's disappointments.

"Nothing special," added Mma Potokwane.

Mma Ramotswe's smile broadened. "Of course not. Nothing special."

Mma Makutsi had been listening. Now, as she placed Mma Ramotswe's cup of red bush tea before her on her desk, she asked what Mma Potokwane's business might be.

"I suspect that something has cropped up in one of the children's lives," said Mma Ramotswe. "Sometimes there are issues with relatives. In some cases they try to get the children back, even if there is nowhere for them to go. Mma Potokwane has to resist things like that."

"They want to get them to work," said Mma Makutsi. "I've seen that sort of thing, Mma."

Mma Ramotswe nodded sadly. "You're right. They hear that there is some nephew or niece whose parents are late, and they think that this is their chance for an unpaid maid or herd boy."

"And that's the end of their schooling," added Mma Makutsi.

Mma Ramotswe sighed. It was occasionally the case that Mma Potokwane was the only defence against a grim future for some innocent child. It was an unfortunate fact of life that there was no shortage of people who were prepared to exploit others, and had no compunction in using every trick or device in their grasp to achieve their ends. It was possible that Mma Potokwane had stumbled across such a case, and that her invitation to Mma Ramotswe to visit the Orphan Farm was nothing to do with birthdays or the presents that went with birthdays. And as she thought this, Mma Ramotswe gently upbraided herself for construing the invitation in such a way. It was not in her nature, not really, to think of herself, and she realised that what she should do was forget about this birthday of hers and think about other things.

And that was what she did as she drove out along the road to Tlokweng. I do not need to celebrate my birthday, she said to herself. Having a birthday is in no sense grounds for congratulations. All you have done is become a year older, and all of us, even the weaker brethren, manage that with very little trouble at all.

The weaker brethren . . . The phrase came to her mind because a few days earlier, as she had sat in her usual pew in the Anglican cathedral opposite the hospital, she had heard a visiting clergyman, a man from Malawi, talk about the weaker brethren and their struggles. "We should not be too quick to censure the weaker brethren," he had said, "because it is not necessarily their fault that they are weak. We must support them. We must offer them our hand. We must allow them to lean upon our shoulder as we make our way through life. If the hand on your shoulder is that of one of the weaker brethren, then do not brush it away, but allow it to remain there until you reach the other side."

Mma Ramotswe had reflected on this, as she sat there, and had wondered whether she would be as supportive as she should be if one of the weaker brethren were to come up to her and put his hand on her shoulder. And even more difficult might be the walk thereafter, with the member of the weaker brethren impeding one's step. She looked about her. Were the weaker brethren in the cathedral even as this homily was being delivered? Were they embarrassed if they thought that people resented their hands upon their shoulders? The weaker brethren, she imagined, were more or less everywhere, and although many of them deserved support, she suspected that some might perhaps be encouraged not to be so weak and to do something about their condition. But that sounded a bit unsympathetic, and so she stopped herself thinking along those lines. She would put up with the hands of the weaker brethren on her shoulders, should it come to that, because she would never turn away anybody in need. How could one? she asked herself. How could one

say no to somebody in their desperation? One had to do something.
One had to do what one could to help.

She drove past a small store on the open verandah of which
two men were sitting in the sun, drinking beer. The weaker brethren, she thought. The weaker brethren enjoying themselves. They
looked happy enough, untroubled by their weakness. Perhaps,
thought, Mma Ramotswe, the weaker brethren do not really know
that they are weak. And, if that were the case, should one *tell* them?

CHAPTER TWO

I HAVE A DAUGHTER, MMA

MMA RAMOTSWE KNOCKED on the outer door of Mma Potokwane's office, and waited for a response. After a short while, the
door was opened, and there stood Mma Potokwane's new secretary,
all efficiency and smiles. They had yet to meet, and so Mma Ramotswe introduced herself, exchanged the necessary courtesies, and was
then ushered into the office.

"Mma Potokwane is on the phone," the secretary said, "but once
she has finished I will take you through. She is very keen to see you,
Mma." And then, after a short pause, she continued, "I hope you
are having a good day."

Mma Ramotswe nodded. "I am, Mma," she said, wanting to
add, "in spite of everything," but not doing so.

"That is very good," said the secretary. "Mma Potokwane has spoken to me about you. She says that you are a very cheerful person—
even when things are not going well. She said that to me."

"I am just like everybody else," said Mma Ramotswe.

"She says you are not," said the secretary. "She says you will
always look on the bright side."

"Well, it's probably . . . probably a bit brighter on that side," Mma Ramotswe admitted.

"That is very true, Mma."

"You are new here?" asked Mma Ramotswe.

The secretary nodded. "This is my second job. I was with a firm of distributors before this. They had those very large trucks. They took things up north—to Francistown, to Maun—to places far from everywhere. They fired me because they said they had too many secretaries. It was very hard for me, Mma. I thought: How can there be too many of me? I am only one person. That is the way I looked at it."

Mma Ramotswe expressed her sympathy. "It cannot be easy—losing your job."

"It is not, Mma. It is very bad."

Mma Ramotswe looked thoughtful. "And it never seems to be the people at the top who go, does it? There never seem to be too many of them, I think."

The secretary smiled. "I think you are right, Mma Ramotswe. That's because they make the decisions. And when somebody comes along and says, 'You are going to have to save money because there are too many people on the payroll,' the people at the top never say, 'Oh, I am one of those too many people.' They never say that. They say, 'Look down there—yes, there are plenty of people down there.'"

Mma Ramotswe laughed. "What do they say about the chickens in the yard, Mma? When it's time to make chicken stew, you never get any of the chickens coming up and saying that they would be tasty." She paused. "Still, a bad thing can lead to a good thing, I think. You used to send trucks off here and there, and now you're helping Mma Potokwane to make these children happy. Maybe this is a better job in some ways."

The secretary was quick to agree. "I sit here, Mma, and I hear the children playing outside the window, and I think the thing you have just said. I think . . ." She raised a finger in the air. "I think that Mma Potokwane has finished on the phone. Yes, she has finished talking."

The door leading from the outer office into Mma Potokwane's sanctum now opened.

"Ah, Mma Ramotswe, I thought I heard you. And . . ." Mma Potokwane stopped. "Your dress . . . You are looking very good, Mma. Not that you don't normally look very good, but today you seem to be looking even better than usual."

The secretary chimed in. "It is a lovely dress, that one, Mma. I was about to say something myself."

"Still," said Mma Potokwane. "We mustn't stand around talking about dresses. If men heard us, they'd say, 'There go those women talking about dresses again.' They do not know that we have many things to talk about."

"More things than they do," the secretary contributed. "Men talk a lot about cars and football. I have a brother like that. Cars, cars, cars. Then football, football, football. Every day."

"But is he happy?" asked Mma Potokwane with a smile.

"He is very happy," said the secretary.

"If there are things that make you happy," Mma Ramotswe suggested, "then there is no harm in talking about them."

"That is true," said Mma Potokwane. "But there are some things that are not so happy, and sometimes we have to talk about those things too." She gave her visitor a serious look. "I want to take you to meet one of the housemothers. She has been speaking to me about something. I think you should hear what she has to say."

Mma Ramotswe nodded. Mma Potokwane's invitation had nothing to do with her birthday: that much was quite clear now. This was going to turn into a working trip. It was a working birthday—

a working birthday in a dress that would be suitable for a party, but there was going to be no party after all. But then Mma Potokwane said, "And then we can have a cup of tea, Mma Ramotswe, and a piece of special fruit cake that I've made for your birthday. Happy birthday, by the way, Mma."

"Oh!" exclaimed the secretary. "Is it your birthday, Mma? Happy birthday. You must be very happy."

Mma Ramotswe thought for a moment. "I am," she said. "I am very happy, Mma."

And she was; or at least she was happier than she had been earlier that morning. Her birthday was not going to go entirely un-marked and there was the additional prospect of tea with a slice, or even more than one slice, of Mma Potokwane's justly celebrated fruit cake. There is always a silver lining, thought Mma Ramotswe—or almost always. The trick was to recognise the silver lining when it came. That was what needed to be done. Sometimes you had to look quite hard and the silver lining might not appear until rather late in the morning, as was the case that day. Still, it was there, and Mma Ramotswe felt grateful for it as she made her way with Mma Potokwane, her old friend, past the vegetable gardens where the children grew their carrots, their onions, their cabbages, towards the small building at the edge of the Orphan Farm where the house-mother, Mma Ikobeng, was waiting for them to arrive.

MMA IKOBENG WAS, like the secretary, a recent addition to Mma Potokwane's staff. Mma Ramotswe had not yet met her.

"This lady," Mma Potokwane confided as they approached the house, "is a real find, Mma Ramotswe. When I interviewed her, I could tell immediately that she was right for the job. She is a very kind lady—and that's what we need round here, you know."

Mma Ramotswe nodded. She had heard enough stories of the

children's backgrounds to know that kindness, more than anything else, was the thing most often lacking in their lives. For many of them, it was only when they were taken in at the Orphan Farm that they started to count for much in the life of anybody else.

"And she is good at so many other things," Mma Potokwane continued. "She is a first-class seamstress. She has made beautiful outfits for the children she looks after—dresses for the girls, and shirts for the boys. They all look very smart."

"A talented lady, then," said Mma Ramotswe.

"Mind you," said Mma Potokwane, "I have had to speak to her about a little failing she has."

Mma Ramotswe raised an eyebrow, but saw that whatever this failing was, it had obviously not been enough to dent Mma Potokwane's high opinion of her.

Mma Potokwane lowered her voice, as they were now close enough to be overheard from within the house. "She spoils the children, Mma Ramotswe. She gives them far too many sweet things. She can't help it, I'm afraid, and the children love her for it. You know how children are: offer them something sweet, and they'll eat it."

"Rather like us, Mma Potokwane," whispered Mma Ramotswe.

Mma Potokwane seemed uncertain whether to laugh at this, or to disapprove. Glancing at Mma Ramotswe, she made her decision. "That may be so, Mma Ramotswe," she said, with a conspiratorial chuckle. "But remember that we are traditionally built ladies, and we are allowed certain things. It is different for children. They should not be traditionally built."

"You're right," said Mma Ramotswe. "But these poor children—they probably were never given anything sweet when they were small. And now . . . well, there's this kind lady making it up to them. The world will not come to an end just because of that."

Mma Potokwane felt that she had to agree. It was difficult being the matron of the Orphan Farm: one had to be firm, but one also had to remember when to ease up, when to make exceptions. And if these exceptions involved a little extra something for the children, then there was nothing wrong with that—not in the overall scheme of things.

THEY SAT AROUND the kitchen table in the small house in which Mma Ikobeng presided over the welfare of nine young charges. On the cooking range against the wall, a large pot of stew simmered, the children's dinner for that night. A tempting aroma of good Botswana beef, mixed with carrots and onions, permeated the small kitchen— enough to make Mma Ramotswe's mouth water.

"Mma Ikobeng is a very good cook," said Mma Potokwane. "You can always tell the children from this particular house. They are sleek and . . . well, sleek and fat, and very happy."

Mma Ramotswe made an appreciative gesture. "I can imagine that, Mma. If their dinner smells like this, then they will be very happy children."

Mma Ikobeng basked in the praise. "Thank you, Mma Poto-kwane," she said. "I think the nicest moment in this job is when the children stop crying. When they first come, some of them cry, cry, cry—you know how it is—but then they gradually stop, and you know that something is working."

"That something is love," said Mma Potokwane. "That is what it is."

"And good food," added Mma Ikobeng. "That is important too."

There was general agreement—and a brief silence. Then Mma Potokwane said, "I have told Mma Ramotswe that there is something you would like to talk to her about."

Mma Ramotswe nodded. "I am very happy to listen, Mma Iko-beng."

Mma Ikobeng looked at her visitor. There was clearly something worrying her—something that made her hesitate. It did not take Mma Ramotswe long to decide what that was.

"You do know, Mma," she said, "that anything you say to me is private. It is very private. You need not worry."

Mma Potokwane added her authority to this. "That is true, Mma Ikobeng. Mma Ramotswe is not one of these ladies who can't keep a secret. She is very good at secrets."

Mma Ramotswe smiled at this. "As are you, Mma Potokwane. You never pass on any secrets, except that one about . . ."

Mma Ikobeng's eyes widened.

Mma Potokwane laughed. "Mma Ramotswe is only joking, Mma," she reassured the housemother. Then she continued, "You should tell her what you told me. Please go on."

Mma Ikobeng, who had been tense, now relaxed. "I have a daughter, Mma. She is almost thirty. I am forty-seven, Mma. I had her when I was very young, and then I had three more children. I am very proud of them, and they have looked after me very well."

Mma Potokwane explained. "Mma Ikobeng's husband is late, Mma. He became late in a car accident over at Ghansi. It was very sad."

Mma Ramotswe inclined her head. She was thinking of her father. Where was he? She never really thought about that, because she wanted to believe he was still somewhere not too far away, not too far from his beloved Botswana and the cattle that he had adored. That was a consolation—the thought that her late daddy, as she called him, still kept some sort of eye on the cattle. That was probably not true, she admitted to herself, but it was important to hope that something was true, even if you knew that it was unlikely. There was always work for hope to do.

"My daughter is my first-born," said Mma Ikobeng. "She has a job in a bank in Gaborone. She is well paid and she has bought a small house. She is very proud of that."

"She is lucky," said Mma Ramotswe. "It is hard for people to buy their first house."

"Yes," agreed Mma Ikobeng. "But she has no husband, Mma Ramotswe. She has a house, but she has no husband."

Mma Ramotswe shrugged. "There are many people these days who have no husband—or no wife, Mma. It is more common than it used to be. People are happy to be single."

"I have heard that," Mma Ikobeng said. "But my daughter is not one of those people. She would like to have a husband."

Mma Ramotswe waited.

"But she has not been lucky in that department," went on Mma Ikobeng. "There seems to be a shortage of men."

Mma Ramotswe sighed. "There has always been a shortage of men—or at least of *suitable* men."

"There are many unsuitable men," said Mma Potokwane. "I can tell you many stories about unsuitable men. They all begin, 'Once there was a man, and he was very unsuitable . . .'"

"Hah!" said Mma Ramotswe. "I think I have heard that story before, Mma."

Mma Potokwane kept the conversation moving. "You tell Mma Ramotswe what happened," she encouraged.

Mma Ikobeng took a deep breath. "My daughter—Alice—read an article in the paper. It was about a new club that had been set up in one of the hotels. It said that this club, which met every Friday and Saturday evening, was for single people."

"I have heard of clubs like that," said Mma Ramotswe. "They have singles bars too, in some places. They are for single people."

"Yes," said Mma Ikobeng. "The idea is that if you go to one of these clubs, then you will meet other people like you, who are looking for somebody to marry. That is what you think, Mma."

Mma Ramotswe considered this. "Well, I suppose that you need to meet people somewhere. The person you are going to marry doesn't just come and knock on your door." She closed her eyes briefly and imagined hearing a knock on the door and answering it to a caller who says, "I would like to marry you," adding, out of politeness—one hoped—"if you don't mind." And you would say, "Please come in, Rra," or "Please come in, Mma," depending on the circumstances, and you would introduce yourself and offer a cup of tea, and possibly discuss the preliminaries of marriage, such as when the two families might get together and discuss the tricky issue of bride price.

"You're smiling, Mma," said Mma Ikobeng.

Mma Ramotswe opened her eyes. "I was thinking. Please carry on, Mma Ikobeng. I am always thinking—maybe too much. And then I forget that other people may be wondering why I am thinking so much."

"There is nothing wrong with thinking," interjected Mma Poto-kwane. "I could give you a list, Mma Ramotswe, of people I know who could do with thinking a bit more. Oh yes, I could give you quite a long list of those people."

They waited for Mma Ikobeng to continue. Now she went on, "My daughter Alice is a very nice young woman. She is polite, and she is attractive. Maybe she is not attractive-flashy, if you see what I mean. She is not one of these ladies who spend all their time looking in the mirror, braiding her hair, and putting on creams and whatnot. No, she is not one of those, but she is nice-looking, I think."

"She is very nice," said Mma Potokwane reassuringly. "She is a homely girl."

Mma Ikobeng frowned, and Mma Potokwane immediately corrected herself. "When I say homely, I mean she is one whom men would like to take home. I use homely in that sense."

Mma Ramotswe encouraged Mma Ikobeng to continue. Mma Potokwane, she thought, has many good points, but she could sometimes be tactless. You forgave her that, of course; you forgave her almost anything, because of what she did for the children. She fought for their interests every moment of the day, Mma Ramotswe reminded herself—every moment of the day. And if anything counted for anything in an increasingly selfish world, then it was that.

"Alice decided to go to this club," Mma Ikobeng continued. "She told me about it—we have no secrets from each other. She said, 'Mummy, I'm going to this social club, you see. It is for single people. There was an article about it in the newspaper. It is very respectable.' That was the word she used—*respectable*. And I said to her that I would never object to her going to a respectable club. It would be different if the club was not respectable—then I would say, 'Please do not go to that club,' or something like that."

"Any parent would do that," Mma Potokwane said. "If you saw your daughter going to a club that was not respectable, then you would warn her. You would say, 'There are people there who may not be respectable. There may be untrustworthy men there.'"

"Of course, that is what I would have done," agreed Mma Ikobeng. "We all know about these untrustworthy people. You see them when you go out these days. There they are. You can't miss them."

Mma Ramotswe was not so sure. It was too easy, she thought, to dismiss people with inadequate evidence. Even those who did not impress might have qualities you did not know about. And there were few people without some redeeming features somewhere. But she did not say this, as she wanted to hear what had happened to Alice Ikobeng.

"Please go on, Mma," she urged.

"Well, she went to a meeting of this club," Mma Ikobeng continued. "There was a band, she told me. Not a big band, but a man on a keyboard and a man with a guitar. They were playing dance music. You know the sort. La, la, la—that sort of thing. And there were tables where groups of people could sit and talk. And Alice said that it was a very pleasant place to be."

"And were there enough men for the women?" asked Mma Potokwane. "That can sometimes be the problem: too many women and not enough men, because the men are all off somewhere, evading their responsibilities. That is a big problem these days."

"There were plenty of men. Fifty-fifty, Alice said. And she danced with this man who said he was called Johnny. He did not give her a Setswana name—he said that he was just called Johnny."

Mma Potokwane frowned. She exchanged a glance with Mma Ramotswe, who was already alerted by the name. She was thinking along the same lines as Mma Potokwane was: very few people, in her experience, were called Johnny—not really. They might call themselves that, but if you asked for evidence, they muttered something about nicknames. It was the same with men called Elvis. You had to be very careful about men who called themselves Elvis. That was well known, she thought.

"She liked Johnny. He said that he worked for the Bank of Botswana, which is always a good sign. She told him that she also worked for a bank—the Standard Bank, in her case. He said, 'Then we are both bankers, which is a good thing.' And she said that she thought it a good thing, too. And it is, I think, Mma. If two people can talk about banks, then that will help them to get to know one another."

Mma Ikobeng hesitated. It was as if she were reaching a painful stage of the story—which she was.

"She met this Mr. Johnny later that week. They went to the cinema and then they went to that place that sells hamburgers. Then she met him that weekend, and he took her for a ride in his car. They talked a lot, she said. He was very amusing. He had many jokes, and he would tell her about his travels. He had been to Johannesburg and to Lusaka. He told her about those places." She hesitated. "I think she began to fall in love with him, Mma. You know how it is."

Mma Ramotswe looked down at the floor. She sensed where this story was going, and she felt sorry for Mma Ikobeng. It could not be easy for a mother to tell such a story about her own daughter.

"There was something that Alice noticed, though," Mma Ikobeng went on. "She said that Johnny did not seem to know any of the people she knew who worked in the Bank of Botswana. She became suspicious. And she was also suspicious that he would not tell her where he lived. He mentioned a part of town, but that was all. When she asked him the name of the street, he just laughed and tapped the side of his nose and said, 'Ask no questions, be told no lies.'"

"But of course, he was lying all the time," Mma Potokwane exploded. "One big lie from start to finish. Name? Mr. Liar. Job? Nothing to do with the Bank of Botswana. Home address? Not disclosed. That was the picture, wasn't it, Mma Ikobeng?"

The housemother nodded miserably. "It was, Mma. And, of course, she eventually found out what I could have told her right at the beginning."

"Married?" asked Mma Ramotswe. It had to be that. It was an old and very familiar story.

Mma Ikobeng nodded. "She found out from a friend at work. The friend said that she knew somebody who had seen the two of them together. And this person who had seen them actually lived a couple of doors away from Mr. so-called Johnny . . ."

"And his wife," prompted Mma Potokwane.

"Yes, and his wife. And his three children. And his mother-in-law, whose husband is late."

Mma Ramotswe shook her head. "This is a very sad story, Mma Ikobeng. It must be painful for you to tell it."

"It gets worse," Mma Potokwane said. "Tell Mma Ramotswe, Mma."

"She knew one of the other ladies who went to this singles club. And she had exactly the same experience—not with Johnny, of course, he was busy deceiving Alice—but with another man. She found out that he was married too."

Mma Ramotswe sighed. "This is very bad, Mma."

"It is," said Mma Ikobeng. "But you know what she found out too? There was something else. She found out that Johnny had paid a lot of money to go to the club—much more than the advertised charge."

Mma Potokwane took over again. "And the reason for that, Mma Ramotswe, is that the organisers knew that he was married. So they deliberately make money out of married men who want to go to the club to meet ladies who think that they're single."

The three of them fell silent. Then Mma Ramotswe asked what Mma Ikobeng would like her to do.

"I think that somebody should do something about this club." She looked at Mma Ramotswe. "Somebody somewhere is making money out of all this deceiving of ladies. And who's doing anything about it? Nobody is, Mma. People just stand by and let that sort of thing happen. Go to the police? What will they say? It is no business of ours if married men are deceiving ladies. This is a free country, and one of men's freedoms is to deceive ladies. Well, I say that we should fight back, Mma."

Mma Ramotswe felt that there was little she could add to that—

other than to agree, of course, because the desire for justice was very strong and people yearned for it, no matter what odds there were against them. But she knew that Mma Ikobeng would be expecting her to say that she would look into this matter, and she knew that she would have to say yes because she could not refuse this sort of request, especially with Mma Potokwane standing by, looking at her with the air of one who thinks there can be only one possible answer.

She drew in her breath. Not a great deal of breath was required to say yes—less, perhaps, than was needed when you said no. And the reason for that, of course, is that when you say no, you usually have to say something else—to explain why you have said no—whereas when you say yes, no further explanation is expected.

"Yes," she said. But she felt that she needed to say something else, and so she said, "I shall do what I can."

Mma Potokwane turned to the housemother and said, a note of triumph breaking through her voice, "You see, Mma? You see—just as I told you, Mma Ramotswe is a very kind lady."

Mma Ramotswe was embarrassed by the compliment. "I am not kind," she said. "You are the kind one, Mma Potokwane. And you too, Mma Ikobeng." She gestured about her—at the kitchen, at the pot of stew on the stove, at the many signs of kindness that you would find in a house such as this. "Yes, you are the kind ones, I think."

Mma Potokwane rose to her feet. "Let's not argue," she said, straightening her skirt. "It's time for some birthday fruit cake, Mma Ramotswe—and Mma Ikobeng, of course. Let us not delay this important matter one second longer."

Mma Ikobeng moved the pot of stew to the side of the stove; it did not do to overcook a stew, she explained. Then the three of them went outside, and walked in quiet companionship back to Mma Potokwane's office. Several of the smaller children were working in the garden, watering their plants carefully, as children who live in dry countries are taught to do, making sure that each drop goes to the thirsty roots of the plants they are nurturing. The children were being supervised by two of the women who were in charge of the gardens. They were gentle with their charges, watchful of what they did, making sure they did not damage the plants, encouraging them in their efforts.

CHAPTER THREE

PERI-PERI CHICKEN

MMA RAMOTSWE WENT HOME EARLY, as there was not much to do in the office—they were going through a quiet patch— and because she felt that her birthday, her one special day in the year, was slipping through her fingers. She would return to the house, she decided, where she would treat herself to a cooling bath with a small pinch of the bath crystals she had been hoarding for some months now, after having been given them by a grateful client. That had been another of these errant husband cases; there were far too many of them, Mma Ramotswe thought—although that particular case had been shown not to involve a misbehaving husband at all, and had become, rather, a matrimonial counselling matter. The husband had been spending unaccounted-for time away from home, and had been suspected by his wife of conducting an affair. As it turned out, he had simply been going to a bar with a group of male friends, to escape his wife's constant nagging. Once she had diagnosed the problem, Mma Ramotswe had had a heart-to-heart talk with the wife, had reassured her of her husband's fidelity, and had managed to persuade her not to try to manage every minute of his time.

"The secret to keeping men happy," she had confided, "is to give them a bit of room to be themselves, Mma. Men sometimes like just to be left alone for a while."

"But surely they will get into mischief then," the woman objected. "You will have heard the expression, Mma: the Devil finds work for idle hands to do. That is true in general, I believe, Mma, but especially true when it comes to men."

"That may be true to an extent," said Mma Ramotswe. "But it is also true that men like just to sit in a chair and look up in the air. Or to do the same thing while standing up." She paused. "How many times have you seen a man just standing there, looking at nothing in particular? Many times, I suspect, Mma. This very morning I saw a man like that, standing in his garden, looking up in the air. It is very important to men that they should be able to do that from time to time."

"But surely that's a big waste of their time," the woman had objected.

"But it is *their* time, Mma," Mma Ramotswe had pointed out. "*Their* time."

Her advice had eventually been taken, and the husband was left more to his own devices, which resulted in an immediate improvement in his relationship with his wife.

"The less you see of him," said Mma Ramotswe, "the more you'll see of him."

It had worked, and in her gratitude, both for the result and for the very small fee that Mma Ramotswe charged, the woman had given Mma Ramotswe a box of lavender-scented bath crystals. And it was in a bath scented by these precious salts that she now luxuriated. She closed her eyes and thought of her birthday, and of how it had been not a complete disaster, but almost. She felt let down by Mr. J.L.B. Matekoni, and by Mma Makutsi too. If you are with somebody virtually every day of the year, year in, year out, as they were, then surely it was not too much to expect them to remember your birthday. Or was it? People were so busy these days, cramming their lives full almost to the bursting point with leisure activities and social commitments, that surely they might be forgiven for forgetting other people's birthdays. And if you forgot something—genuinely forgot—then were you to be blamed at all? You couldn't blame people for things over which they had no control, and forgetting might be just that—something they could not help but do. And now that she had reminded herself of that, her sense of disappointment with both Mma Makutsi and Mr. J.L.B. Matekoni seemed to diminish. They were human, after all—as we all were—and it was incumbent upon us to forgive the human failings of others. Her birthday had been a damp squib, but there would be other birthdays, she hoped, and next year she might gently remind them in good time.

The bathwater had been tepid when she had stepped into it, and now it was getting cold, which was what she needed. If she lay there for a few minutes longer, shivering just a little, then by the time she was dressed again, she would be pleasantly cool. And the worst heat of the afternoon was over now, the mercury shrinking in the small maximum-and-minimum thermometer she kept outside the kitchen window. She poured herself a cup of red bush tea, picked up a magazine, and seated herself in the shade of the verandah. She would not think about dinner just yet; she would find something in the fridge, something simple, and prepare it for the two of them later on. There was no hurry. Today was evidently a busy day for Mr. J.L.B. Matekoni, and on such days he often did not return until just after seven in the evening. They would eat at seven-thirty, after he had had a bath, and so there was plenty of time.

He returned earlier than she had anticipated, just before six-thirty, during that brief, beguiling time between afternoon and evening. As Mma Ramotswe stepped out of the house to greet him as he parked his truck, she looked over to the west where, above the Kalahari, the sun was sinking below the horizon. There was a line of roofs, indistinct in their detail, dark shapes against the copper glow in the sky, while here and there, in the foreground of the sunset, the branches of acacia trees were outlined against the sky. And there were birds, too, small black dots, darting homewards, excited in their chatter.

She noticed all that, familiar and yet so arresting, and then she saw him, her husband, getting out of his truck and looking surprised to see her coming out to meet him. He hesitated, and then ran towards her, and for a few moments she thought there was something wrong, that perhaps he had seen that she was about to step on a snake in the dimming light and was rushing forward to save her. There were snakes, of course, and this was just the time that they might be moving about on that snake business of theirs; it could be that.

But of course it was not, and when she heard him, she knew immediately what it was. "Oh, my Precious. Oh, I am so sorry. I am so sorry."

Mr. J.L.B. Matekoni was not a demonstrative man. Working with engines, as he did every day, he did not need to say as much as some people needed to say. And when away from his garage and its demands, and, in particular, when he was with Mma Ramotswe, who somehow seemed to manage his world for him—in the nicest possible way—he felt that he did not need to burden others with his observations on things. But now, in the toils of what seemed to be insupportable regret, he blurted out the words that he had been preparing as he drove home from work that evening. He had imagined himself delivering them in the kitchen, even as Mma Ramotswe stood at the stove making the final preparations for their dinner, but she had chosen to come outside to meet him, and the apology would not wait.

"I am sorrier than I can say," he continued, as he reached out to clasp her hands. "I am the most forgetful man in all Botswana." That sentence had been weighed, approved, and practised. It sounded somewhat theatrical to his ear—he would never say such a thing spontaneously—but out it came now, and it did not sound too extreme, he thought. No, it sounded about right, and so he repeated it.

"I am the most forgetful man in all Botswana, because I only remembered your birthday twenty minutes ago. I am so sorry."

Her hand was in his. She pressed it. "It doesn't matter," she said. "It really doesn't."

"But it does," he insisted. "How can a husband forget his wife's birthday? What sort of hopeless, useless—"

She stopped him. "You are not hopeless, Mr. J.L.B. Matekoni. You are not useless. Definitely not."

"But I am."

She gave his hands another squeeze. "I forgot it myself." That was not true, and it was not typical of her to tell a lie. But there were occasions, she felt, when a lie was justified to protect the feelings of another, when a lie would do no harm to anybody, and this surely was one of those. Another such occasion, she suddenly remembered, had occurred when, a few days earlier, Mma Makutsi had arrived at work wearing a dress that was festooned with ridiculous pink bows, and she had asked Mma Ramotswe what she thought of it. It had required an almost physical effort to answer that question and to say that she thought it a very attractive dress—to the obvious delight of Mma Makutsi. She had said it in spite of thinking that it was the most inappropriate dress that Mma Makutsi could possibly have chosen, even for one of those fancy-dress parties where you are specifically invited to look ridiculous. You could not wear a dress with multiple pink bows when you were over the age of twelve, she thought—and even then, that might be pushing it.

This was such a lie, and Mr. J.L.B. Matekoni, forgetting that the right response to such an attempt to protect one's feelings was to go along with the well-intentioned deception and to pretend to believe the unbelievable, should have said, "Well, that's a relief, Mma, and it makes me feel much better. Still guilty, of course, but much, much better." Instead of which, he said, "Surely not: people don't forget their own birthdays, Mma."

"Well, I did, Rra, but let's not talk about it."

And with that, the subject should have been dropped. But it was not.

"Did you not remember what date it was today?" he asked. "Did you think it was the twelfth rather than the eleventh?"

She led him back towards the house. "I don't know," she said. "I just forgot. Let's not . . ."

"Very strange," he said, shaking his head. "But I suppose, Mma, you are always thinking of other people. And when you are thinking of other people, it might be only too easy to forget about yourself . . . and your birthday."

She made a non-committal noise.

"So, you weren't cross with me?" he asked. "In spite of it?"

She felt a momentary irritation. She wished he would say no more, as his questions were asking of her half-truth upon half-truth, if not direct lie upon direct lie.

"I'm never cross with you, Mr. J.L.B. Matekoni. You are my husband, and you are a good man. Why should I be cross with you?"

"Because I forgot your birthday," he replied. "And that is not what a good husband does."

"There are more important things than birthdays," she said, now sounding, perhaps, a bit short.

They had reached the house.

"Have you made dinner?" he asked.

"It is on the stove. It will not be long."

He stopped her. They had just gone inside, and he took her hands again. "Can you put the dinner in the fridge?"

She looked puzzled. "But it is already hot. It will be ready when I cook the peas. That will only take a few minutes."

He shook his head. "We will not have dinner here, Mma. Our dinner can be put in the fridge. It can become tomorrow's dinner— cooked today, but eaten tomorrow."

She wondered whether he had already eaten. Sometimes he had been known to stop at the food stall near the crossroads, because he was unable to resist the pleasure of a fat cake. That happened occasionally, especially after a demanding day. Had that happened this evening?

"I'm feeling a bit hungry," she said. And then she added, "All I had today was a piece . . ." She hesitated before continuing, ". . . a piece or two of Mma Potokwane's fruit cake. She made a special one for my birth . . ."

The words died on her lips. He might not have noticed, she told herself, but that comfort was short-lived.

"For your birthday?" He looked at her. And then, with the air of one upon whom an entirely regrettable truth is dawning, he went on, "So you didn't forget your birthday, Mma. And neither did Mma Potokwane."

She looked down at the floor. The deception she had sought to practise—well intentioned though it might have been—had not lasted long. "I'm sorry," she confessed. "I was only hoping to save your feelings. I did remember. I remembered right from the time I woke up."

He let out a small cry of anguish. "So you remembered when you woke up. And I had already gone to work, and you were alone in the house and you remembered. Oh, this is terrible, Mma."

She shook her head. "It is not terrible, Mr. J.L.B. Matekoni, and I don't think we should talk about it any longer. You forgot, and then I told you something that wasn't true, and now you're feeling miserable, and I am too. And all of this is happening on my birthday, or on what remains of my birthday." She paused. "I even think it would be good if midnight came more quickly tonight, so that today would be yesterday and we could stop thinking about all this."

They stood for a few moments in silence. Then Mr. J.L.B. Matekoni clapped his hands together. "We're going out for dinner," he said. "I have already telephoned them. That peri-peri place. They are keeping a table for us. It's all arranged."

She looked at him in astonishment. They had not been out for dinner for years. She would have liked to have gone out for dinner, but there had been no invitations, and so it had never happened.

"Are you sure?" she asked.

"I am very sure, Mma. I am very hungry and I think you are too. We will have peri-peri chicken, I think, and some ice cream too—afterwards."

She smiled at the thought. Peri-peri chicken was a hot dish, and was the perfect prelude to ice cream. And the luxury of being cooked for by somebody else, when your life consisted of cooking every single day, without let-up! Even if their going out tonight was a precedent for no more than a single dinner outing each year—on her birthday—then that would still give her something to look forward to.

The restaurant was not far away, and they drove there in Mr. J.L.B. Matekoni's truck, engine parts and tools rattling about in the back.

"It's busy tonight," said Mma Ramotswe, as Mr. J.L.B. Matekoni nosed the truck into its parking place.

"That's because it's your birthday," he said, switching off the ignition.

She laughed. The tension that had arisen on his return had completely disappeared, as had the sense of disappointment she had felt earlier in the day. She was going out to dinner with her husband, as so many wives no doubt were doing at this precise moment, in towns and cities elsewhere, although there were so many, of course, for whom this would be an impossible, unattainable treat. She thought of Mma Potokwane, just as an example: nobody ever took her out to dinner, although if ever anybody deserved it, it was her. Or Mma Ikobeng. She would treat both of them to lunch at the President Hotel, she decided. They would go, the three of them—three ladies out for lunch—and they would talk about the things that ladies going out for lunch liked to talk about. There was never any shortage of subjects for such occasions, and they would probably end up doing no more than scratch the surface of the topics they considered.

They were shown to their table by the proprietor himself. He knew Mr. J.L.B. Matekoni, and had entrusted his car to him on several occasions. He offered his hand, and Mma Ramotswe shook it.

"Special occasion?" the proprietor asked, as he seated them.

"My wife's birthday," said Mr. J.L.B. Matekoni.

The proprietor clapped his hands together. "Happy Birthday, Mma. Well done!"

Mma Ramotswe acknowledged his good wishes. "Thank you, Rra. It doesn't seem like a year since the last one—but that's the way things are, isn't it? The days speed up the older you get."

The proprietor, practised in compliments, said, "But Mma, you are one of those people, I suspect, who look younger with each year that goes past—even now that you've reached your mid-thirties."

Mma Ramotswe wagged a finger at him. "You're just saying that, Rra. You're flattering me."

"She is much older than that," said Mr. J.L.B. Matekoni.

Mma Ramotswe gave him a discouraging glance.

"I can hardly believe that," said the proprietor, quickly. "But tell me, Mma, what presents did you get for your birthday? I hope you got something nice."

There was a brief and rather awkward silence. Mr. J.L.B. Matekoni picked up the menu and started to study it assiduously. Mma Ramotswe bit her lip.

The proprietor was perceptive. "But let's not talk about all your presents," he said briskly. "Let's talk about what you'd like for dinner."

"I like peri-peri chicken," said Mma Ramotswe. "And so does my husband."

"Then you have come to the right place," said the proprietor, adding, "with chips or mashed potato?"

Mma Ramotswe hesitated. Then she said, "Chips, I think."

Mr. J.L.B. Matekoni looked relieved. "I think chips would be best," he added.

"A very good choice," said the proprietor. "It's not as if either of you has a weight problem."

The silence returned, and continued until Mma Ramotswe asked, brightly, "When do you think the rains will come back? Soon—do you think?"

THE PERI-PERI CHICKEN LIVED UP to its reputation, but they both made sure to leave just enough room for a three-scoop helping of ice cream topped with double-chocolate sauce.

"I'm not sure what double-chocolate means," said Mma Ramotswe, as she dealt with the last few spoonfuls of the delicious concoction. "Perhaps it means a double helping."

"Or much richer chocolate," suggested Mr. J.L.B. Matekoni. "I think chocolate may be like motor oil. You get different grades, you know, depending on what your engine requires. It's viscosity, you see. Viscosity decides how the oil moves through the engine. An engine oil with a low viscosity will flow very easily through an engine—it will be more liquid."

He looked at her through the candlelight. It was very romantic, he thought.

"High viscosity," he continued, "means that the oil is sluggish. If your engine runs cold, then you want to have low viscosity, so that the oil gets round as it should. If your engine runs at a high temperature, then it's best to use high-viscosity oil. Otherwise, you get more wear and tear on the moving parts." He finished the last of his ice cream and its high-viscosity chocolate sauce. "I'm always telling people that, Mma. I'm always saying to them, 'Never, *ever,* use the wrong grade of motor oil.' There are some people who don't seem to care. They'll put anything into their engine. They really don't know what they're doing."

"Even chocolate sauce?" asked Mma Ramotswe. "Would chocolate sauce do the trick if you didn't have engine oil?"

Mr. J.L.B. Matekoni thought for a moment before he gave his considered response. "I don't think so, Mma. I think it would break down. No, I would never put chocolate sauce in a motor engine."

Mma Ramotswe smiled. Dear Mr. J.L.B. Matekoni, she said to herself, with his engine oils and whatnot. We have to mother them, she thought. We have to look after these poor men, who would otherwise be so adrift . . . In her mind's eye she saw a whole crowd, a host, of men, milling about aimlessly, waiting for women to come and claim them.

Her reverie was interrupted by the arrival of the proprietor, who bent down beside her and whispered, "Sorry to disturb you, Mma, but there is somebody at another table who asked whether you are the Mma Ramotswe who runs the No. 1 Ladies' Detective Agency. You are that lady, I think."

Mma Ramotswe nodded. "I am, Rra. That's me."

"It's just that this lady said that somebody had pointed you out to her. She wonders whether she might have a word with you."

Mr. J.L.B. Matekoni frowned. "But she's not working at the moment, Rra. It's her birthday, and we're out to dinner."

The proprietor made a placatory gesture. "You're absolutely right," he said. "I shall point this out to her."

But Mma Ramotswe stopped him. "It's all right, Rra," she said. "I am happy to speak to her."

Mr. J.L.B. Matekoni sighed. "But it's your birthday, Mma . . ."

She shook her head. "It's no trouble for me to speak to people, Rra. Please tell her that is all right."

Mr. J.L.B. Matekoni made to protest, but evidently thought better of it. As the proprietor went off to fetch the other customer, Mr. J.L.B. Matekoni lowered his voice and said to Mma Ramotswe, "You are too soft-hearted, Mma. You cannot take all the problems of the world onto your shoulders."

"You cannot be sure that this lady wants to talk to me about a problem."

He shook his head in disbelief. "But she must do," he argued. "Why else would somebody who doesn't know you want to speak to you in the middle of a restaurant?"

"For any number of reasons," said Mma Ramotswe, although she was struggling to think of one.

Mr. J.L.B. Matekoni looked unconvinced, but did not argue, as the proprietor was now returning with a woman walking behind him. He reached the table and introduced his customer to Mma Ramotswe.

"This lady is a visitor from America," he said.

The woman came up to the table and reached out to shake hands with Mma Ramotswe.

"I'm very sorry to be intruding like this, Mma," she said.

She turned to Mr. J.L.B. Matekoni and offered her hand. "Please forgive me. You go out to dinner and an American lady comes up and you must think, Oh dear."

Mr. J.L.B. Matekoni shook his head. "Not at all, Mma. I do not think that at all."

Mma Ramotswe gestured to the spare chair that the proprietor had thoughtfully drawn up for the visitor. "You must sit down, Mma. It is easier to talk if you are sitting."

The woman sat down. "My name is Julia Cotterell, Mma. I am from a place called Bloomington. It is in the United States. In Indiana."

Mma Ramotswe looked up. "Indiana, Mma? I met somebody from Indiana. There is a place there called Muncie."

Julia smiled. "Muncie? Of course, there is. It's about a hundred miles north of us."

Mma Ramotswe absorbed this. "So you may have been there, Mma?"

"Yes, I've been there," Julia replied. "Not very often, but once or twice. There's a college there—not as big as the college we have in Bloomington, of course, but I had a niece who went there. I went to her graduation."

"The person I know wrote a very famous book," said Mma Ramotswe. "You may have heard of it."

Mr. J.L.B. Matekoni intervened. "It's called *The Principles of Private Detection*. It is a very important book about that subject."

Julia seemed interested. "I can imagine it's quite a book."

"Yes," said Mma Ramotswe, "it is. The author is a man called

Clovis Andersen. Perhaps you met him when you went to Muncie. The world is very small, I think, and you might know him."

Julia shook her head. "Regretfully, no. That is not an area I have read much about."

"His book has been very useful to me in my profession," said Mma Ramotswe. "And then I had the great honour of meeting him when he visited Botswana. I had never thought that somebody like him would come here, but he did, and saw our sign. He came to visit us in the office."

Julia said that you should never rule out anything happening. There was nothing, she thought, that might not happen if you waited long enough.

There was now a brief but polite silence. Then Julia said, "I have heard of you, Mma Ramotswe."

Mma Ramotswe bowed her head modestly. Gaborone was the sort of place where everybody knew everybody else's business, but she had never imagined that people might have heard of her over there in . . . where was it? Bloomington? She liked that name; it would be a good name for a daughter, if one was stuck. Surely, they could not be talking about her over there in Bloomington unless . . . yes, that might be it. Perhaps Clovis Andersen had returned to America and spoken to people about his visit to Botswana and happened to mention that he'd met her. That must be it. And then the people to whom he had spoken had in turn mentioned to others that there was a person in Botswana who had a detective agency known as the No. 1 Ladies' Detective Agency, and that she was called Mma Ramotswe, and lived on Zebra Drive with her mechanic husband. That's how news got around after all, whether it was in America or in Botswana. A lot of news was not all that far removed from gossip, and we all knew how quickly gossip spread—every bit as quickly as one of those bush fires where the dry grass went up in flames so quickly and was soon a long line of flame licking at the land.

Mma Ramotswe thought about that, but it was Mr. J.L.B. Matekoni who asked directly, "Where did you hear about Mma Ramotswe, Mma? Was it in your place over there?"

Julia shook her head. "No, it was through a lady called Mma Potokwane. She's the matron of a children's home just outside town here, that I visited on behalf of my church back in Bloomington. We had a collection for it."

Mma Ramotswe was momentarily crestfallen. It was one thing to be talked about in Bloomington, Indiana, and quite another thing to be talked about in Tlokweng—even by no less a person than Mma Potokwane. Her moment of possible international fame had been brief—and illusory—but she saw the humour in the situation, and smiled. "That is more likely," she said. "I was thinking that perhaps . . . No, that is much more likely, Mma. Mma Potokwane and I are old friends, you see. I talk about her, and I suppose she talks about me. That is how it is with old friends, I think."

"Oh, it is," Julia agreed. "Sometimes, you know, I pick up the phone to call my old friends—just to see that they are still there. I may have nothing to talk to them about, and they may have nothing new to say to me, but I say hi and they say hi in return."

Mma Ramotswe nodded. "You do not need to say much more than that to old friends."

Mr. J.L.B. Matekoni joined in again. "That is because you have already said everything you have to say to those old friends. They've heard it all before—many times, in some cases."

Julia laughed. "That may be so," she said. "But then every so often a friend says something new, and your answer is also something new, and you go away thinking, how interesting. That happens too." She paused. "Mma Potokwane showed me an article from the newspaper. It was about your business, and there was a picture of you standing in front of the building with another lady—a lady wearing glasses."

"That's Mma Makutsi," said Mma Ramotswe.

"What a lovely woman," said Julia.

Mma Ramotswe nodded. She would tell Mma Makutsi that. People loved to hear compliments about themselves, and Mma Makutsi was no exception. She would appreciate that because she was sometimes embarrassed by her glasses and by her slightly problematic skin, which was much better these days, anyway, after she'd stopped using those creams. Mma Ramotswe had felt obliged to tell her that she thought the creams just made it worse, and she had been proved right.

"Anyway," Julia continued, "that was how I recognised you here—from your photograph."

Mma Ramotswe waited. She was not sure where the conversation was going. She thought there might be a request, but it was also possible that this was simply a social conversation. She had heard that Americans liked to talk, and of course people in Botswana liked to chat as well. If there was a Talking Olympics, then America and Botswana would both get gold medals, she imagined, while some other, silent countries—countries you had never heard of, because they never said anything—would go home without any medals at all. That was a pity. She had always felt that anybody who got as far as the Olympics should get *something,* even if it was only a very small medal made of some recycled, cheap metal.

It turned out to be a request, and it was a request of a sort that she was accustomed to receiving. "I wondered if you might be able to find somebody," said Julia. "I was hoping, when I arrived in this country, that I would find a business just like yours—a business that had experience in tracing people. So I was very excited when

Mma Potokwane mentioned you, and showed me the article. I was going to seek you out, in fact, and then I saw you here in the restaurant. I was very pleased when that happened, Mma."

Mma Ramotswe smiled encouragingly. The agency was not very busy, and this sounded like regular work rather than a request for a favour. "We do a lot of that sort of work," she said. "We are often asked to find—"

"Husbands," interjected Mr. J.L.B. Matekoni. "If you are looking for your husband, Mma—if he has run away—then Mma Ramotswe is just the person to help you."

Mma Ramotswe gave him a sideways look. That was not at all tactful, she thought. If a woman's husband had deserted her, you never broached the subject directly: you let them come up with the story in their own way, in their own time. And you never said "ran away," you said "gone somewhere else" or "away from home pro tem."

Julia did not take offence. "No, I am not looking for my husband, Rra. I know exactly where my husband is. He's back in—"

"Bloomington?" supplied Mr. J.L.B. Matekoni. "He is looking after the children?"

Mma Ramotswe caught her breath. This was too bad: Mr. J.L.B. Matekoni was trying to be helpful, but he was completely out of his depth here. He was very good with gearboxes and suspension issues, but when it came to the psychology of client relations, he had a great deal to learn.

Julia looked down at the floor, and Mma Ramotswe knew immediately that the question had hurt her. Her husband *had* run away; of course he had, and now Mr. J.L.B. Matekoni's tactless question and the assumption behind it had cut to the quick. And not only would there be no husband, she thought—there would be no children either.

Julia looked up again. "No, my husband is in Cleveland. He is not in Bloomington."

Mr. J.L.B. Matekoni nodded. "He is away at the moment?"

Mma Ramotswe caught her breath again. She imagined a few sentences that might be inserted as a note in Clovis Andersen's book: *Never take your husband with you on an enquiry. Remember that he is an unqualified person, and that he might ask embarrassing or even counter-productive questions. Tell him to stay at home. That is an important rule.*

She heard Julia begin to answer, "My husband and I are separated, Rra. He lives permanently in Cleveland, but I have stayed in Bloomington."

Mr. J.L.B. Matekoni nodded. He did not seem to be feeling in the slightest bit awkward. "So, you are not looking for him, then. You do not need to look for somebody if you know where he is."

Julia shrugged. "I guess you don't."

Mma Ramotswe seized the initiative. "I'm sure we shall be able to help you, Mma—whoever it is that you are looking for. We are experienced in tracing people, not just husbands"—she gave Mr. J.L.B. Matekoni a warning look—"but also other sorts of people. Perhaps you would tell me who it is you are trying to find. Then we can see about helping you." She paused. "All our resources will be at your disposal, Mma."

She thought about that. *All our resources* sounded rather grand, but what did their resources actually amount to? To herself, Mma Makutsi, and Charlie (on a part-time basis)? And the tiny white van, of course, and the extra teacup that they kept for the use of any client who came to the office? Was that more or less it?

Julia looked at her gratefully. "Thank you, Mma," she said. "Perhaps it would be best if I called on you at your office. Then we can talk in pr . . ." She stopped herself before she uttered the word *private*, but Mma Ramotswe knew what she meant. This was women's business, and she did not want to discuss it with Mr. J.L.B. Matekoni present. That was perfectly understandable.

After they had agreed "It is much easier to talk in the office," Mma Ramotswe said quickly, "It is just me there—and my associate, Mma Makutsi."

"The lady with the glasses?"

"Yes, that lady."

Julia seemed relieved. "May I call round tomorrow?" she asked.

"I shall be waiting for you, Mma," said Mma Ramotswe. "Do you like tea?"

"I certainly do."

"Then there will be tea ready for when you arrive."

Julia rose to her feet. "Now, I should leave you to get on with your birthday," she said, then added, "Thank you, Mma Ramotswe."

She left after Mma Ramotswe had told her how to get to the office, and they had agreed a time to meet. Then Mr. J.L.B. Matekoni leaned forward to say, "That was interesting, Mma. Very interesting, I think."

Mma Ramotswe had toyed with the idea of telling him, as tactfully as possible, about what to avoid in a conversation with a client, but she refrained. The main reason for that, she thought, was because it was her birthday, and there was little left of it now. And a secondary reason was that there were occasions when it was best not to try to tell men what to do. Half the time they never listened to you, and the other half they did the opposite of what you said. She looked at Mr. J.L.B. Matekoni. No, he was not like that. He was a good man, and he was always prepared to listen to her, and indeed to follow her advice. He was, in a sense, one of these *new men* that you read about. But then, when you looked at his khaki trousers and at his battered suede boots with their oil stains, and at his truck, you realised that he was not quite there yet. But whatever and wherever he was, he was still one of the best men in the country, and she knew that she would never meet a kinder or more considerate husband. Ever. That was well known, she thought.

CHAPTER FOUR

CAUTION: MARRIED MEN INSIDE

WHEN MMA MAKUTSI ENTERED the office of the No. 1 Ladies' Detective Agency the following morning, she did so with the demeanour of one who had realised only that morning that she had forgotten her colleague's birthday the previous day. Such a demeanour is unmistakeable, and Mma Ramotswe noticed it immediately. She took no pleasure in it. Had she been of a vindictive nature, she might have enjoyed her colleague's discomfort, as a sop for injured feelings; but that was not how she was, and so she simply waited for Mma Makutsi to speak.

"I have a big apology to make," Mma Makutsi began, even before she sat down at her desk.

Mma Ramotswe spread her hands out in front of her in a gesture of understanding and forgiveness. "Mma, who among us has not forgotten somebody's birthday? We have all done it. We are all human."

Mma Makutsi shook her head. "We are all human," she said. "Yes, we are all human, Mma, but sometimes we are more human than we are at other times. I have been very human. I forgot your birthday. There is no excuse."

Mma Ramotswe raised a hand. There was no need for Mma Makutsi to feel as bad as that—forgetting a birthday was a small thing in the scale of human failings. "Oh, come now, Mma Makutsi," she said. "It was not an important thing. I shall have other birthdays— I hope."

She made a joke of the wish, but Mma Makutsi was too beset by guilt even to smile.

"I hope you have many, many more birthdays," said Mma Makutsi quickly. "And I hope that I forget none of them. That is what I sincerely hope, Mma."

"Let's not talk about it any longer," said Mma Ramotswe. "Yesterday is yesterday, and today is today. That is what I always say, Mma."

Mma Makutsi considered this. "And tomorrow is tomorrow, Mma."

Mma Ramotswe nodded gravely. "That is very true, Mma—very true."

There was then a short silence, eventually ended by Mma Makutsi, who said, "I do not have your present yet, Mma Ramotswe. But the matter is in hand."

"But you need not bother," Mma Ramotswe said quickly. "Really, Mma, you don't need to buy me a present."

But, even as she said this, she found herself wondering what Mma Makutsi was planning to give her. The last birthday present she had given her had been those lace handkerchiefs and that Turkish delight, but the year before it had been a rather odd flower pot, painted in the national colours, blue, black, and white, but of a rather curious shape—and, what was more remarkable, somewhat unstable. Even with earth in it, the pot's centre of gravity was too high, with the result that it toppled over at the slightest provocation, spilling out earth, roots, and the rest of the plant. It had not been a success and had been relegated to the small shed that Mma Ramo-

tswe had at the back of her vegetable garden. There it had quickly
been colonised by small rat-like creatures that had used it to bring
up their sprawling family. A snake had put an end to their unstable dynasty, and the pot had after that remained empty. It had not
been a successful present in any sense, and Mma Ramotswe wondered whether Mma Makutsi was planning a similar gift this year.
Gifts can very quickly become traditional, with people giving one
another the same thing year after year, establishing a form of private
custom—anticipated or dreaded, according to the suitability of the
present.

"I think you will like it," Mma Makutsi now said. "I spoke to
them on the telephone this morning, and they said it had not arrived
yet. They are having to order it, you see. They want to be sure they
get the right one."

Mma Ramotswe nodded. "It is best to get it correct." She wondered what it was.

"And the right colour, too," Mma Makutsi added.

"Oh yes," agreed Mma Ramotswe.

"But I mustn't ruin the surprise," said Mma Makutsi. "It will
come in the next two weeks, they said. Sometimes it takes a bit
longer."

"As long as I am not too old for it when it eventually arrives,"
said Mma Ramotswe.

Mma Makutsi laughed. "Don't worry, Mma. It will come."

Realising there would be no further disclosures, Mma Ramotswe turned to the business of the day. There were a few minor issues
to be resolved first—matters connected with concluded investiga-
tions, issuing of invoices, payment of bills, and the like—and then
she turned to the question of Mma Ikobeng.

"When I went out to see Mma Potokwane yesterday," she began,
"I had a word with one of the housemothers out there—or, rather,

she had a word with me. She's only recently taken on the job—I don't think you've met her. She's one Mma Ikobeng."

Mma Makutsi thought for a moment. "I do not know that name, Mma. I have met people called Obeng, but I do not think they are the same people."

"No, she is Ikobeng."

"But sometimes," Mma Makutsi continued, "you find that people are related if there is just a very small difference in their names. That happens, you know, Mma. Way back—maybe sixty, seventy years ago—somebody makes a mistake in writing down a name, and the mistake sticks. And then you have a different name."

"That is possible, but—"

Mma Makutsi was warming to her theme. "There are people called Makotsi, you know. They use an *o* rather than a *u*. They live up that way—not in Bobonong itself, but not far away. They are a very bad class of person, I'm afraid, Mma. They are cattle thieves, I think, although they deny it. But where did their cattle come from, I ask? Why have their cattle often got torn ears—where the identity tag would be? Why have they lost skin where the brand would have been? Accidents? I don't think so, Mma. Cattle don't come from nowhere."

Mma Ramotswe shook her head. Of all the property crimes in country districts, stock theft was the most widely condemned.

"They say that we are their cousins," Mma Makutsi continued, "and we say that we are not. They say that we have made a spelling mistake. They are very rude."

Mma Ramotswe agreed that these were not the sort of cousins anybody would wish to have. Spelling, she said, could be important in such cases.

"So, I do not think I'll know any of this Mma Ikobeng's people," Mma Makutsi decided, then added, "What did she want, Mma?"

It was at this point that Charlie came into the office. Since he had stopped his full-time mechanical apprenticeship, his time was divided between helping Mr. J.L.B. Matekoni in the garage and working for the No. 1 Ladies' Detective Agency in a capacity that had been left undefined, and was the subject of some doubt, at least in Mma Makutsi's view. Charlie described himself as an assistant detective, but, whenever he did so, was promptly corrected by Mma Makutsi. He was, in her opinion, an apprentice-assistant detective, indeed a junior-apprentice-assistant detective, to which description the word *temporary* might be added.

This lowly status did not prevent Charlie from coming into the office with a certain jauntiness and offering, cheerfully, to lend a hand.

"Need anybody to follow anybody?" he asked. "Need any discreet enquiries made?"

Mma Makutsi looked disapproving. "You should not talk about our work like that, Charlie. It is not a game, you know."

"Oh, I know that," said Charlie. "I know this is very serious work. That is why I am suitable for it."

A thin beam of morning sunlight fell from the window and caught Mma Makutsi's large glasses. They flashed in a burst of silver: a bad sign, thought Mma Ramotswe.

"You have a lot to learn, Charlie," she snapped. "You do not know just how much you have to learn about this profession."

"You teach me, Mma," retorted Charlie. "You're the big expert, after all. Even Mr. Clovis Andersen himself could learn a lot from you, I think."

Mma Ramotswe sighed. She did not like this bickering. It was by no means constant, but it arose from time to time, and she disapproved of it. Mma Makutsi should know better, she thought, than to rise to the challenge of Charlie's remarks. Young men liked to wind people up, and she should realise by now that the best way of dealing with such behaviour was to ignore it. She looked at Charlie: he just wanted to be part of what was going on; he wanted to be appreciated, as most young people did. It must be frustrating for him, she thought, to be put down by Mma Makutsi, who seemed intent on blocking him. We should do everything we can to encourage those at the start of their careers—after all, each one of us was in exactly the same position ourselves not that long ago. Perhaps she should remind Mma Makutsi of the fact that she herself had struggled to assert herself when she had first come to the agency. She had promoted herself from secretary to assistant-detective, or whatever it was she had called herself, and Mma Ramotswe had not stood in her way—nor had she objected to her subsequent self-propelled ascent of the ladder. We all have to begin somewhere.

She made her decision. She would involve Charlie in the Iko-beng enquiries—whatever form they eventually took—because not only would this be a boost for him, but it was also the sort of situation where a male detective might be useful. She further decided that she would appoint Charlie to take charge of the case—something he had not yet been allowed to do. She was not sure if he was entirely ready for that, but he had to make a beginning some time. It was like a pilot's first solo flight, she thought. Mr. J.L.B. Matekoni had mentioned to her recently that one of his customers had been taking flying lessons and had recently been told by his instructor that he was ready to take the plane up himself. He had been apprehensive, but it had all worked out well, and he had landed safely after a ten-minute circling of Kgale Hill. Charlie would have to learn how to handle an enquiry from start to finish if he was to make any progress, and this one, which of course involved no fee, might be just the place to start.

Mma Ramotswe cleared her throat. "I was about to tell Mma Makutsi about something," she began. "I think you should listen to what I have to say, Charlie." She paused. "I think this might be a suitable case for you to take on."

Charlie's eyes widened. "Me, Mma? For me?"

"Under supervision," interjected Mma Makutsi. "I think Mma Ramotswe means that you can be involved under supervision, Charlie."

Mma Ramotswe shook her head. "No, Mma, I think that Charlie might handle this himself. Or he should at least be the main investigator. You and I will be available, of course, to support him. But Charlie can be the one in the driving seat."

Mma Makutsi drew in her breath. "Mma Ramotswe," she said, struggling at the reckless boldness of the suggestion, "I'm the last person to suggest that Charlie is useless. I'd never say that, Mma."

Charlie turned to her. "But you have said it, Mma. Remember ten days ago when we were talking about some business or other and you said that I was useless? Those were your exact words, Mma. You said, 'Charlie is very useless.' You said it. And Mma Ramotswe told you that I was not, and you just answered, 'But he is.' And now you're saying that you never said any of that, although I heard it, Mma. I wasn't dreaming."

Mma Makutsi looked uncomfortable under the accusation. "I was only joking, Charlie. We all sometimes say things about our friends that we don't mean. Can't you tell the difference between something that is meant seriously and something that is just . . ." She waved a hand in the air. "Just a bit of nothing? Can't you?"

Mma Ramotswe gestured for Charlie to sit down. "You sit there, Charlie, and I'll tell you about a conversation I had with a lady called Mma Ikobeng. Then we can all discuss what we can do about it."

She looked at Mma Makutsi, who evidently felt that the matter had been decided and was not worth arguing over. "If that's what you want, Mma Ramotswe."

"And perhaps we can have tea," suggested Mma Ramotswe. "Mma Makutsi, do you think you could get some tea going? It is almost time for the first tea break." She looked at Mma Makutsi. "And remember, Charlie, that Mma Makutsi is only trying to help you. She is a kind lady at heart, you know, and she only wants to help."

It was a technique that Mma Ramotswe had long applied. You did not change people by shouting at them, nor by criticising their behaviour too stringently. You changed people by praising them, and by giving them something to which they might aspire.

And her words had an effect on Charlie, just as much as on Mma Makutsi. "I am sorry, Mma Makutsi. I should not have said that you called me useless. I know you didn't mean it."

"That's all right, Charlie," Mma Makutsi replied. "We all make mistakes."

"And I'm ready to listen," said Charlie. "See: I have my notebook ready. You'll see that I can take notes. Everything can be recorded."

Mma Ramotswe smiled. Charlie's enthusiasm was heartening, even if he had a tendency to be impetuous. But who isn't impetuous at Charlie's age? Who isn't keen to get on with things and show the world what he or she can do?

Mma Makutsi made the tea, and even managed a smile as she passed Charlie his mug. He responded well, thanking her in the proper manner, and telling her that in his opinion there were very few people in Gaborone, and indeed in all Botswana, who could make as good a cup of tea as she could. This was well received, and so it was in an atmosphere of almost tangible concord that Mma Ramotswe began to tell her two colleagues the story that Mma Ikobeng had narrated the previous day.

"so," concluded Mma Ramotswe, "that is what Mma Ikobeng told me."

"And you think we should do something about this?" asked Mma Makutsi.

Mma Ramotswe replied that she did think that.

"But there are always married men who will deceive women," said Mma Makutsi. "Only the other day Phuti was telling me about somebody he knows who was deceiving two ladies at the same time. Actually, three: his wife, and then two ladies with whom he was having an affair."

"At the same time?" asked Charlie. "He was having two affairs at the same time, Mma?"

Mma Makutsi nodded. "He had one lady in Old Naledi and one lady in a house near the golf course. He would go to see these ladies on alternate days. Monday, the Old Naledi lady; Tuesday, the golf course lady; Wednesday, back to the Old Naledi lady . . ."

Charlie whistled. "He must have been a very strong man. Three ladies! He must have eaten a lot of meat to be so strong. Meat for breakfast, lunch, and dinner. He would need it, I think."

Mma Makutsi gave him a disapproving look. "It is not that simple, Charlie. We do not know what went on when he went to see these ladies. They may have just talked together."

Charlie sniggered. "I don't think so, Mma. You don't keep a lady near the golf course just to go and talk to her about this, that, and the next thing. That is not the way things are. I am a man, Mma. I know how men think. And I know that if you go to see a lady near the golf course and you are a married man, then there is only one reason for your visit. Oh yes, I know about these things, I can tell you."

Mma Ramotswe sensed an impending argument. "Let's not waste our time on that man and his affairs," she said. "The point is this: Mma Ikobeng's daughter was deceived by a married man. We all know that there are men like that—many of them, I think—whether or not they have girlfriends who live near the golf course, or whatever. That is not the point. The important thing is that this happened to her daughter, and she thinks there is something fishy going on."

"You mean that there is somebody helping these married men?" asked Mma Makutsi.

"Yes," replied Mma Ramotswe. "She thinks that this is a commercial business. She thinks that there is somebody who has decided that they can make money out of a club like that. You call yourself a singles club, or whatever. You let women think that the club is really for single people, so that it will be a good place for them to go and meet men who might turn into nice husbands."

"While all the time," interjected Charlie, "the men who go there are already husbands—but husbands of other ladies altogether."

"Exactly," said Mma Ramotswe.

"It is a very clever idea," mused Charlie.

Mma Makutsi stared at him. She was not sure whether she had seen a look of envy in his expression. It would not be surprising, she thought: Charlie had always had an eye for the ladies, and although he was now, and fairly recently, married, old habits often lingered, she felt.

"Very wicked," she said, giving Charlie a challenging look. "These poor ladies are being deceived. And then they find out the truth and they must feel very bad about things."

"It is very bad," said Charlie, shaking his head in disapproval.

"You are quite right, Mma," said Mma Ramotswe. "Ladies who find themselves with a married man are usually very disappointed.

They feel tricked—as anyone would in those circumstances. Certainly, Mma Ikobeng's daughter felt like that, apparently."

Mma Makutsi looked thoughtful. "But what does she expect us to do? Why doesn't she go to the police?"

Charlie burst out laughing. "The police? They'll say this is no business of theirs. They cannot stop men from looking for ladies, even if they are married."

Mma Makutsi defended her suggestion. If people were being harmed, did it matter by what means the harm was being caused? She thought it did not. "A broken heart is as bad as the bruise you get when somebody hits you with a stick," she said. "If the police chase after the person with the stick, then why can't they do something about the men who go round breaking hearts like this?"

Mma Ramotswe was careful to give full consideration to what Mma Makutsi said, but decided that it was frankly impractical. "These are things that people have to deal with themselves," she said. "The police cannot look into every part of people's lives, Mma. I just don't think they can."

Mma Makutsi reluctantly conceded that there was probably no point in burdening the police with this information. "But what does she expect us to do? Go and stand outside the door of this club with a sign saying: 'Caution: married men inside?'"

Charlie raised a hand. "I could make that sign," he said. "I have some red paint left over. I could paint that, Mma Makutsi."

Mma Makutsi sighed. "I was only joking, Charlie. I wasn't seriously suggesting that."

"I think that she would like us to find out who is behind this," Mma Ramotswe said. "Then perhaps we can think about what to do about it. You can only do that sort of thing if you have proof."

There followed a silence. Charlie scratched his head; Mma Ramotswe stared at the surface of her desk, as if in the grain of the timber the solution might be found; while Mma Makutsi took off her large round spectacles and polished them.

It was Charlie who spoke first. "I have an idea, Mma Ramotswe," he began. "We go to this place and we observe. Doesn't your Clovis Andersen book say something about that? Doesn't he say something about observation?"

Mma Makutsi replaced her glasses. "He does, Charlie. You're quite right. He says, *Remember the importance of looking: observe, observe, observe.* He says that. Three times. *Observe, observe, observe.*"

"So we go there and observe," said Charlie.

Mma Ramotswe unfolded her hands. "I need more tea," she said. "I cannot deal with a complex case like this without another cup of tea."

"I agree," said Mma Makutsi, rising from her desk. "I shall put the kettle on, and while we wait for it to boil, we can all think hard."

Tea was made, and served. They thought. Then Mma Ramotswe said, "I don't think we can all go to this place. It would look very odd, I feel. There would be all those singles . . ."

"Many of the men will not be singles," Charlie pointed out.

Mma Ramotswe corrected herself: "Well, there will be all those people. And they will be busy talking to each other and dancing and so on, while we are looking around. They will think: Who are these people looking around like that?"

Charlie nodded his agreement. "Mma Ramotswe's right. But it will not be just because we're looking around that they will be suspicious. No, they will spot us the moment we come in—or, they will spot you two ladies straightaway."

Mma Makutsi frowned. "Why should they spot just us? What about you, Charlie? You'll be there with us. What about you?"

He looked smug. "I won't stand out so much, Mma."

Mma Ramotswe saw what he meant. It was a question of age,

she imagined. She and Mma Makutsi would not describe themselves as old, but equally would not be so unrealistic as to describe
themselves as young. She was somewhere in-between, she felt—
somewhere in that vague, forty-ish territory that people could
inhabit for years, for decades even, after their fortieth birthday.
Mma Makutsi was a bit younger, but not by all that many years,
and was, Mma Ramotswe felt, in roughly the same boat as she was.

"I understand," she said to Charlie. "You are much younger and
will merge with the crowd."

Charlie smiled. "It's not just that, Mma," he said. "It's not just
age. It's . . ."

Both Mma Ramotswe and Mma Makutsi waited. Mma Maku-
tsi's glasses flashed in the sunlight from the window on the other side
of the room. Charlie, however, seemed impervious to the warning.

"It's just that the people at a place like that will all be cool, you
see. The people who go to a singles club are definitely cool."

Mma Makutsi exchanged a glance with Mma Ramotswe, and
then trained her gaze on Charlie. "So Mma Ramotswe and I are not
cool, then, Charlie? Is that what you're saying?"

It was a moment of considerable danger, and Mma Ramotswe
sought to defuse it, and largely succeeded in doing so, with some
deft footwork.

"Oh, I am certainly not cool," she said. "I'd never claim that.
Never. I am the opposite. And what is that? What is the opposite
of cool? Hot?"

Charlie gasped. "No, Mma, you mustn't say that. That is not
what I think you mean."

"Well, whatever the right word is, I'm definitely not cool.
Mma Makutsi is a bit more fashionable than I am. I think she might
be a bit cool."

"Well, I don't know," began Mma Makutsi. She was not displeased by the compliment, but Charlie's insinuation still rankled. "I don't think we would look as out of place as Charlie suggests."

Mma Ramotswe felt that it was time to be decisive. "I think that Charlie should go there by himself," she said. "We should stay out of it, Mma Makutsi."

Charlie beamed with pleasure. "I shall do that, Mma. I shall go undercover." He dwelt on the last word: *undercover.* He had been waiting for just such an assignment for a long time. *Undercover!* It was a dream come true.

Mma Makutsi sniffed. "Of course, Rra, you are a married man. I take it that you will remember that."

Charlie looked back at her reproachfully. The days when Mma Makutsi could tell him much were over. He was virtually a junior detective, and was no longer an ordinary apprentice mechanic; he did not have to be reminded of what was what by Mma Makutsi, of all people. "No married man forgets that he is married, Mma."

The retort was intended for Mma Makutsi, but was intercepted by Mma Ramotswe. "Some do, I'm afraid, Charlie," she said gently.

"Yes," said Mma Makutsi grimly. "Some married men are very forgetful—in that particular department."

CHAPTER FIVE

WHAT DRESSES SAY

THE DISCUSSION of the Ikobeng matter, along with asides and excursions, lasted for a good forty minutes, fuelled by a further cup of tea, constructive suggestions, and excited enthusiasm on Charlie's part. Even Mma Makutsi was caught up in Charlie's relish for the job, and she found herself nodding in agreement with him and offering advice as to how to proceed.

"Think carefully, Charlie," she counselled. "Imagine yourself in the shoes of the person you're pretending to be. Then you'll look the part. It's called method acting. Many famous film stars are method actors."

Charlie looked thoughtful. His usual expression when Mma Makutsi addressed him—one of bored bemusement—was replaced by a look of frank interest. "Yes," he said. "That is what I will do. I will think that I am a married man who is fed up with his wife. I will look like this." And with that he affected a deep frown, clenching and unclenching his fists in a display of intense frustration.

The two ladies watched in astonishment. Struggling not to erupt in laughter, Mma Ramotswe said, as gently as she could, "I think it might be best not to do any of this method acting, Charlie. Just be yourself."

Charlie looked to Mma Makutsi for support. "But she said . . ."

"I think Mma Ramotswe is right, Charlie," said Mma Makutsi. "Don't draw attention to yourself. That is something that Clovis Andersen says time and time again. Merge with your surroundings, he says. Don't stand out from the crowd."

Charlie seemed disappointed, but only briefly, as he was distracted by a tactfully reassuring comment from Mma Ramotswe to the effect that those who were so obviously *cool* should have no difficulties in simply being themselves. "Being yourself," she said, "goes a long way if you're cool." And then added, to underline the point, "That is well known, Charlie." That imprimatur should be enough for anyone, and it was for Charlie, who nodded appreciatively and left behind him any regrets at his short-lived career as a method actor.

Once the discussion was over, Mma Ramotswe started to attend to a few administrative tasks that had been hanging over her and that she had been putting off, as one does with those niggling little things that have to be done, though not quite yet. There was a letter from the bank, pointing out a minor mistake on their part; there was a file to be updated before it was consigned to Mma Makutsi, the undisputed doyenne of filing; there was a bill to be itemised before being sent to the client—small matters, and none of them urgent, but all needing to be attended to at some point. But her heart was not in it, as she knew that in a couple of hours she had the appointment that the American woman had arranged with her in the peri-peri restaurant the previous night. This was new work, and new work always seemed more intriguing than the odd, unresolved scraps left by old work. She looked at her watch, sighed, and made her decision. She did not like to put things off unduly, but she could not settle, and she felt that she might as well acknowledge the fact.

"I am going to go over to the supermarket," she announced to Mma Makutsi. "I have to buy potatoes."

It was true: she needed potatoes for the stew she was proposing to make for dinner that night. She had enough time not only to buy potatoes, but also to drop in for a cup of tea and chocolate cake—a rare treat for her—at the small café beside the supermarket. There was always the chance of meeting a friend there, or, if not, simply spending a few minutes watching the procession of passing shoppers.

"If you need potatoes," Mma Makutsi replied, "then you need potatoes. That is what I always say, Mma."

Mma Ramotswe did not recall Mma Makutsi ever saying that, but nodded nonetheless, and prepared to leave. "I shall be back in time for my appointment," she said. "I shall not be late, Mma."

"I have plenty to do," sniffed Mma Makutsi, in the slightly long-suffering voice she used when the situation called for an element of reproach. Potatoes were important, yes—but so were the tedious office chores that needed doing. If everyone went off to buy potatoes on a whim, then would those less glamorous tasks ever be done?

A few minutes later, with her van parked in the car park alongside more modern, more gleaming vehicles, Mma Ramotswe made her way into the supermarket. Her shopping list had expanded, and now included cooking oil, peanut butter, and the chilli flakes that she knew she would need if she were to make peri-peri chicken at home—a decision she had reached as she was driving in to work that morning. She would surprise Mr. J.L.B. Matekoni, perhaps the following day, with the dish. He would be expecting something more mundane—macaroni cheese, perhaps—and she would produce peri-peri chicken instead. Of such little moments of unexpected joy is a contented marriage made.

The supermarket was not busy and it did not take Mma Ramotswe much time to find the items she needed. The chilli flakes took longest, though, and she almost missed the small red and orange container nestling among the curry powder and the mustard grains. Once she had all her items and had spent a few minutes engaged in chat with the woman at the checkout—the daughter of a friend of a friend—she found that she had a good hour and a half in hand before her meeting with Julia. That meant there was plenty of time to order tea and cake at the nearby café before making her way back to the office.

But she was to be sidetracked. Just before the café was a dress shop run by Mma Mogatusi, a woman whom Mma Ramotswe knew slightly—she was a distant cousin of Mr. J.L.B. Matekoni, on his mother's side—and although they did not see much of one another, the sense of family connection, even if it was remote, meant that they would sometimes exchange snippets of news. Now, as Mma Ramotswe headed to the café, it was Mma Mogatusi who rushed out of her shop to intercept her.

"Mma Ramotswe," the shopkeeper began, "I am very pleased. It has arrived at last."

Mma Ramotswe returned the greeting, but was puzzled as to what had arrived. "I am not sure what has arrived, Mma," she said. "But it is certainly a good thing when something you have been waiting for eventually arrives. That is better . . ." She paused, before continuing, rather lamely, "than when it does not arrive."

Mma Mogatusi shook her head. "No, Mma. I am not the one who has been waiting . . . although I have, perhaps, been waiting on behalf of somebody else. This thing, you see, is not for me."

Mma Ramotswe absorbed this in silence. This was one of those conversations that was going nowhere, and when a conversation was going nowhere, or going round in circles, then she felt it was best not to say anything and to wait to see where, if anywhere, once it started to go somewhere, it went—although even as she thought that, it occurred to her that there might be better ways of thinking that particular thought.

"No, Mma," continued Mma Mogatusi, "this thing that I have been waiting for is for you. You are the person for whom it is intended. It is the order that your assistant—that lady from Bobonong . . ."

"Mma Makutsi?"

"Yes, Mma Makutsi. It is the order that she came to place on your behalf."

Mma Ramotswe's puzzlement continued. "But I have not asked Mma Makutsi to order anything," she said, adding, "Not as far as I know."

Now it was Mma Mogatusi who looked confused. "But she said it was for you."

"What was for me, Mma?"

"That dress. The one she looked at for you. That one. We didn't have the right size, and so I ordered it, and now it has arrived. I have been waiting and I almost called the suppliers to tell them that they should hurry the order up, but you know what they're like, Mma Ramotswe. I suspect you know."

Mma Ramotswe shook her head. "I am not sure who these people are," she said. "And I am sure that I never ordered a dress."

"I didn't say you ordered it yourself," protested Mma Mogatusi. "But it is certainly for you, Mma. It is your size, you see, rather than Mma Makutsi's. It is a size eighteen, which is what you must be . . ." She allowed her gaze to run over Mma Ramotswe. ". . . at least, Mma. Mma Makutsi is a twelve—if that. She is less . . . less . . ."

"Less traditionally built?"

Mma Mogatusi clapped her hands together. "Oh, Mma, that is a very good way of putting it. Less traditionally built. Certainly."

Mma Ramotswe looked thoughtful. "Is this dress red, by any chance, Mma?"

Mma Mogatusi replied that it was. There had been some debate about the choice of colour, she recalled, and Mma Makutsi had said something about Mma Ramotswe having a preference for red. "There are many ladies who choose red," said Mma Mogatusi. "It is a colour that sends a message of confidence, I think. Red is like a traffic light—which is red too. Red says: 'stop and look.' That's what it says."

It was now clear to Mma Ramotswe what had happened. This dress—this red dress—was the present to which Mma Makutsi had referred. So Mma Makutsi had bought her a dress, which was kind of her, although there were surely risks in buying a dress for somebody else, even for a close friend. Clothing was a very particular matter, and you could never be absolutely sure that a gift of clothing would be to the recipient's taste.

Mma Ramotswe sighed. The situation was complicated—and perilous. If she did not like the dress that Mma Makutsi had chosen, she would hardly be able to tell her that. Mma Makutsi was sensitive, and this was exactly the sort of situation in which she might take offence. And if she did not like the dress, Mma Ramotswe would still be expected to wear it from time to time, or risk being thought ungrateful.

It seemed to Mma Ramotswe that there was no easy way out and that she would at least need to see the dress before she reached any decision as to what to do. She smiled at Mma Mogatusi. "I think I should try this dress on," she said. "Then we shall know whether we need to let it out or take it in."

Mma Mogatusi agreed. "I think it is more likely that it will need to be let out," she said, and then, almost immediately, apologised. "I'm sorry, Mma—I did not mean to suggest that you are always letting your clothes out. I am sure that doesn't happen very often. Things shrink, of course . . ."

Mma Ramotswe assured her that offence had not been taken.

"We all grow outwards a bit, Mma. It is to do with gravity, I think. Gravity is always pulling us downwards, and that means that we expand in an outwards direction. It is not something we can do much about."

She accompanied Mma Mogatusi into her shop, where an assistant, a young woman wearing bright red lipstick—far too bright, thought Mma Ramotswe—produced a dress on a hanger.

"This is the outfit," said Mma Mogatusi. "It is very fine quality, as you will see, Mma Ramotswe. One hundred per cent cotton, and twenty per cent polyester. That is a very good mix, you know. It is washable, which means you don't have to go to the dry cleaners all the time. That is a big selling point with this range of dresses."

"That is one hundred and twenty per cent," observed Mma Ramotswe, feeling the fabric between her fingers. "That is a very high specification."

"Yes," said Mma Mogatusi. "Once you're over the one hundred per cent mark, then you're into very high quality."

Mma Ramotswe smiled. She was more than a little surprised; Mma Mogatusi was the owner of a business. She presumably had to place orders and pay invoices. She should be familiar, surely, with how percentages worked, and yet here she was making a basic error. Of course, people talked loosely about these matters, she reminded herself; they talked about being two hundred per cent committed to a cause, about being one hundred and fifty per cent behind people, and so on. These were just casual expressions that were not meant to be taken too literally.

She stood back to survey the dress as the assistant, looking slightly bored, held it up on its hanger.

"It's very fashionable," said Mma Mogatusi. "There are many dresses in that style these days. If you go to any of the big cities—Nairobi, Johannesburg, and so on—what are the ladies wearing? I'll let you in on a secret, Mma: they are wearing versions of that dress. That is all you'll see these days. That dress."

Once again, Mma Ramotswe smiled. She was not one to correct people in the way they talked, but, having made a bad mistake with percentages, Mma Mogatusi was now compounding error with contradiction: If people were wearing this style of dress openly in the big cities to which she referred, then how could this fact be a secret? Quite the opposite, she thought: it would be something that was well known. But she resisted any temptation to point this out, remembering Mr. J.L.B. Matekoni's advice that you should not tell people that they are wrong, except where absolutely necessary, lest you hurt their feelings unnecessarily. "People have the most peculiar ideas about engines," he had once remarked to her. "They have no idea what an alternator is, for instance—just to give you one example, Mma. Can you believe that? Not knowing what an alternator is?"

She could, because she herself was completely unaware of what alternators did. She assumed that there was one in her van, but she did not know where it was, and what it did.

"Alternators?" she said, trying to sound surprised at the ignorance of others. But then she relented, and confessed. "Actually, Mr. J.L.B. Matekoni, I myself may be one of those people. In fact, I *am* one of them. I have never heard of this thing that you mention."

He had looked surprised, and then laughed. "But Mma, without an alternator, you would go nowhere—nowhere at all." He paused. "I should not laugh at you. There are many things you know about that I do not know. You know more about cattle, for example. Yes, that is one area in which you know much more."

She accepted the compliment graciously. "That is only because of my late daddy," she said. "He knew everything about cattle— everything."

"He did," said Mr. J.L.B. Matekoni. "It was a great gift. They still talk about him up there in Mochudi, don't they? If there is any problem with cattle, somebody will say, 'It is a pity that Obed Ramotswe isn't here any longer—he knew all about this. He would tell us.'"

Mma Ramotswe looked away. She was touched by this tribute to her father, which she knew was true. He had known everything there was to know about cattle. But more than that, he had felt for cattle in a way that was unusual, even in a country where cattle were so important. When she was a young girl, she had even believed that her father could talk the language that cattle understood. And that, she imagined, must be a version of Setswana, because cattle would never master English, with all its strange rules. She had asked him about that, and he had smiled, and explained to her that cattle talked with their eyes, and with the way they moved their heads, and that after you had spent a long time with them you suddenly realised that you understood what they were wanting to tell you.

But now she stopped thinking about her father and cattle—and alternators, although it was difficult to think about alternators when you did not know what they looked like or what they did. She thought, instead, of the dress that Mma Mogatusi's assistant was showing her, and she was wondering how she could possibly get out of the difficulties that she saw looming ahead of her. This was no little cloud in an otherwise bland sky: this was a towering thundercloud, engorged and purple, ready to bring with it peals of thunder and bolts of lightning. She had made up her mind. She did not like the dress.

"It is very bright," she said.

Mma Mogatusi nodded; she was not deterred by the detectable note of caution in Mma Ramotswe's voice. "This sort of dress is definitely very bright, Mma. This is what we call a statement dress.

This dress is saying, 'The lady wearing this dress is going places.' That is what this dress says, Mma."

Mma Ramotswe thought: but I don't want to go places. I am happy where I am—right here in this town, where I have my house and my family and the work that I do. Why go anywhere if you are happy where you are? Nobody needs the whole world. Nobody needs more and more of everything, or a bigger and better job— nobody needs to always be going places. What was wrong with clothes that said, "This person is going nowhere—she is staying where she is?" That, perhaps, is what the clothes currently in her wardrobe would say if she were ever to ask them. They would say, "We are clothes of a person who is happy to stay where she is. We are non-competitive clothes."

Mma Mogatusi turned to the assistant, who was still holding the dress up on its hanger and who was still looking bored. "You like this dress, don't you, Mma?"

The assistant, who had clearly been thinking of other things, nodded vaguely. "Big time," she said. "I like this dress a lot."

"And do you think it's Mma Ramotswe's colour?" asked Mma Mogatusi. "I think so, I must say."

The assistant transferred her gaze to Mma Ramotswe. "The colour's all right," she said. "But it's too small."

Mma Mogatusi looked concerned. "It's size eighteen. Show me the label."

The assistant shrugged as she looked for the label at the back of the neck. She read it lazily. "Size eighteen. Yes. Eighteen. But this lady, Mma, is not size eighteen. She's a twenty, at least."

Mma Ramotswe stared at the assistant. This was typical of what was happening, she thought. People were losing their manners, or, more probably, they had never been taught any. She pursed her lips. There was no point allowing yourself to become annoyed at the way the world was going, because that did not help. If you became annoyed, then you would end up seeming ill-mannered yourself. Tolerance and patience—and the occasional sigh—were the responses that best suited this sort of decline.

"Perhaps I should try it on," Mma Ramotswe suggested. "If you think that something may not fit, then you should try it on, don't you think?"

Mma Mogatusi was quick to agree. With a glance of disapproval at her assistant, she took the dress and handed it over to Mma Ramotswe. "That is our fitting room over there," she said. "Behind that curtain. You can take your time, Mma."

Mma Ramotswe crossed the shop floor and entered the tiny fitting room. There was a chair on which she placed the dress she took off, and she thought, as she put it down, that it looked washed out. It was not an old dress, but it had seen considerable use, and its colours had begun to fade. That was the sun, she thought; the sun faded clothes, draining them of their colour even as it dried them on the washing line. Would that happen with this new dress, and its vivid red? Would the statement that the dress made be changed as the sun toned it down?

She began to slip the new dress over her head. With her head covered by the material, the world was suddenly red. And there came to her that lovely smell of new cloth, so unmistakeable, so redolent of a moment of freshness; if only that lingered, but it never did, never survived its first experience in the washing machine. She tugged at the cloth, attempting to ease it down over her figure, as one might try to envelop a teapot in a cosy that was just too tight. It moved—but only reluctantly, it seemed, and she had to pull harder. Perhaps the bored assistant was right; perhaps it was too small. But then, even the clothes she wore every day seemed at times to be a bit too small for her, and so she persisted. Material gave, once you encouraged it—it stopped being so uncooperative once you let out your breath, which is what she now did, and the dress responded on cue, sliding down over her hips until it fitted snugly round her shoulders and her middle. Possibly too snugly, for now she breathed in, and she felt the material press in on her once more.

She caught her breath, and exhaled, which provided temporary relief. But she could hardly hold her breath indefinitely, and this time, when she drew air into her lungs, she felt something at the side give way. She heard, accompanying this, an unmistakeable ripping sound, and for a moment her heart stopped.

"Is everything all right in there?" called out Mma Mogatusi, from the other side of the flimsy curtain.

Mma Ramotswe turned so that she could examine the damage in the full-length mirror on the wall behind her. There it was— a long split in the side of the dress, a jagged wound in the cloth, where a seam had given way. More than that, the material had torn in such a way that it would take more than a stitching of the seam for the dress to be repaired.

She did not take the dress off, but drew back the curtain and showed the damage to Mma Mogatusi. "I'm afraid the dress was too tight. It gave way almost immediately. I didn't even move, Mma."

From the other side of the room, they heard the assistant mutter, "Who said that would happen? I did. I told you, Mma Mogatusi."

Mma Mogatusi shot a look of irritation in the direction of her assistant and then turned back to Mma Ramotswe. "It will be easily fixed," she said. "It looks very good on you, Mma."

Mma Ramotswe shook her head. "I think it's too small, Mma. And anyway, the material has torn. It's not just a seam that's come away. Look at this."

She pointed to the place where the rip had occurred, and Mma Mogatusi let out a small wail. "Oh, this is very bad, Mma. That is going to be hard to fix."

"I don't think it can be fixed at all, Mma," said Mma Ramotswe.

A silence ensued. Then Mma Ramotswe said, "I am very sorry this has happened, Mma. I think I should get back into my ordinary clothes." She paused. "But what are we going to do about . . ." She gestured to the red dress. "What are we going to do about this dress?"

Mma Mogatusi looked glum. "The people I ordered it from are very difficult, Mma. They have a no-returns policy. They refuse point blank. They say that once a dress leaves their premises, that's it. They demand payment in advance too."

"Ow!" said Mma Ramotswe. "That is no way to run a business."

Mma Mogatusi sighed. "I suppose I can see why they do this. There are special problems in the clothing business. There are some people who order a dress because they have to go to a wedding or a special party. They wear it to the occasion, and then they bring it back the next day and say that it doesn't fit. They ask for their money back."

"You should refuse," said Mma Ramotswe.

"It's not that simple, Mma. I have to allow customers to return things if they don't fit, and most people don't abuse that system. It is only a few people who take advantage of us." She paused. "I can think of one bad case, Mma. There is a certain lady who bought a dress from me because she was going to a big wedding down in Lobatse. It was a very expensive dress, and it fitted her perfectly. But she still brought it back and said that she had decided not to wear it after all. She said I should take it back because it was completely unworn. But it wasn't, Mma. It had been worn. You can always tell."

Mma Ramotswe waited.

"There was a food stain on the front of the dress," said Mma Mogatusi. "When she gave it back to me, she had folded it so that the stain could not be seen. But when I put it on the hanger, it was obvious. It was a very dishonest thing for anybody to do, Mma. Really dishonest."

For a moment Mma Ramotswe was silent. She was thinking. There was one person she could imagine doing this, and now, as she nodded her agreement with Mma Mogatusi's verdict on such behaviour, she uttered the name. It came as a question, but she felt that she already knew the answer. "Violet Sephotho?"

Mma Mogatusi had clearly not expected this. Her eyes widened as she struggled to respond. "Possibly, Mma . . . perhaps even probably. In fact, more or less definitely . . . But how did you know that, Mma?"

Mma Ramotswe smiled. "Don't worry, Mma Mogatusi. I know that you wouldn't normally gossip about your customers—even a customer like that one."

Mma Mogatusi nodded appreciatively. "This is a delicate business," she said. "Buying clothes is a private matter and there are many ladies who do not want the whole world to know about their purchases. There are many ladies, in fact, who do not want their husbands to find out what they have been spending in shops like mine."

Mma Ramotswe agreed that there were some men who did not understand these matters. Some did, though, and Mr. J.L.B. Matekoni was one of them. He encouraged her to spend money on herself, which was such an endearing trait in a man, even if he spent next to nothing on his own needs. He needed new shoes, for example, but he would never go out and buy them for himself—she would have to do that. And as for his trousers—they were well past the normal lifespan of trousers, but he steadfastly refused to treat himself to a new pair.

"I won't mention it to anybody," she assured Mma Mogatusi.

And then, cautiously, she went on, "What are we going to do about this dress, Mma?"

Mma Mogatusi hesitated for a few moments before answering. "I don't think we can do anything," she said at last. "Mma Makutsi will not be pleased. Nobody likes to pay for something that has been damaged."

Mma Ramotswe grimaced. "You don't mean that she . . ." She did not finish. It was out of the question that Mma Makutsi should have to pay for this dress that she, Mma Ramotswe, had ruined. And yet the damage was in no way the fault of Mma Mogatusi, although Mma Ramotswe reminded herself that her assistant had warned her that the dress was too small. Perhaps they were both to blame—Mma Mogatusi for allowing her to try on a dress that she should have realised was too small, and Mma Ramotswe herself for persisting with the fitting even after she experienced difficulties in getting the dress over her head and shoulders. Many disasters were like that: they came about as a result of fault on the part of more than one person. And in such cases, she imagined, the fairest solution was for the cost to be shared between those responsible.

"I don't think I should shoulder the cost," muttered Mma Mogatusi. "I didn't do anything wrong here, Mma."

"No," said Mma Ramotswe, "you didn't, Mma. But then, it's not Mma Makutsi's fault."

From across the room, the assistant intervened. "She ordered the size eighteen, remember. That lady with the big glasses—she ordered that size. That is her fault. If you're ordering a dress for a very large friend, then you know what size that friend is."

Mma Mogatusi shot her a discouraging glance, but the assistant had more to say.

"I have a friend who is very big," she continued. "Not quite as big as this lady here, of course, but she said to me the other day that she was a size fourteen. I said that she wasn't. I told her. I said, 'You're at least a sixteen, maybe more. Eighteen even, for comfort.' That's what I said. And you know what? She went out and bought herself a size fourteen and she put it on and she couldn't sit down—it was that tight. She went to a bar with her boyfriend and she pretended that she wanted to stand the whole night. And when he asked her to dance, she couldn't move properly, because the dress was too tight. She was like one of those sausages you see in the supermarket. You know the sort—with very tight skins, and when you put them in the frying pan, the skins burst—"

"Thank you, Mma," said Mma Mogatusi.

"Perhaps I should pay, Mma," said Mma Ramotswe. "That might be the best solution."

Mma Mogatusi greeted this with silence.

"I really don't mind," Mma Ramotswe went on. She looked at the price tag, still attached to the dress. "It is not too expensive." It was not; but neither was it cheap.

"I cannot allow you to pay," said Mma Mogatusi. "I cannot allow that." She paused. "And when Mma Makutsi comes in to collect it, Mma," asked Mma Mogatusi, "what then?"

Mma Ramotswe was at a loss. "I suppose . . ." But she had no idea what to say.

"I cannot lie to her, Mma," said Mma Mogatusi. "I cannot mislead her."

"Of course not," said Mma Ramotswe hurriedly.

"Oh dear," sighed Mma Mogatusi.

Mma Ramotswe looked at her watch. She had to get back to the office to meet Julia, who was due to arrive in twenty minutes. The dress, and the problem of what to do about it, would have to wait: not every problem could be solved immediately, and decisively—some had to be left, to be mulled over, to be considered from every angle before a solution suggested itself, or did not, depending. So she said goodbye to Mma Mogatusi, who also seemed keen to shelve the problem for a while.

As Mma Ramotswe left the shop, she heard the assistant muttering, "Big problem, Mma; big problem."

She hesitated. There were many problems in this life, and not a few of them were far bigger than the one they were now facing. It was important, she thought, to keep a sense of perspective, and not to imagine that minor problems were larger than they really were. She thought she might point this out to the assistant—gently, of course—but she decided against it. Instead, she simply smiled, said goodbye, and stepped out of the shop into the sun. She looked up at the sky; it had witnessed so much: a torn dress and a social dilemma as to what to say to Mma Makutsi were nothing by comparison with what it had seen. That thought made her feel much better, and she set off on her journey back to the office in a cheerful mood, ready to hear what this new client, this woman from America, had to ask of her.

As she drove back, she reflected on what had happened in the dress shop. I am definitely still size eighteen, she thought. Definitely.

CHAPTER SIX

TEN THOUSAND MEN OF AFRICA

WELL, MMA RAMOTSWE," said Julia, looking around the premises of the No. 1 Ladies' Detective Agency, "this is a very fine office. It looks so . . ." She searched for the right word, and alighted on *organised.* "It looks so organised. I have a study at home that is always full of papers and things that I should put away, but never do."

"I can take no credit for that," said Mma Ramotswe, gesturing towards Mma Makutsi, who was sitting at her desk, smiling at their new client. And, of course, the compliment widened the smile, and brought a positive flashing of light from the large glasses.

"Mma Makutsi, you see," Mma Ramotswe went on, "is the No. 1 filing champion of Botswana."

Mma Makutsi made a self-deprecating gesture. She would not argue, though, with that particular plaudit, which she believed, with all due modesty, was quite true. After all, you would never—*never*—get ninety-seven per cent in the final examinations of the Botswana Secretarial College without being completely on top of any filing task the examiners might choose to quiz you on. In her case, the filing questions had been particularly challenging, involving issues of classification of partly paid invoices—whether these should be placed under *unpaid* or under *pending matters*—and questions of cross-entries in matters concerning more than one party. These were fine points, and in order to get full marks, a candidate had to explain why a particular option was chosen. Luck or habit alone would not do: there had to be an understanding of the rationale behind a filing system.

The American woman turned to Mma Makutsi. "It's a great skill, Mma. I just stuff things into drawers."

Mma Makutsi shook her head. "Oh, Mma, that will never do. Perhaps I can give you some lessons. A good filing system can change your life. There are many cases in which that has happened."

"I would love that," said Julia. "Maybe one day I can have a lesson."

"Right now?" said Mma Makutsi quickly.

Mma Ramotswe intervened. "I think that Mma Julia wants to talk about other matters first," she said. "Perhaps there can be a filing lesson some other day."

"That would be very kind," said Julia. "I shall be here for some time, I hope. Perhaps next week—if that suits you, Mma Makutsi."

Mma Makutsi nodded. "I am always here, Mma."

"In the meantime," said Mma Ramotswe, "it might be a good idea to have some tea."

Mma Makutsi sprang from her chair to switch on the kettle.

"Tea *and* filing," said Mma Ramotswe. "Mma Makutsi is in charge of more than one department, you see." And then she added quickly, "As well as carrying a full load of investigative duties."

"That is so," said Mma Makutsi. "I am a co-director here, actually."

Strictly speaking, that was not true. The No. 1 Ladies' Detective Agency was not an incorporated company—as Mma Ramotswe had explained to Mma Makutsi on more than one occasion—and there were therefore no directors. Mma Ramotswe thought that Mma Makutsi should know that, as she claimed to have studied business organisation at that college of hers, and surely a basic part of any business organisation curriculum would explain the differences between the various forms of trading bodies. But these things did not matter much, thought Mma Ramotswe; if Mma Makutsi wanted to see herself as a director, then she had no objection. It did not matter what you called yourself, after all; what mattered is what you were *inside,* and Mma Makutsi's heart was in the right place—there had never been any doubt about that.

Once Mma Makutsi had made tea, Mma Ramotswe invited Julia to tell them what it was that she wanted to talk about. "We are happy to help you, Mma. You told me in the restaurant that you were looking for somebody."

Mma Makutsi cleared her throat. "We have found many people over the years, Mma. If there are any needles in the haystack, then we will find them."

Mma Ramotswe thought that claim was perhaps a bit exaggerated, and so she qualified it with a simple, "If we can, Mma. We do not always succeed—"

"But we will look under every stone," interjected Mma Makutsi.

"In a manner of speaking," said Mma Ramotswe.

"I am sure you will be very helpful," said Julia. "But should I tell you about why I am here?"

Mma Makutsi reached for a piece of paper. She had learned shorthand, and liked to keep it up. She would make notes. "Could I have your family name?" she asked. "For filing, you see."

"Of course. Hadden. That is my married name. That is the name I still use, although, as I think I told you, my husband and I are no longer together."

Mma Makutsi made a note on the piece of paper. Then she said, "Are you divorced, now, Mma?"

Julia looked down at the floor, and Mma Ramotswe recognised her regret.

"Yes. We are divorced. I never wanted that to happen. In many partings, you know, there is one person who doesn't want to say goodbye . . ."

Mma Ramotswe inclined her head. "I am so sorry, my sister. I am so sorry." She reminded herself of Note Mokoti, and of the sorrow he had brought into her own life; but she quickly banished these thoughts. She had forgiven Note, and an important part of forgiveness was allowing the past to fade, like an old photograph exposed to the sun.

Julia looked up, surprised, perhaps, at being addressed as "my sister." But it was not the first time that she had been spoken to in this way since she'd arrived in Botswana, and it moved her. She looked down again.

"Thank you, Mma. I'll tell you about it—about everything."

"We are listening, Mma," said Mma Ramotswe.

"I'm an American," said Julia, "as I think I told you, Mma Ramotswe. I'm from Vermont, in the north-east. That's where I was born, and where I spent most of my life. I like it because, well, because it's my place. We all have somewhere that we think of as our place—and that place stays with you, I think, all the way through your life. I'm lucky, because the place I have is a beautiful one, and I like the people. I wouldn't like to live in a big city, I'm afraid. I know that some people like it, but I find it too noisy, and I think I'd always long to see hills when I looked out of my window, or forests. And I'd like to recognise at least some of the people I met when I went out in the street.

"My father was from Antigua, which is why, as you can see, I have a bit of Africa in me. He came to work in the US and that's where he met my mother. She was half French, half German, and so you see our background is a bit complicated. Sometimes I think of myself as being half American, half history—as many people are, don't you think? We all have history in our veins.

"The easiest way of telling you the story, though, is to start with my grandmother. That's where this all began. No, perhaps it didn't. Perhaps I should start even earlier, and start right here, Mma Ramotswe—and Mma Makutsi, of course. Right here in Botswana, a long time ago, in 1941, when you were called something different, weren't you? You were the Bechuanaland Protectorate, of course, and you had a commissioner who ran things from Mafeking, with your chiefs, of course. And although I imagine most of you would have wanted just to be left alone, at least the British stopped South Africa from swallowing you up, which some over there would have been only too happy to do. Or so I've read.

"In 1941, the British were running out of men and they wanted to get people from their colonies to help them fight a war in which they weren't coping very well. So they looked over here and they encouraged the chiefs to recruit men from their people to send over to the war. Some of the chiefs were particularly keen to do this. They wanted to make sure that the British would remember their loyalty and would not let the South Africans take the land. It was partly for this reason that they cajoled their men into agreeing to join the war effort. Many men were unwilling to go—and who can blame them? This was not their war, and they did not like the idea of being sent off to die for somebody else, even if they were offered a few cents a day to do so. Many ran away, buying railway tickets to travel over the border into South Africa, where they could get jobs in the mines. The mines were only too happy to have them, because you know how hard and dangerous that work was, and how they said that the mines ate men. That was better, though, than going a long way away to be shot at by Germans and Italians. Men may be prepared to die to protect their wives and children, and their land, too, but they are not so ready to die to protect other people's wives and children, and a land they have never seen. Who can blame them for that? I can't.

"In spite of people not wanting to go, this country sent ten thousand men. That was a big number, Mma Ramotswe, bearing in mind how small the population was in those days. How many adult males were there then? Fifty thousand—that's all. So that meant that one in five men joined up, which is a lot.

"One of these was a man called Khumo. He was eighteen when the call came, and he was signed up none too willingly. His father, who was a relative of a chief, made him go because it would not look good for him if his own son ignored the chief's appeal. He was sent, along with a whole lot of other men, down to Durban, on the Indian Ocean, where they were given some basic training.

"Can you imagine how it felt? Here was this eighteen-year-old, who had lived with his parents until then, being absorbed into an alien military world, taught how to fire a rifle and to respond to commands shouted at him by intimidating superiors. He had never seen the sea, and now he and his companions were herded into ships and taken to the battlefields of North Africa, with all that dust and tanks and screaming aeroplanes. He and his fellow Batswana were put into what they called the African Pioneer Corps. They were not intended to be used as fighting troops, except in emergencies; they were destined to be the labourers, the diggers of fortifications, the mixers of concrete, the loaders and unloaders of army cargo. It was the least glamorous of military tasks, and they were expected to perform them under the fierce heat of the Egyptian sun.

"Khumo was moved from place to place, as happened in wartime. He was briefly in Palestine, and then back in Egypt. Then, in 1943, he and a number of other African Pioneer Corps men were sailing from Alexandria on a troop carrier called the *Erimpura*. This was attacked by a German warplane and sunk, with the loss of many hundreds of men. He managed to escape the wreckage, and he was picked up by a naval vessel that took them back to Alexandria. From there he was eventually taken to Italy, where he served, travelling painful mile after painful mile up the length of the peninsula, until the Germans were defeated there. He thought he was going to be sent home immediately, but that did not happen, and he decided to desert. He had had enough, and he thought he would never see home again. So he left his unit, which was then in the far north, and walked over the border into France. He managed to board a train, hiding in a luggage van, and eventually ended up in Normandy, in a small market town. He had no idea where he was and how the war was progressing—if it was still going on at all.

"He found his way to a farm, where he was taken in by the farmer, who needed somebody to help him with the dairy herd. He knew Khumo was a deserter, but he protected him, giving him food and clothing. The farmer had a daughter, who was barely twenty. She had become involved with a German soldier and had borne his child. With the Liberation, women who had taken up with Germans were vilified. They had their hair cut off and were paraded in the streets as traitors. This woman was called Francine, and she was my grandmother. The baby was called Thérèse, and she was my mother.

"Khumo and my grandmother became friends. She taught him French, and he started to teach her English, which he could speak quite well, as he had spent several years in a missionary school at home. I think that they wanted to get married, but could not do so because of attitudes at the time. And Francine's mother was opposed to the idea. She wanted to send her daughter and grand-daughter away, to a place where the disgrace of having given birth to a German soldier's child would not hang above her. She had a cousin in Quebec, and somehow they managed to get my grand-mother and my mother berths on a passenger ship to Canada. That was in 1946. They thought that Khumo would stay in France, or somehow get back to Africa, but the following year he succeeded in working his passage on a cargo vessel sailing to Nova Scotia. From there, he made his way to the town in Quebec where my grand-mother was now living with her female cousin.

"They never married, but she and Khumo were devoted to one another. To my mother, as she grew up there in Quebec, he was her step-father. They were all living on a farm, and Khumo was the only man. He did everything and effectively kept the farm from going bankrupt. They loved him.

"In 1969 my mother went to live in Vermont, where she had been offered a job as a nurse. It was there that she met my father, who, as I said, was from Antigua. He was good to her, and they married. I was born in 1975.

"Because Quebec and Vermont are not far away from one another, I was often taken up there in school holidays. I knew Khumo for the first seven years of my life. I thought of him as my grandfather. I remember him singing to me. I remember his kindness. I remember his smile and his gentleness. I remember how bereft I felt when he died.

"I went to school in Vermont and took a job as a book-keeper. When I was twenty-five, I met a man called Tony, who had an engineering equipment rental business. He was lively and good-looking. I did not have to think about it for long once he asked me to marry him. I was in love with him. I loved him so much, Mma, that it hurt. You can do that, you know—you can love somebody so much that your heart aches. It really does.

"Unfortunately, I could not have children, Mma Ramotswe, and although I came to terms with that, Tony did not. Six years ago, Tony left me for a woman who worked in his office. She already had two children, and so I suppose there was no doubt as to her ability to have a family. My world seemed to end like that. One day, I was happy—I had a husband and a future. The next, I had nothing. Just emptiness.

"I tried my best to get over the sorrow I felt. I put more time into the job I had; I signed up for courses; I volunteered to help in a literacy programme. All of this was to fill the time, because I knew that if I was not doing something, I would be thinking of Tony and of what I had lost. Most painful of all was the thought that he was with another woman. At breakfast, I thought: he will be sitting at the breakfast table with *her;* if I went shopping, I thought: he will be out shopping with *her;* if I saw a man playing with children, I thought: he will be playing with the child *she* has given him.

"It became less painful after a couple of years had passed. I am not saying that it went away—the sorrow, that is: it is still there, I think, but it is buried a bit more deeply. I started to think more about my family, about who they were, and about the past. I still have cousins up in Quebec, and there are some very distant cousins in France whom I don't really know. I tried to find out a bit more about my father's side, the Antigua people, and I went there once. There were some relatives there who were polite enough, but not really interested in me, and we lost touch after I came home. That left Khumo. I thought a lot about him, and I realised how important he had been to my grandmother and my mother. I had heard about his past from them, but now I found that I wanted to know more about this kind and gentle man whose personal story had been such an extraordinary one. In particular, I wanted to find out more about where he had come from and to see whether I might find some members of his family here in Botswana. I wanted to touch that part of my history—if you see what I mean. I wanted to close a book that I think had never been closed. Does that sound strange to you? Does it seem odd that somebody should want to connect in that way with a particular world, even after so many years have passed? I suppose you might even say that I wanted to say thank you to him. You never think of saying thank you as a child, and then much later, of course, it may be too late.

"That is why I am here, Mma Ramotswe. I want to find some of Khumo's people. I want to be able to tell them about him. I want to tell the story of a man who was just one among many, many who were never made much of in spite of what they did. I don't think those people should be forgotten, Mma Ramotswe—I really don't.

"But I don't know where to start. I have only a vague idea where he came from—that is all I know. There is a place called Mochudi, I believe. That is the place he spoke about from time to time: Mochudi. I believe it's not far from where we are now. Do you know it, Mma Ramotswe?"

She stopped and looked enquiringly at Mma Ramotswe, who blinked, almost unable to believe what she had heard.

"That is my place, Mma," Mma Ramotswe whispered.

"Oh."

Mma Makutsi dropped her pencil, which fell off the side of her desk onto the floor below. "Oh, goodness," she said.

CHAPTER SEVEN

AT THE COOL SINGLES EVENING CLUB

CHARLIE TOOK SOME CARE in preparing himself for his assignment. He had not been married for long, but his wife had already succeeded in sorting out some of his clothing, passing on to the church clothing bank several shirts that she deemed unsuitable for a married man, and throwing out altogether several oil-stained overalls that were beyond rescue. Men, she observed, keep their clothes far too long, and, in a world of limited storage space, you should not be too sentimental about older garments. But several smart outfits remained—including the one he now donned. This consisted of a tightly cut sports coat, the label of which pronounced it part of the *Mr. Special Collection*. Charlie was inordinately proud of this jacket, which he wore only to weddings and funerals, but which was now taken out of its zip-up bag and brushed down, ready for use. This was complemented by a pair of jeans, pristine in the stiffness of their blue denim, and a plain red shirt. The shoes were two-tone and made of black and white patent leather, scuffed here and there—Botswana could be hard on shoes—but entirely suitable, Charlie thought, for an evening that might include, if not dancing, at least a certain amount of toe-tapping.

He explained to his wife that he was dressing for an assignment, and that he needed to look his best. She said that she understood, but further explanation was required when he slipped his wedding ring off his finger. That was an awkward moment, but it passed once he had told her about the Cool Singles Evening Club. "I am glad you are doing something about people like that," she said. "You are a very brave man, Charlie."

Charlie had no car, but was allowed by Mma Ramotswe to borrow her tiny white van for work purposes, and the van was now parked outside, ready to be driven to the hotel just off the Lobatse Road where the Cool Singles Evening Club was hosted every weekend. Taking one last look in the mirror, Charlie closed his front door behind him and walked out to Mma Ramotswe's van. He was pleased with his appearance and was looking forward to what seemed to him to be an ideal investigation. He was grateful to Mma Ramotswe for entrusting this case to him, and for offering him, too, a special out-of-hours payment. This was particularly kind of her, he reminded himself, as he knew that this was not an enquiry for which she would get a fee. Mma Ramotswe, although one of the most talented investigators in the country—and possibly the only one, but that was not the point—was nevertheless not the strictest of businesswomen. As Mr. J.L.B. Matekoni once succinctly put it, the problem was *heart*. Mma Ramotswe had too large a heart to be successful in business. Being generous and warm-hearted did not always sit well with being firm in the charging and collection of fees; on far too many occasions, she acted *pro bono,* taking on clients who would have been happy to pay a fee, but who might not have the money to do so. As a result of this, word had got round that there was always a sympathetic ear at the No. 1 Ladies' Detective

Agency and that any justice the agency might be able to bring to its clients was always affordable, whatever the circumstances of the supplicant.

Charlie slipped into the van. It was a pity that it was only a tiny white van and not a more suitable vehicle for one dressed as he was—a two-tone convertible, for instance, with twin exhausts and a throaty roar, or even something more modest than that, but still not a van: a red Volkswagen, for instance, would have been perfectly adequate. But no matter: the important thing was that here he was, a private investigator, smartly dressed, setting off to an assignment in a nightclub. This was a long way away from the earlier days of his apprenticeship, he reflected, when, wearing his oil-stained khaki overalls, he would lie for hours under vehicles, draining sumps and checking suspension. Things were definitely improving, he told himself. And if this enquiry went well, he might even raise with Mma Ramotswe the possibility of his being taken on full-time as a fully fledged private detective. He had acquired a fair amount of experience now, and he had read Clovis Andersen's *The Principles of Private Detection* sufficiently closely to remember much, if not all, of the advice that the great American authority had to impart. The profession required no examinations, he believed, and presumably a certificate composed and signed by Mma Ramotswe would suffice as evidence of fully fledged status.

The evening traffic was light, and it did not take Charlie long to negotiate the route to the hotel. This was a long two-storey building, more of a motel in its appearance, but with an extension at the end housing a bar and a dance area. This was the location of the Cool Singles Evening Club, and the club was announced not only by a poster attached to the door but by the sound of throbbing music emanating from the open windows to either side of the entrance.

There were several vacant parking spaces near the front door, but Charlie refrained from choosing one of these as he did not want to be seen emerging from the van. He noticed that the cars around the door were shiny and expensive, one of them being fashionably but impractically low-slung. That was a mistake, he thought: cars like that were completely unsuited to many of the smaller roads in Botswana. On the other hand, if you were a man about town who intended to spend his time at clubs like this, there was no need to have a more practical vehicle.

He parked the van at the far end of the hotel's parking, and then made his way back to the entrance to the bar.

"Excuse me, Rra."

Charlie stopped. A well-built man, wearing a lapel badge marked *Security,* had appeared in the doorway.

Charlie looked up. This man was considerably taller than he was and exuded an air of authority. "Is this the club?" Charlie asked.

He felt the man's gaze running up and down him, taking in the two-tone shoes before returning to the red shirt and the tightly fitting jacket.

"Cool Singles?" asked the man.

"Yup," said Charlie. He had not intended to say "yup," but somehow it had come out.

"Could be," said the man.

Charlie was not sure what to say next. It occurred to him that the club might be members only, and that this could end his enquiry before it had even started.

He cleared his throat. "I'd like to join, Rra," he said.

"Join what?"

Charlie hesitated. "The club. The Cool Singles Evening Club."

"You don't have to be a member," said the man. "You can just walk in."

Charlie waited. If he could just walk in, then what was this security man doing blocking the door?

"Excuse me," said Charlie politely. He felt his neck becoming warm. This happened when he was embarrassed, and it was happening now.

The man seemed to be taking pleasure in the exchange. "Excuse you from what?" he asked, and then laughed. "You've done something, Rra?"

Charlie forced a smile. "Hah! That is very funny, Rra. No, I have not done anything. I was just wanting to go into the club."

The man grinned. "Oh, I think I might be in the way. That is very rude of me, Rra. Please come in, although . . ." He held up a hand. "Are you single, Rra? This is a singles club, you see."

"Of course I am," said Charlie.

The man fixed him with a humorous gaze. "In that case, you'll probably be the only single man in the building." And with that, he laughed in a lewd, belly-laugh sort of way, and stepped aside for Charlie to go through the door. As he did so, he told Charlie that although his first visit would be free, thereafter he would have to pay to get in. "But it's worth it, Rra," he added. "In view of the quality of the ladies, it is definitely worth the money."

Charlie entered. This encounter with the security man had irritated him, and he felt that the investigation was starting off on entirely the wrong foot. He had envisaged making a rather different entrance into the Cool Singles Evening Club, gliding across the floor in his two-tone patent-leather shoes, acknowledging, with a slight nod of the head, a greeting here and there, brushing off the attentions of barmen and waiters until he was ready to order a drink. And that, of course, would involve discretion: as a condition of lending him her van, Mma Ramotswe had made him promise that he would not drink anything alcoholic.

"You are driving, Charlie," she admonished him. "Remember that. That means no beer in that club—understand? Just something soft."

He had readily agreed, but now, as he entered the bar, he realised that this undertaking—which he fully intended to honour—might complicate his cover. It was all very well being as smartly dressed as he was, but men who wore tight-fitting jackets and two-tone shoes tended not to go into bars such as this one to order an orange juice or equivalent. They drank short and powerful drinks, served to them in squat, ice-filled glasses, with names known only to the denizens of bars such as this. They did not come into a place like this and order . . . milk. For that was what Charlie, had he been free to fol-low his instinct, would have liked to order: he loved milk, and if he was not to have a cold beer, a glass of chilled milk was exactly what he would have chosen.

He looked about him, his eyes taking a moment or two to become accustomed to the darkness of the dimly lit bar. The room was quite crowded, with two distinct clusters of people—one around the bar, and the other on the dance floor, where couples were dancing under a rotating mirror light. Charlie had always liked these fixtures, and the small points of light that they cast on the ceiling and walls as they turned on their axis. He stood now for a while and watched the circling specks of light play on the dancing couples, trying to estab-lish whether he recognised anybody.

And he immediately did. For there, locked in a shuffling embrace with a young woman in a shiny red dress, was none other than the deputy principal of the school that Charlie had attended before he began his mechanical apprenticeship. He gave a start, and looked again. There was no doubt about it: it was Mr. Modise, the popular and much-admired deputy principal, who had been in office when Charlie had been at the school some years earlier, and who was still there. It was the same Mr. Modise whom he had seen featured in the newspaper only a couple of weeks ago, pictured showing the Minister of Education round the school's new science block.

And who was the young woman? Charlie did not recognise her, but he could see that she was somewhere in her early twenties, not much more, and that, by the way she was dancing, she was not the quiet, home-loving type. Suddenly, unbidden, he heard Mma Makutsi's voice, full of disapproval, using the expression she occasionally used to describe such women: *a bad, bar-type girl.* This was a bad, bar-type girl—there could be as little doubt about that as there was that Mr. Modise was a *respectable, deputy principal-type man.*

Except he was not. Mr. Modise may have been a pillar of the community, but here he was in the Cool Singles Evening Club dancing with a *real* single, while Charlie, and half the town, knew that he was married to Mma Modise, a traditionally built lady—as Mma Ramotswe would put it. The teacher's wife had long been secretary of the local winter blanket appeal, a worthy cause that collected blankets to give, during winter, to those in need of extra warmth. It was a popular charity, and Mma Modise's photograph appeared in the newspapers at the start of each winter, accepting donations of blankets from various local businesses.

It was a moment of shock for Charlie, and it took him several minutes to recover his composure. Mr. Modise would not remember him, of course . . . or would he? Charlie suddenly thought that he might, because six months or so earlier he had brought his car into the garage for a service one morning. Mr. J.L.B. Matekoni had been off in his tow truck, and Charlie and Mr. Modise had spoken. Mr. Modise had remembered him then, greeting him warmly, although he had not been able to put a name to the face. But the teacher had remarked on how pleased he was to see that Charlie was doing well and had said something about remembering him as a good performer in track events at school. That had been so, and Charlie had basked in the pleasure of being remembered in that way. He admired Mr. Modise, and it pleased him that he should have made an impression in this way when there were so many youngsters at the school and he was just one of them.

Spotting Mr. Modise momentarily put Charlie off his stride. His feelings were mixed: on the one hand he was amused to see an authority figure of such importance in an unseemly setting like this; on the other, he was dismayed at the embarrassment that both he and Mr. Modise might feel if they came face to face. That would be an uncomfortable moment for the teacher, Charlie thought, and he would not wish that on somebody he had always liked and admired. There were other teachers—the woodwork teacher, for example—whom Charlie would not have minded seeing embarrassed, but not kind Mr. Modise. That woodwork teacher, Charlie now remembered, had always taken a delight in testing the constructions that the class made—the three-legged stools, the bathroom shelves, the wooden pot-stands—and testing them to destruction. He particularly enjoyed lowering his not insubstantial frame onto a student's painstakingly constructed chair and waiting for the inevitable collapse of the joints. At which point, with the surprising litheness sometimes shown by the bulky-figured, he would leap to his feet and shout triumphantly, "There—that has failed the stress test!"

But this was Mr. Modise, not that mean-spirited woodwork teacher, and Charlie decided that he would have to take great care to ensure that he was not spotted. He would go to the bar while the teacher was on the dance floor, and then make sure that for the rest of the evening he remained at the edge of the crowd, as far away from Mr. Modise as possible. It was not how he had envisaged himself in the Cool Singles Evening Club, but fieldwork, as Clovis Andersen was at pains to point out, required one to adapt to a changing situation on the ground. Reminding himself of that, he felt rather better, and readier for any challenges the evening might hold.

Reaching the bar, Charlie ordered himself a glass of lemonade.

"Anything in it?" asked the bartender, a grumpy, middle-aged man with a rather disapproving look.

"Ice," said Charlie. "And a slice of lemon, please, Rra."

The bartender looked down his nose. "Lemonade already has lemon, you know. There's a clue in the name: *lemon*ade."

Charlie tried to smile. "Oh, very funny, Rra."

The bartender frowned. "I wasn't trying to be funny. I'm just pointing it out to you."

Charlie bit his lip. Some words of Clovis Andersen came back to him: *Don't draw attention to yourself. Go with the flow. Blend in, even if you have to stop yourself from saying what you want to say.* This was clearly a situation, he decided, in which that advice applied.

"No lemon, then, Rra. Just lemonade, please. I'm driving, you see."

The bartender seemed to like these emollient words. "It's good," he said, "that at least somebody round here obeys the law." He paused, and as he opened the chilled can of lemonade, he asked, "So what business are you in, Rra?"

Charlie was pleased to have defused the situation. He almost replied that he was a detective, but stopped himself in time and said, instead, "Security. I'm a security consultant."

The barman nodded. "Everybody's a consultant these days. I'm a drinks consultant, I think."

Charlie hesitated. It occurred to him that the barman could be a *source*. Mma Makutsi was always going on about *sources*, and Charlie had never had one, as far as he could work out. This man, though, was an obvious source, as barmen knew everything there was to know, not just whether or not there was lemon in lemonade.

He made up his mind. "Actually, Rra," he began, "I'm just a trainee security person. Nothing big. I'm also a mechanic." He paused, and added, "I didn't finish my apprenticeship in the garage, you see. So, I do various things."

The barman looked at him with new respect. "Well, you're honest. That's a good thing to come across in a place like this. I like that very much." He poured the lemonade into a glass, and then carefully selected a couple of ice cubes from a small bucket. "You wouldn't be looking for a part-time job, would you?"

Charlie took the glass of lemonade. His heart thumped within him. This was a *lead*—another term that Mma Makutsi used from time to time. I have never had a lead, he thought, but now I do—and all within a few minutes of entering the Cool Singles Evening Club.

"What sort of job, Rra?" he asked.

The barman nodded in the direction of the front door. "We always have somebody out front. There are three of them we use, but that man out there tonight is going to live up in Maun. He's got a job in one of the hotels up there. So we—or rather the outfit that runs this place—needs somebody to replace him."

Charlie knew what his answer would be, but was careful not to appear too eager. "And the hours, Rra?"

"I'm not sure of the exact arrangement; I think they do one night a week, but it's divided into shifts." He fixed Charlie with a questioning gaze. "Can you handle trouble?"

Charlie nodded. "No problem." And then he asked, "What sort of trouble?"

"Undesirables trying to get in. Undesirables being thrown out.

Undesirables being sick in the toilets. Undesirables making the ladies feel uncomfortable."

Charlie said that he had no problem with undesirables.

"Some of these undesirables," the barman warned, "can be *very* undesirable."

Charlie shrugged. "I can control my temper," he said.

The barman thought for a moment. Then he said, "I know the manager will be pleased."

"The hotel manager?"

"No, the manager of the club. The club rents this room from the hotel. I'm on the hotel staff. These people can't tell me what to do."

Charlie absorbed this information. Then, as casually as he could, he asked, "Who's the manager, Rra?"

The barman did not answer immediately. Suddenly he became guarded. "Are you interested—in the job, that is?"

Charlie nodded.

"In that case," said the barman, "Go outside and sit on the bench. I'll get him to come out and have a word with you. He doesn't like to conduct business inside the club."

Charlie lifted up his glass of lemonade.

"No glasses outside," said the barman. "Sorry. I can keep the drink for you, though. For afterwards."

Charlie slid the glass back over the bar.

"Although you should pay first," the barman continued. "Policy, you see. All drinks to be paid for. No glasses outside. There aren't many rules, but those are two of them."

CHARLIE SAT on the bench outside the hotel, only a few yards from the door to the Cool Singles Evening Club, but far enough away to allow a private conversation. The bench was overhung by a large bougainvillea, its lower branches just above the head of anybody seated below. Charlie was wary of such bushes, in spite of their attractive floral displays: he had heard that snakes liked to lurk in them, and had himself once seen a boomslang elegantly draped across just such a branch as the one that overhung the bench. The thin green snake had been quite still—it might have been an innocent branch itself—and it would have been easy to miss, but its bite was particularly lethal. There was an antivenom, but it was rare and expensive, and it had to be injected quickly. Charlie had heard, though, that it was hard for the boomslang to bite you, as its fangs were well back in its mouth. But he would not care to take any risks, and now, as he sat on the bench, he looked up into the bougainvillea to check that there was no suspicious movement.

A figure emerged from the door and conferred briefly with the doorman. Charlie looked down at his hands: he was nervous, and he wondered whether this would be obvious, even in the darkness. It was all very well being dressed as he was, but what if his hands were shaking? That was the sort of thing that would be noticed and would weaken the effect of any disguise. You did not have to be Clovis Andersen to know that.

The figure came over and bent down to look at Charlie in the shadows. It was Mr. Modise.

Charlie looked up. For a few moments he was unsure what to think, but then it occurred to him that this was an unfortunate coincidence. Mr. Modise had been dancing—fairly energetically— and had come out to get some fresh air. And now, having avoided the teacher inside, he was meeting him outside. These things were embarrassing, but they happened.

Mr. Modise stared down at Charlie. For a few moments he looked uncertain, but then he broke into a broad grin. If there had been any embarrassment, or even dismay, on his part, then it was quickly and expertly concealed. "Now then," he began. "Don't tell me; don't tell me. Let me see if I can remember your name. Yes. Yes. You're Charlie, aren't you?"

Charlie rose to his feet, only to be pressed back down by Mr. Modise, who now sat down on the bench with him.

"I don't always remember names," the teacher said. "I try, but there are so many. But I remember you, all right. You made people laugh back in those days." He paused. "You became a mechanic, didn't you?"

Charlie nodded. He was confused. Mr. Modise seemed completely unfazed by being seen in the Cool Singles Evening Club—and he a married man, and a deputy principal to boot.

"I must get you to look at my car one day," Mr. Modise continued. "It's developed a rattle. I've done my best to find the source, but I can't. Perhaps you'll be able to find out what's causing it."

"Rattles are very annoying," said Charlie.

Mr. Modise rubbed his hands together. "But that's not what we should be talking about. Our barman said you might be interested in working with us. He said you have some security experience."

The revelation was astounding, and it took Charlie all his self-control not to gasp with surprise. Mr. Modise was not just a casual visitor to the Cool Singles Evening Club—he was the manager. This was a monumental disclosure; this stood everything—everything—on its head, and it took Charlie a while to find his voice. But he reminded himself of the fact that he was on duty, he was a field officer of the No. 1 Ladies' Detective Agency, and he must be professional. He remembered that now and said, in what he hoped were measured tones, "Not very much. A bit, though. Some experience . . ." And then he added, rather weakly, "Here and there."

"It's not the hardest of jobs," said Mr. Modise breezily. "Most of our clients are well behaved, but every so often you get some young man who gets a bit out of hand. That doesn't happen very often, though."

"I would like that sort of work," said Charlie. "I am good at throwing people out." I am not, he thought: I have never thrown anybody out of anything.

Mr. Modise seemed pleased. "I see no reason why we can't take you on, then. I'll have to check with the person who owns the club, of course. I'm just the manager. I don't see any problems, though."

Charlie expressed his thanks. Then he asked, "Who owns the club, Rra?"

Mr. Modise hesitated. "You'll find out in due course."

Charlie waited, but nothing further was said. Then he asked, "Are you still teaching, Mr. Modise?"

"Am I still teaching? Of course I am. I'll never give up teaching. Never. It's in my blood."

Charlie nodded towards the inside of the club. "So this job is just part-time?"

"Very part-time," said Mr. Modise. "The club is only open a couple of times a week. I come here at five in the afternoon and stay until midnight. That's it. For the rest of the time, I'm busy with my day job, so to speak. Same old, same old, but there we are. There's a pension at the end of it, and I enjoy it."

Charlie took a few moments to absorb this. It astonished him that a respectable deputy principal would openly run a club like this—in the past, that would never have happened. He decided to ask a question. "Does anybody ever say you shouldn't be running a nightclub? *I* don't say that, of course, but I wondered if there were other people who would say such a thing."

Charlie had half expected an angry reaction, but that was not what he got. Rather, Mr. Modise smiled as he gave his reply. "But why would they say that, Charlie? Why would they show any interest in what I do in my spare time?"

Charlie frowned. "You do not expect a deputy principal to—"

Mr. Modise interrupted him. "Deputy principal during the day, Charlie! During the day! This is night time, and that is different." He paused, as if waiting to see if his perfectly obvious point had been taken. "Same as you, I think. Mechanic during the day—man about town at night!"

Charlie said nothing. Now Mr. Modise continued, "Can you start next week?"

He could, and Mr. Modise stood up, extending a hand to shake on the arrangement. "I must say that I am pleased you'll be joining us, Charlie," he said. "It's hard to get reliable people these days."

Charlie remembered why he was there. "When will I meet the owner?" he asked.

Mr. Modise looked at him with an expression of slightly guarded amusement. "You seem keen to do that," he said.

Charlie shrugged. "It's just that I like to know who I'm working for."

Mr. Modise hesitated before he replied, "I suppose that's fair enough. Well, we can set it up, I suppose. Next Monday? Are you doing anything then?"

The proposal was quickly accepted.

"As it happens," said Mr. Modise, "I'll be meeting the boss on Monday. Here at the bar."

Charlie made an effort to appear nonchalant. "Oh yes?"

Mr. Modise laughed. "Ladies are running just about every business these days, Charlie. There's not much left for us men to do, is there? Other than to whisper sweet nothings to the ladies." Then he grinned—in much the same way as a schoolboy would grin over a half-understood salacious reference.

Charlie drew in his breath. What had happened to Mr. Modise? Where was the sense of probity that was still expected of deputy principals? Did the Ministry of Education know that somebody who occupied such a senior position was spending his evenings running a *nightclub,* and an apparently disreputable one at that? Did people no longer bother about that sort of thing?

Charlie collected himself. There would be time to reflect on all this when he reported back to Mma Ramotswe and Mma Makutsi. They would be shocked, he imagined—particularly Mma Makutsi, who had pronounced views on how people should behave. He had heard her talking about the standards that the community expected of people in important positions—doctors, policemen, and teachers—and graduates of the Botswana Secretarial College, of course. People looked up to you, she said, if you had been given the advantage of an education, and you should not disappoint them.

Clovis Andersen said: *When asking an important question, make it sound casual. Don't give the impression that you really need to know the answer. If you do, the other person will have leverage over you. Be careful.* Charlie remembered that now, and so he said, "Oh, there are many ladies running things these days, Rra. And they do it very well, I think. I'm sure this lady will be one of those . . . what's she called, by the way, Rra? Not that I'm likely to know her, but if I meet her, I should know her name—just out of politeness, of course."

Mr. Modise nodded. "It's important to call people by their names. I always say that you should give your full name and not just your first name, as many people are doing these days. They say: 'Oh, I'm called Tsepo, or John, or whatever,' and I think: 'And what's your other name? Are you just like a dog or a cow that only has one name?' That's what I say, Charlie, and I don't care if they take offence. People have to be told how to behave sometimes."

Yes, thought Charlie—but what about you? What about you, Mr. Deputy Principal? What about *your* behaviour? He did not say that, of course, but waited for Mr. Modise to continue.

"Violet Sephotho," said the teacher.

CHAPTER EIGHT

THE NO. 1 HUSBAND-STEALER

HAD IT BEEN DISCLOSED that the Cool Singles Evening Club was being run by the Secretary-General of the United Nations or even by the Pope himself, Charlie could not have been more shocked than he was to discover that not only was a deputy principal the manager, but that behind him stood the figure of no less a person than Violet Sephotho. Charlie knew who she was, of course: he knew only too well that this was the person who had in the past been involved in more than one questionable enterprise, who enjoyed a considerable reputation as a husband-stealer, and who was the would-be nemesis of Mma Makutsi. On several occasions Charlie had heard Mma Makutsi listing Violet's perfidies—they went back many years, those two, right back to the days when they had been contemporaries at the Botswana Secretarial College. And when he told Mma Makutsi that it was Violet who owned this rackety nightclub—or *evening club,* as it called itself—he could imagine how righteous would be her indignation, how determined she would be to deal a blow to this sordid little business. Of course, Charlie, as a young man, was less inclined to be censorious of people wandering off the straight and narrow, but this was going just a bit too far. In particular, he had been disappointed to discover the involvement of a teacher to whom he had looked up. Young men need heroes, and when their heroes are shown to have feet of clay, their disappointment can be acute.

When he left the hotel that evening, shortly after the conclusion of his meeting with Mr. Modise, he drove home with his head full of what he would tell Mma Ramotswe and Mma Makutsi the following morning. Mma Ramotswe had told him that he could hold on to the van overnight and bring it to the house on Zebra Drive first thing the next day. Then he could ride in to work with Mr. J.L.B. Matekoni, and she would drive the van in a little bit later. As he parked outside his house that night, Charlie reflected on how he would make his report—he would do it slowly, he decided, painting a picture of the club and its atmosphere and then dropping in, with a ringmaster's sense of theatre, the astonishing information that he had garnered. They would be aghast, but Mma Ramotswe and Mma Makutsi would both realise that he had put his evening undercover to very good use indeed. At one stroke, he had found out not only about the management of the club, but also about its ownership. Now they knew everything they needed to know before taking the next step, whatever that might prove to be.

But when he arrived at Mma Ramotswe's house the next morning, Mr. J.L.B. Matekoni emerged to tell him that he should just leave the tiny white van under the shade of a tree and that he should accompany him in his truck to Tlokweng Road Speedy Motors, where there was a minibus waiting for its suspension to be renewed. "They cram people in," Mr. J.L.B. Matekoni said disapprovingly. "They overload—all the time. Never overload a vehicle, Charlie. Never. A vehicle is like a donkey—load it with too many sacks of mealies and you break its back." He had paused, and then added, "Of course, donkeys don't have suspension." This was a joke, and Charlie had smiled politely. Mr. J.L.B. Matekoni did not often make jokes, and sometimes Charlie and Fanwell missed them altogether, although this remark about donkeys and suspension had been correctly identified for what it was.

As they got into the truck, Mr. J.L.B. Matekoni had explained that Mma Ramotswe would not, in fact, be coming into the office until that afternoon, or perhaps not even until the following morning, as she was planning to go to Mochudi. And as for Mma Makutsi, she was tied up with some Radiphuti family business, and would definitely not be in the office until later that day. "So I shall have much of your time today," said Mr. J.L.B. Matekoni cheerfully. "We have that minibus and two cars in for services. We shall be kept very busy, I think."

"I have something very important to tell Mma Ramotswe," said Charlie, a note of wistfulness in his voice. "I was conducting an investigation last night, as Mma Ramotswe might have told you."

"She did say something," said Mr. J.L.B. Matekoni. "She said you were going to a bar or somewhere like that."

Charlie explained that it was a club and that his investigation had been particularly successful. "I found out who runs it," he said. "And I also found out who owns it."

Mr. J.L.B. Matekoni did not seem particularly interested, but they had become involved in an incipient traffic jam and, as they waited, he asked what Charlie had to report.

"You will find this hard to believe, Boss: it's run by a teacher," Charlie replied. "He is a deputy principal called Modise. I remember him from when I was at school."

Mr. J.L.B. Matekoni frowned. "I know who that man is. I look after the car of the people who live next door to him. They speak very highly of him. He keeps his yard immaculate." He paused. It really was very puzzling. "That is very odd, Charlie. What is a deputy principal doing running a . . . what was it called?"

"The Cool Singles Evening Club."

Mr. J.L.B. Matekoni snorted. "What a name! Cool Singles. Cool this, cool that. Cool nonsense." And then he continued, "Who's cool? Am I cool, Charlie? I don't think so. Are you cool? No, I don't think so. It is a very silly word."

Charlie might have taken offence. *I*, at least, am cool, he thought. But he did not press the point.

"He is definitely the manager," said Charlie.

Mr. J.L.B. Matekoni shook his head, either at the traffic, at the fact that a deputy principal should be mixed up in such matters, or at the state of the world in general—it was hard for Charlie to tell.

"And there's another thing," Charlie went on. "Mr. Modise is the manager, but the club is owned by somebody else—by a woman. Modise is the boss, but the boss has a boss."

Mr. J.L.B. Matekoni said that he was not surprised. In business, he told Charlie, it is often the case that the person you think is in charge is actually given instructions by somebody else altogether. "That applies even at the very top," he went on to say. "You have a prime minister or a president, or whatever, but who do you have beyond that, Charlie? Do you have any idea?"

Charlie scratched his head. "A king, maybe. If there's a king knocking around, then maybe he can tell the prime minister what to do."

Mr. J.L.B. Matekoni looked amused. "Kings don't knock around, as you put it, Charlie. And that's not the way it works. No, I was thinking of the wife. That's the person with the real power, you see. The wife is the real boss if the prime minister or president is a man, and if she's a woman . . ."

"If the wife's a woman?"

"No, if the prime minister or what have you is a woman, then perhaps the husband will be in the background . . ." He stopped. "No, I do not think so. I think that if the prime minister is a woman, then she will be making all the decisions."

Charlie looked thoughtful. "If Mma Ramotswe was the President of Botswana," he said, "would you be telling her what to do in the background, Boss?"

It did not take Mr. J.L.B. Matekoni long to answer that question. "I do not think so," he said. "I think Mma Ramotswe would make up her own mind on most issues. She'd listen, of course— she is always happy to listen, but the decisions would be hers." He paused. "With, maybe, a bit of input from Mma Potokwane . . ."

Charlie agreed that Mma Potokwane would be a valuable presidential advisor. But then it occurred to him that having Mma Makutsi as president would be rather different. "If Mma Makutsi were to be elected as president," he said, "I think she might be a dictator, Boss. I can just see her sitting there in that big office, glaring at people through her big round spectacles. It would be a very frightening government, I think, Rra."

Mr. J.L.B. Matekoni could not encourage such openly seditious talk, but secretly he agreed. A Mma Makutsi government would be an uncomfortable one. But now he remembered how they had got onto the topic of powerful women. "You said that the club was owned by somebody else—by a woman. Do you know who that is?"

Charlie looked pleased with himself. "As a matter of fact, Boss, I do. It's Violet Sephotho. You know, that—"

"I know exactly who she is," Mr. J.L.B. Matekoni interjected. The traffic was beginning to move, and he took out his feelings for Violet on the gearstick as he inched the truck forward. "Any trouble in this town—any trouble at all—and when you scratch the surface, whose name crops up? I'll tell you: Violet Sephotho—that's who."

He shook his head. "Just think: husband-stealer No. 1, as they call her, setting up a club for cheating husbands. Perhaps we shouldn't be surprised. No leopard ever changed its spots."

"I can imagine how Mma Makutsi will react when I tell her," Charlie mused. "She'll go ballistic. I'll have to peel her off the ceiling."

"You must not give Mma Makutsi a heart attack," said Mr. J.L.B. Matekoni. He shook his head in disbelief. "Just think, that woman . . ." He stopped. "There must be something going on."

"There is," said Charlie. "Violet Sephotho is running a club for married men to meet ladies. That's what's going on, Boss."

"Yes," said Mr. J.L.B. Matekoni. "But what interests me is this, Charlie: how did Mr. Modise become involved in this?"

Charlie could offer no suggestion.

"You might make some enquiries," suggested Mr. J.L.B. Matekoni.

Charlie looked thoughtful. "Yes, I could, Boss. But . . ."

"But what?"

Charlie shifted uncomfortably in his seat. "I'm not sure how I'd do that."

Mr. J.L.B. Matekoni glanced at him. He was fond of this young man, in spite of his past irresponsibility, his ogling of girls, his youthful, puppy-dog manner. I was like that too, he thought—a long time ago. I also liked to watch girls. I also liked to talk nonsense with my friends. I used to dream about being all sorts of things I never could be.

"Would you like me to help you?"

Charlie hesitated. Then he said, "Yes, Boss. That would be good." To which he added, "But how?"

Mr. J.L.B. Matekoni tapped the side of his nose. "You know what Mma Ramotswe says?"

"She says many things," said Charlie.

"Yes, she does. And all of them, I think, are true, don't you agree?" This was said as a mixture of tribute and warning—and Charlie did not argue.

"Mma Ramotswe says: ask the neighbours," Mr. J.L.B. Matekoni said. "She says that is what you should do if you want to find anything out. Neighbours know."

Charlie had to admit that this was probably true. Now that he thought about it, he remembered Mma Ramotswe saying something about speaking to neighbours.

"I told you that Modise lives next to somebody whose car we look after," Mr. J.L.B. Matekoni said. "It is that bad silver-coloured car. You might even remember it, Charlie. It is a very bad car, I think."

Charlie did remember the car. "Oh, that one, Boss. Bad news. Bad brakes."

"Bad brakes, bad suspension, bad transmission," said Mr. J.L.B. Matekoni, with the air of a doctor reviewing a grim X-ray report. "It is not his fault, of course—nobody deserves to have a bad car." He shook his head. "I know that man. He is Modise's neighbour. A quiet word with him might be helpful, I think."

They were now nearing the garage, and Mr. J.L.B. Matekoni was preparing to turn off the main road.

"I think that is a very good idea, Boss," said Charlie. "And thank you."

"That's all right, Charlie. I'm on your side, you know. I always have been."

Charlie knew this was true, and he gave expression now to his feelings of gratitude. "You've done so much for me, Boss. Right from the beginning."

"I was only doing my job."

"You have been my father," said Charlie.

Mr. J.L.B. Matekoni swallowed. He was pleased that Charlie said this, because in many respects it was how he felt. He had a son, of course—Puso, whom he and Mma Ramotswe had fostered. He loved Puso and Motholeli with all his heart, but that was the strange thing about hearts: there was always room for somebody else. And if he had fostered or adopted Charlie too, then he was sure that he could have been a father to him as well. Of course, Charlie had one or two faults, including a tendency to use a hammer on machinery, but nobody could specify the children they had: you took what arrived, and Charlie was at heart a good young man. Fanwell was a better mechanic—he had never been in any doubt about that—but Charlie had flair, and made the world a brighter place for that.

"We can go to see this person this evening," Mr. J.L.B. Matekoni said. "We can go to his place after he has finished work."

"Maybe you're becoming a bit of a detective yourself, Boss," joked Charlie.

"Only to help you," said Mr. J.L.B. Matekoni. "I think it's best for me to stick to fixing cars and for Mma Ramotswe to stick to making enquiries—or whatever it is she does."

Charlie burst out laughing. "Mma Ramotswe would keep cars going through kindness," he said. "Cars would do anything for her."

Mr. J.L.B. Matekoni liked that. But then he thought of Mma Makutsi. No car would dare defy her, he imagined.

AT THE END of their day's work, Mr. J.L.B. Matekoni drove over to the house of Mr. Gideon Maponde, owner of an uncooperative silver car, and neighbour of Deputy Principal Modise. It was in one of the middle-range suburbs that had sprung up around Gaborone, within the reach of those on good, but not over-generous government salaries, or those in middle management who looked forward to being able to afford a larger, more sought-after house, even though they might not be able to afford it just yet. The houses that lined the street had been built closer together than those on Zebra Drive, where Mma Ramotswe and Mr. J.L.B. Matekoni lived—domestic plots had been wider and deeper in those days, when it seemed unlikely that there would ever be any shortage of land. And there was still an abundance of undeveloped bush, stretching out to the distant horizons of the Kalahari, but there was a sense now of its finite nature, because everybody knew that there was not enough of everything and that what there was would not last forever.

They found the plot number, which was 5409, painted on a small metal plate attached to the front gate. A fence marked the perimeter of the yard, and on the other side of this a small flock of chickens, scrawny and disconsolate, pecked at the barren earth. The Maponde house itself seemed in need of a coat of paint, and one of its gutters was hanging off the roof at a drunken angle.

"He is a very untidy man, our friend Maponde," muttered Mr. J.L.B. Matekoni. "Untidy car, untidy house, untidy man."

Charlie noticed the infamous car, parked under an acacia tree beside the house. It had been reversed into position and was facing them, its grille a mocking mouth, its headlights malevolent eyes.

"There's that car of his, Boss," said Charlie.

Mr. J.L.B. Matekoni threw a glance towards the parked vehicle. "He could easily afford a new car, you know. But he holds on to that wretched vehicle in spite of everything."

Charlie grinned. "Perhaps it has something on him, Boss," he said. "Perhaps the car is blackmailing him."

Mr. J.L.B. Matekoni looked askance at Charlie. "That's ridiculous, Charlie."

"I wasn't serious," protested the young man. "I was joking, you see."

"I did not think it very funny," said Mr. J.L.B. Matekoni. "Maybe I'm slow with these things. Maybe I'm old-fashioned."

"You, Boss?" exclaimed Charlie. "You are very modern and up to date. No, I'm not just saying that. Sometimes people who look very old-fashioned are the most modern of all . . ." He trailed off, as Mr. J.L.B. Matekoni was staring at him, and he felt disconcerted as a result. Perhaps he should not have described Mr. J.L.B. Matekoni as looking old-fashioned—even if he was. So he continued, "I'm not saying you look old-fashioned, Rra. I'm not saying that at all."

Mr. J.L.B. Matekoni brushed the protestation aside. "Stop going on about nothing, Charlie," he said. "We must go and speak to Maponde."

As they approached the house, a door linking the verandah to the interior opened, and a woman emerged. She looked intensely at her visitors before saying, "You're the mechanic, aren't you? You're Mr . . . Mr . . ."

"Mr. J.L.B. Matekoni. Yes, I am that person, Mma. I have come to see your husband—if he is in. If he is not in, well, then I shall not see him, I think."

"Maponde is here," said the woman. "He never goes out these days. He just sits in the house and complains about what is happening. That is all he does."

"About what is happening, Mma?" said Mr. J.L.B. Matekoni. "About what is happening where?"

She replied with the air of one who had been called upon to explain something that was perfectly obvious. "About what is happening in the world," she said. "About all the problems that the government has; about unemployment; about what the Bank of Botswana should do—that sort of thing."

Mr. J.L.B. Matekoni sighed. "There are many problems, Mma.

But then every government has its problems, doesn't it?" He paused. "I hope that your car is not giving you trouble."

This triggered a sound that was a combination of a snort of disgust and a disapproving clicking of the tongue. "He should get rid of that wretched car!" she exploded. "How many times have I told him that, Rra? I have lost count. Yes, I have lost count. Once you have said something over one hundred times, you do not remember how many times you have said it." She lowered her voice. "You know something, Rra? I think that car has had a curse put on it."

She fixed Mr. J.L.B. Matekoni with a stare, as if to challenge him to contradict her. When he did not, but instead nodded politely, she went on, "Some people say that it's impossible to put a curse on a car. They say that you can only put a curse on a person and that you cannot do it with a car because a car has no soul."

She seemed to expect a reaction, and so Mr. J.L.B. Matekoni nodded. He knew what she meant, but that was not to say that he agreed, or not entirely. A car had a personality, which was not quite the same thing as having a soul.

"But I don't think that is true, Rra," Mma Maponde continued. "I think there are people who can curse *things* as well as people. I think that happens." She paused. "That is why I think that somebody has used *muti* to make that car behave the way it does."

Charlie was less tactful than Mr. J.L.B. Matekoni. Now he said, "I do not believe any of that old-fashioned nonsense, Mma. There is no such thing as witchcraft. *Muti,* medicine, what have you—that is ancient nonsense."

She rounded on him. "Oh, that's what you think, Mr. Modern-Modern. Well, I can tell you that I have seen things you wouldn't believe. I have seen people trembling with fear—right here in Gaborone, in bright sunlight, because they know that some witch doctor somewhere has put a curse on them and that if they shake hands with somebody they will make that person get sick and maybe even die. Oh, I have seen that sort of thing, young man. It is something that is still happening, I can tell you."

Mr. J.L.B. Matekoni made a non-committal gesture. "You may be right, Mma—you may be right."

"I *am* right, Rra," she snapped. "All the time—I'm right."

Mr. J.L.B. Matekoni looked down at his feet. He was wondering what it would be like to be married to a woman as opinionated as this. He was so fortunate having Mma Ramotswe, who listened to what other people had to say, who was quite ready to admit that she was wrong. This Mma Maponde was a sort of turbo-charged Mma Makutsi—that's what she was. Ninety-seven per cent in the final examinations of the Botswana Secretarial College, he thought—and smiled to himself.

Mma Maponde looked at him suspiciously. "You have thought of something amusing, Rra?"

He shook his head quickly. "No, Mma, I was just thinking of how right you are. That is all. And I was wondering, too, whether you could tell your husband that we are here."

She hesitated, but then said, "You can come with me, Rra. My husband is always sitting in his chair. He is always there. I never have to look for him."

She led them into a corridor that ran into the cool interior of the house. Somewhere the whirring of a fan explained the draught Mr. J.L.B. Matekoni felt touch his arms. At the end of the corridor was a room that looked out over the back yard—not a large room, but spacious enough for a sofa, two easy chairs and a table on which a handful of loose change lay scattered. On one of the easy chairs, a middle-aged man wearing a scruffy open-necked shirt was sitting, paging through a lawnmower catalogue. He looked up as the visitors arrived and sprang immediately to his feet. He seemed pleased to see Mr. J.L.B. Matekoni.

"It's very good of you to come and see me, Rra," he said as he shook Mr. J.L.B. Matekoni's hand. "I have often hoped that you would come to my place one day. I have often spoken about you to my wife. I'm glad that you've had the chance to meet her."

"We have already been speaking," said Mr. J.L.B. Matekoni.

"And I recognise this young man," Mr. Maponde went on. "This is Fanwell, isn't it?"

"No, this is Charlie. He is a part-time mechanic at the garage—Fanwell is full-time."

Mr. Maponde smiled at Charlie. "Many people are part-time these days. I think they like the flexibility."

"That is true," said Mr. J.L.B. Matekoni. "But you have to be careful that you don't become too part-time. Some very part-time people seem to lose the desire to do any work at all."

"Oh, we all know some of those," said Mr. Maponde. "The government should do something about them, I always say. But you know what, Rra? What does the government do?" He made a circle of thumb and forefinger. "Nothing—exactly nothing."

Mr. J.L.B. Matekoni was polite. "You make a very good point, Rra," he said. "But I suppose we should remember how hard it is for the government. If they do something, then there are people who will immediately say: 'You should not have done that.' Or they'll say: 'You should have done something different.' It is not simple being the government."

Mr. Maponde looked doubtful. "I think the government *likes* being the government, Mr. J.L.B. Matekoni. They keep asking us to elect them. They must want to be where they are."

Mr. J.L.B. Matekoni conceded that this was true. But he pointed out that there were still many issues on which it must be rather difficult for the government to do anything that would please everybody. "That is what democracy is all about," he said. "It is not always comfortable."

Mr. Maponde turned to Charlie. "What do you think, Rra? How does it look from the point of view of young people?"

Charlie shrugged. "There is always one thing," he said. "And then there is another."

Mr. Maponde waited. He was looking expectantly at Charlie, as if anticipating further wisdom, but at last he said, "That is one of the truest things I have heard for a long time. You are very right, Rra."

Charlie glanced at Mr. J.L.B. Matekoni, uncertain where this encounter was going.

"Charlie is very good at understanding things," said Mr. J.L.B. Matekoni. He spoke without any trace of irony, and for a few moments Charlie beamed with pleasure.

"The country is in good hands, then," observed Mr. Maponde, smiling at Charlie. "If that is the calibre of our young men."

He invited his visitors to sit down, while Mma Maponde, looking vaguely resentful, went off to the kitchen to make tea.

Mr. J.L.B. Matekoni cleared his throat. "I wanted to ask you something, Rra," he said. "It is a delicate issue."

Mr. Maponde laughed. "Everything is delicate these days," he said. "You can't say anything without somebody saying, 'You shouldn't say that.' It is best not to think at all now—in my opinion, at least. That is only the opinion of one man, Rra, but there you are."

Mr. J.L.B. Matekoni nodded. "People are always ready to wag their fingers at you. It's a bit like the old days in the villages—remember, Rra? Remember there were always people who were watching what you said or did, and they told you off if you stepped out of line. It is the same thing now, but much, much worse. Everyone is a policeman now, I think."

"That is very true, Rra," said Mr. Maponde. He sighed. "It is best not to show your face these days. Sit in your chair. Say nothing."

Mma Maponde returned with three cups of tea. She had sugared them heavily, without asking, and Mr. J.L.B. Matekoni struggled to conceal his distaste for the syrupy liquid.

"This delicate matter?" asked Mr. Maponde.

"My wife," began Mr. J.L.B. Matekoni. "She's—"

He was not allowed to finish. "Your wife's the delicate matter, Rra?"

Charlie giggled at the misunderstanding.

"No, not at all," protested Mr. J.L.B. Matekoni. "What I was going to say, Rra, is that my wife is the person who runs the No. 1 Ladies' Detective Agency. You will have seen her office when you brought your car round to Tlokweng Road Speedy Motors. It is right next door to the garage—in the same building, in fact."

"Oh, I know all about that," said Mr. Maponde. "I have heard that she has helped many people."

This pleased Mr. J.L.B. Matekoni. He was proud of Mma Ramotswe, and there was nothing that gave him more pleasure than to hear that she was of good report in the country at large. "You are very kind, Rra," he said. "And you see, this young man, Charlie here, is learning how to be a private detective from my wife. He is a sort of apprentice."

Mr. Maponde turned to Charlie and smiled encouragingly. "I'm sure you will be very good at that, Charlie."

Charlie was about to acknowledge the compliment, but Mr. J.L.B. Matekoni now continued, "He is involved in an enquiry at the moment that affects somebody you know. I am not saying that this person has done anything wrong—I am not saying that, Rra. But we need to know a bit more about what he is doing. That is why I thought it would be a good idea to come and have a word with you. You may be able to help us, I think."

As he listened to this, Charlie's surprise grew. He had not anticipated that Mr. J.L.B. Matekoni would be so direct; he had imagined that any enquiry about Mr. Modise would be veiled in some way, instead of which here was a direct and unambiguous disclosure of the object of their visit.

And Mr. Maponde was equally forthright. "Who is this person, Rra?"

"Your neighbour," Mr. J.L.B. Matekoni replied.

There followed a brief silence. Outside, in the warm air of the afternoon, a chorus of cicadas whirred in shrill protest. Charlie looked up at the ceiling where a small gecko, albino-white, clung upside down, eyeing a solitary fly.

Mma Maponde had been standing in the doorway, just out of sight. As Mr. J.L.B. Matekoni revealed his hand, she swept into the room. "Modise?" she exclaimed, her voice high with excitement. "You're talking about Mr. Modise? The deputy principal? Our neighbour?"

Taken by surprise, Mr. J.L.B. Matekoni could only reply with a gesture of confirmation.

"Oh, I can tell you a thing or two about that man," said Mma Maponde.

Mr. Maponde looked at her with concern. "We mustn't make up our minds too quickly," he said. "We don't know anything for sure."

Her reaction was to laugh. "Don't know? How can you say we don't know for sure when I have seen them myself, with my own eyes? How many times? Three, four? They think they can go off to the Sanitas tea garden and not be seen by anybody who knows them. Hah! For a clever man, Modise is very stupid. First-class stupid, I'd say. But then, that is what happens to men when their brains go soft. They don't think."

Mr. Maponde was clearly embarrassed by his wife's outburst. He glanced under his eyebrows at Mr. J.L.B. Matekoni, then at his folded hands, then at the floor.

Mma Maponde now went on, "When men get to a certain age,

Mr. J.L.B. Matekoni, something happens to their brains. Scientists know all about it nowadays. There are many articles about it in the magazines."

"What age?" interjected Charlie.

Mma Maponde turned to stare at him. "What age? Not yours, Mr. Charlie. Oh no, not yours. But this will come to you, one hundred per cent, when you are forty-five. That is when it happens. Forty-five. Bang! Big trouble."

Mr. Maponde tried again. "I'm not sure that we should—"

He was not allowed to finish. Mma Maponde was in full voice now, and she would brook no interruption from her husband. "Do you know that woman, Violet Sephotho? Have you heard of her?"

Mr. J.L.B. Matekoni inclined his head. "She is very well known in Gaborone," he said.

"She certainly is," spat Mma Maponde. "Well known for being a No. 1 husband-stealer. Well known for being in on every dubious bit of whatnottery. Well known for being a disgrace to Botswana. Well known for everything, in fact.

"And what do you think happens when Modise reaches that dangerous age for men? I'll tell you: he meets Violet Sephotho, and suddenly he's eighteen again, and behaving exactly as an eighteen-year-old boy behaves. She looks at him—because she looks at all men, Rra—and he thinks, Oh my, that glamorous lady is looking at me. And he forgets that he's a deputy principal and that he has a wife who does a lot of good work for the winter blanket appeal. He forgets all that because he is at that stage of life when men do that sort of thing. And before you know where you are, he's all lovey-dovey with this flashy lady and goodness knows what is happening, although I think I know well enough. Oh, this is a very common story, Mr. J.L.B. Matekoni, I'm sorry to say. It's happening all the time, and these foolish men don't realise what a ridiculous spectacle they are making of themselves. Oh goodness, this is a bad thing—very bad. It is a disgrace to Botswana and to the Ministry of Education. It is a shameful, shameful thing."

She stopped to draw breath, and Mr. J.L.B. Matekoni took the opportunity to ask a question. "Are you saying that they are having an affair, Mma? Is that what you're saying?"

CHAPTER NINE

MY SISTER IS ALWAYS DRINKING TEA

JULIA WAS STAYING in a small private hotel near the old Gaborone Club, a part of the city known as the Village. Here older bungalows, some dating back to the early days of independence, stood cheek by jowl with newer houses, overlooked by the occasional apartment block or school, or government building. It was a quiet area, halfway between the bustle of the centre of town and the timeless somnolence of the hinterland. The hotel catered for guests who wanted privacy and peace, and paid great attention to its dryland garden, with its drought-resistant shrubs and its rockeries of succulents. A small sitting-out area, protected by a panoply of shade netting, had been created at the rear of this garden, and it was there that Mma Ramotswe found Julia sitting that morning, a tea tray on a table at her side, and a magazine open on her lap.

"I know I'm a bit early," Mma Ramotswe said, as she crossed a small patch of discouraged, wilting grass. Water was the issue, it always had been—water was the anxiety at the heart of any dry country. "But in this weather, it's better to start before the sun gets too high."

Julia looked up to greet her visitor with a smile. She addressed Mma Ramotswe haltingly, with the Setswana words she was still struggling to learn. Mma Ramotswe clapped her hands together. "You are speaking so well," she said.

Julia was apologetic. "I know only a few words, and when you have so few, you think you sound like a child."

"You are doing well, Mma," said Mma Ramotswe. "It is always good to hear other people use our language."

Julia thanked her. "That is kind of you, Mma." She paused. "Not everybody is so kind when you try to use their language. I have been in countries where they don't seem to encourage it. You sound odd to them and they laugh."

Mma Ramotswe shook her head. "That would never happen here," she said.

Julia gestured to the chair beside hers and invited Mma Ramotswe to join her for a cup of tea. Mma Ramotswe, though, glanced at her watch, and suggested that they should leave for Mochudi. "We shall be offered tea up there," she said. "Whenever I go to Mochudi, there is tea."

They set off in the white van, following a route through the outskirts of the city before it joined the main highway to the north. In the past, Mma Ramotswe had known every twist and turn of the road, every farm gate, every whitewashed rural store that marked the unfolding miles of this familiar journey, for it was one that she had done countless times before, from her girlhood onwards. She was familiar with every outcrop of rock that could be glimpsed from the road, every cattle enclosure, every tiny graveyard with the wind-blown canopies that people erected to shelter their late relatives from the sun. This was her land, and it was her people who had made their mark upon it. And now, sitting with this new friend of hers, this woman who had come from a place so distant from this Botswana, she wished that she could tell her something of the country around them, but they had lapsed into silence, not because there was any awkwardness between them, but because Julia was looking out on the landscape and seemed to have her own thoughts. There would be the opportunity to speak later—for now, silence seemed somehow right. Had she been able to say anything, Mma Ramotswe thought she might have spoken of her late father, Obed Ramotswe, and of the time she had gone with him to look at some cattle that were being kept not far from this road, on a stretch of land where the grass was thought to be particularly sweet. Her father been called in to settle a dispute between the owner of the herd and a purchaser—an argument that could only be resolved by an expert and dispassionate valuation by one who really knew about cattle, and he, of course, had been that man. She had watched, a shy fifteen-year-old, while the cattle had been driven in front of her father and his famous eye for livestock. She remembered the dust, and the circling of a hawk, and the infected, weeping eye of one of the young herd boys: little things, small memories that even now remained with her, but could not really be explained to her companion, because so much of our life has a flavour that only we, and a few who are with us on our journey, can be expected to understand.

But she felt that she had to say something now, and so she remarked, "I have been on this road so many times, you know. And my van knows it too, I think. Maybe it could do this journey without me."

Julia laughed. "I know what you mean, Mma. When I was a girl, I thought that my bicycle remembered the way. I didn't think I had to steer."

Mma Ramotswe nodded. "That is one of the reasons why I would not like to exchange this van for a newer one," she said. "A new one would know nothing, you see, and I don't know whether I have the time to teach it."

They were now almost at the turning that led off to Mochudi, just visible a few miles off to the east, a skirt of scattered houses around the familiar hill. Now the associations, she knew, would come thick and fast—years had passed since she had left the village, but it was still her place, the spot to which she knew she could return at whatever stage of life she had reached, and belong. That was the definition of home, she thought. Zebra Drive, and the house she had purchased there after she had sold the cattle left to her by her father, was now the place she lived—and she loved it well enough—but it was not home in the sense in which most people in Botswana spoke of home. Home was so often somewhere else, somewhere rather far away, where nobody would ever have to ask you your name—because they would already know, just as you would know theirs.

Mma Ramotswe glanced at Julia. The other woman seemed completely absorbed by what she saw, her expression that of one who is relishing a moment of discovery and delight. "This is the place, Mma Julia," she said. "This is Mochudi."

They stopped at an intersection. A car ahead of them, packed with children in the rear seat, signalled with its indicator light that it would turn left, and then, almost immediately, this changed to right, and then to left once more. "Perhaps that means it will go straight on," said Mma Ramotswe, and they both laughed as this proved to be true.

"Sometimes it's best just to continue in the direction you're already following," said Julia.

Mma Ramotswe agreed. But there were some people, she thought, who were never satisfied with that. These were people who thought that things had to change all the time—that there was something wrong in sticking to the path you were already on. They were often unhappy, she felt; they imagined that people who were going in a different direction to them knew something that they themselves did not know. And this thought led to another thought, which was a memory of Obed Ramotswe telling her about a man he had known who was never happy with the house he lived in and who was always moving to another one, from which, after a very short time, he would launch a search for somewhere that he believed might suit him better. "Never do that," her father had cautioned her. "Look at what you have and say to yourself, 'I am very fortunate to have what I have.' Which is true, Precious, isn't it, don't you think?"

He had been right, of course, although she had not understood that until she was a good bit older. That was how it was, she told herself: it is only when we get a bit older that we realise that our parents knew what they were talking about. For some, it was a disappointing, even sobering discovery, because they had, up until then, been so sure that their parents were wrong about most things—or, if, they were not entirely wrong, still did not understand the ways of the world quite as well as one understood them oneself.

They drove past the small cluster of stores at the heart of the village. There was the general store, onto which extensions had been tacked over the years so that it was now a rambling warren, packed with the necessities of life—rope and plasters and small bottles of aspirin and tins of peaches preserved in syrup and boxes of ten candles and . . . She imagined that the store would smell the same as it had smelled when she was a girl, that aroma of goods as yet unbought, that aroma that was impossible to break down into its constituent parts. Then there was the butchery, on the front of which was the badly painted picture of a chicken in full plumage, with, at its side, a string of sausages. That sign was so familiar to Mma Ramotswe that she only noticed it now because she was looking at the village with the eyes of her new companion. And Julia had spotted it, because she had been about to say something, but had checked herself.

"That sign has been there ever since I can remember," said Mma Ramotswe. "It is a very odd picture, Mma, but I suppose it makes it clear what's for sale inside."

Julia smiled. "That is all it needs to say, Mma Ramotswe."

That was true, thought Mma Ramotswe. The trouble with signs was that many of them set out to tell you what to do, rather than being content to pass on some information. That was what was wrong with so many signs in towns—signs that displayed pictures of things that somebody wanted you to buy, when as often as not, you did not need the item they portrayed. Signs in villages—signs like this butcher's sign, showed you things that you actually *needed,* and there was a difference. There were also signs that could not resist the temptation to lecture you about something, or give you advice, even if you had not asked for it. Government signs liked to do that, telling you what to do or not do. She had once seen a sign that simply said, "Remember to register." Just that, with no explanation of what it was that you should remember to register for. She had mentioned it to Mr. J.L.B. Matekoni, who had laughed and told her of how he had once seen a sign that had simply said, *Beware of* but nothing more. "They must have run out of paint," he said. "Or perhaps they had forgotten what it was they were meant to be warning the public about."

"Yet it was good enough advice as it stood," Mma Ramotswe said. "We must beware of, I suppose, even if we do not know exactly what it is. Better to be safe than sorry."

"Perhaps it was *Beware of lions,*" Mr. J.L.B. Matekoni suggested. "But before the poor man could paint the word *lions,* he heard a noise . . ."

"A sort of growl?" prompted Mma Ramotswe.

"Yes. A sort of growl. Oh, Mma, this is a very sad story, I think . . ."

MMA RAMOTSWE PARKED HER VAN at the back of the hill, under the protective cover of a large acacia tree. Another driver had had the same idea, and there was just enough room for the two vehicles, huddled together in the pool of shade. Getting out of the van, Julia brushed at her jeans and looked up at the cloudless sky. A Cape dove, landing on a branch of the acacia, peered down at the two interlopers before cooing some announcement of its own.

"This is so lovely," whispered Julia, almost to herself.

Mma Ramotswe nodded. She knew this place so well. It was here that she and her friend would begin their walk to school each morning, a walk that took them up a winding path to the school on top of the hill. And there, beside that small boulder of red-brown stone, she had sat with the same friend when school had finished for the day; they had sat there and talked about what they would do once they grew up, as children will do, and with the same sense of boundless optimism that children always feel when they think of the future. She would have a big store in Gaborone, she said, one that sold fridges, and food to put in the fridges, and necklaces and bracelets too, and it would always be full of customers; while her friend would be a doctor in the hospital on the other side of the hill, and would give her patients injections with a large syringe, and would have six children, all girls, with a trailer to put the children in, and a large car to tow the trailer and a husband to drive the car and be helpful and respectful when not driving.

They began to make their way up that path that led to the top of the hill. It was not a long climb, but in parts it was quite steep, and they stopped to get their breath. "I used to be in better shape," said Julia. "But you know how it is."

Mma Ramotswe did know how it was. Mma Makutsi had recently made a few remarks about the importance of shedding a few pounds—and she was right, of course—but there seemed to be so many other pressing matters to deal with, and there was always tomorrow.

And suddenly it was there, the old school that had now become a small museum for the area. It was largely unchanged, a single-storey building with shady verandahs and wide, friendly windows. To the front, beyond a low outcrop of rocks and a small tangle of shrubs, the ground fell sharply away in an almost sheer, several-hundred-foot drop, down to the plains below. These plains stretched, it seemed, forever, interrupted only here and there by small conical hills that rose like islands in a sea of land. The hills and the landscape that surrounded them were of an attenuated blue, and as a child Mma Ramotswe had thought that the distant world, the wider world, must be blue in colour. She longed to travel one day to this intriguing world of blue.

She took Julia to the edge, and they stood there and gazed at the village below, with its meandering dirt roads and its little clouds of dust where a car or a truck made its way to one of the homesteads that made up the sprawling settlement. Mma Ramotswe pointed out to Julia the thin ribbon of water that wound its way through the brown—a few weeks earlier that would have been a dry bed, but there had been some rain now, and it had begun to flow. That insignificant river, so small when viewed from up there, was the beginnings of the Limpopo River, and she told Julia about that now. "We all have to start somewhere, I suppose, Mma," Julia remarked.

They stood in silence, each lost in the sort of thoughts that come to us when we look upon a place we love or are ready to love. Then the sound of cattle bells drifted from below, and Julia turned and looked at Mma Ramotswe and said, in wonderment, "There are bells, Mma." And Mma Ramotswe smiled and pointed towards the place where, far beneath them, cattle moved between the acacia trees. It was a sound that all those raised in Botswana had imprinted upon their hearts: the anthem of the land, the notes of the country. And it reminded her of her father, and of all that he meant to her.

She looked at Julia with fondness. She wanted Julia to be happy. She had detected a feeling of sadness in the other woman, and had been concerned that she might not be able to do much about that. Experience had taught her that there were many people who seemed to be searching for something that they would never find—who might not even know what they were looking for. That, she thought, was because so many of us felt that there must be an answer to the questions we all asked at one point or another—what was the purpose of our lives and why was there so much suffering?—and if we looked hard enough we would find the key to that. That search, although understandable, was one that was more or less destined to fail, and inevitably we were disappointed. The way to deal with the sorrow of the world, Mma Ramotswe thought, was not to think you would ever necessarily understand why the world was the way it was. Rather, you should list the things you felt were good, and work towards bringing those into the lives of others. That would keep you busy enough, because there was always—always—room for more kindness and love (and tea) in our lives, none of which needed any explanation or justification.

THEY WENT into the tiny museum's office, where Mma Ramotswe's friend, Edith Mokotedi, was secretary, treasurer, and director

rolled into one. The two of them were more or less exact contemporaries, and had grown up together in the village. They had
always referred to themselves as sisters, or, as Mma Mokotedi put
it, "sisters who would have been sisters had our parents filled in
the necessary paperwork." Mma Ramotswe had never quite been
sure what her friend meant by that, but laughed dutifully whenever the phrase came up. And she did so now, as, shortly after she
had made the introductions, Edith said to Julia, "This lady, Mma,
is my sister—or would have been, if our parents had filled in the
necessary paperwork. I am very cross with them for forgetting to
do it."

Julia smiled, and said, "You are lucky to have a sister, Mma—
even if the paperwork was never filled in. That doesn't matter too
much, surely."

"You have no sister, Mma?" asked Edith, and then, sensing that
her question was potentially tactless, hurriedly added, "Friends can
be sisters, of course. And there are some brothers, I think, who are
almost as good as sisters."

Mma Ramotswe looked puzzled. "What sort of brothers would
those be, Mma?"

Edith waved a hand vaguely. "Oh, brothers who are prepared to
listen to you. Many men won't do that, you know. They are happy
to talk to you, but they do not listen."

"Many men are unhappy," said Julia. "Perhaps they want to
listen, but they think that listening makes them seem weak. Men
think they need to look decisive."

Mma Ramotswe agreed with Julia. She liked men and did not
take pleasure in the thought that there were men who were unhappy
with who they were. And yet there were many of those, she felt—
men who would like to be able to let themselves feel about things in
the same way that women could; men who would like to be able to
say what was in their hearts.

Edith had been sitting behind her desk, almost concealed by a teetering stack of box files. Papers protruded from these files—press cuttings, letters, official documents of one sort or another, faded by sun, the paper trail of a community's history. Now she rose to her feet, and crossed the floor of the office to a small table on which a kettle, together with cups and a jug, stood in readiness.

"I needn't ask you whether you would like tea," she said to Mma Ramotswe. "That is a question that I think always gets the answer 'yes.' Am I right?"

"You are not only right," replied Mma Ramotswe, "you are *very* right, Mma."

Edith turned to face Julia. "My sister is always drinking tea," she said. "I like tea myself, but sometimes I like coffee. But for Mma Ramotswe here, it's always tea. And not just any tea . . ."

"Red bush," said Mma Ramotswe. "That is the tea I like to drink. It is very good for you, Mma. It helps the digestion—and the brain too, I'm told. It keeps the brain in good order."

"That is important," said Edith. "I have a long list of people who should drink a bit more red bush tea, I think." She tapped her head, to indicate the benefit such people required.

Mma Ramotswe smiled, but looked away. There were people who could do with a bit of improvement, but, for the most part, they were still doing their best—and that was the important thing. Even Violet Sephotho, of whom it was hard to say anything good—even she was probably doing her best . . . Forgiveness, she thought: we *all* need forgiveness for *something* . . .

Edith made the tea, and they sat together in the office, under the slowly turning overhead fan. After a few enquiries as to the health of mutual friends and acquaintances—including those who were recently and "regrettably late," as Edith put it—Mma Ramotswe broached the subject of Julia's search. "So that is why we are here, Mma," she concluded. "We are looking for somebody who was here a long time ago. We are looking for . . ."

"For a late person?" prompted Edith.

"Yes," said Mma Ramotswe. "You could put it that way." And, as she thought of it, it seemed to her that what Edith had said was, intentionally or otherwise, true about so much of what we were looking for in life: we were looking for late people, whether or not we knew it. The moment we started to think about ourselves and about what made us who we were, we were, in fact, looking for the *people* who made us who we were.

Edith was staring at Julia—not in a rude, inquisitive way, but with the sympathy that comes from knowing how the other person feels. Now she put that sympathetic understanding into words. "I can imagine how you feel, Mma," she said. "We all want to know about the people in our past. We need to know such things, I think."

"I'm glad that you understand," said Julia. "I have been worried that people will think I'm foolish for wanting to find out about things that happened a long time ago."

"No," said Mma Ramotswe.

And Edith said, "Tell me who you are looking for, Mma. I cannot guarantee anything, but I may be able to help." She gestured towards the files and the piles of paper. "That is my job, you see. History is my job."

Mma Ramotswe reached out to put a hand on Julia's forearm. "Perhaps you should start at the beginning," she said. And to Edith she said, "This is one of those stories that begins a long time ago, Mma. It starts in Protectorate days."

Edith smiled. "That is when so many things started. Take your time, Mma. We have all the time you need."

Julia began, and it was twenty minutes or so before she reached the point where she encountered Mma Ramotswe in the peri-peri restaurant. "And that is why I am here, Mma," she concluded. "I would like to find out about my grandfather. Because that's what he was to me, you see. I would like to find his people—if there are any left. I would like to meet them and . . . well, to tell them about him."

For a few moments, Edith was silent. Then she said, "Servicemen." Julia watched her.

"Servicemen," Edith repeated. "He was one of the servicemen. They went because the chiefs were keen for them to go. They were not really volunteers—or, some were, perhaps, but not many."

"But they were brave men," said Mma Ramotswe.

"Of course they were," Edith said quickly. "There were some who received medals. They only give medals to brave men."

Julia said, "There must be records."

Edith gestured towards the box files. "There are some records—not many. There are lists of who went, and from what area. Then there are some lists of who came back. But there may not be much else, you know. History doesn't pay much attention to ordinary people—half the time."

Julia lowered her eyes. "I thought that perhaps his family name might suggest something to you."

"It does," Edith said. "Yes, I know that name."

Julia brightened. "They still live around here?" she asked.

Edith nodded. She was cautious, but she confirmed that the family was known to her. "If they are the same people," she said. "You sometimes get people of the same name who are nothing to do with each other."

"Of course," interjected Julia. "But . . ."

"That is because there are not all that many names," Edith warned. "When you have people of the same name, there may be a connection a long time ago, but it may be very distant. At the end of the day, Mma, we are all cousins, but that doesn't make us the same family—if you see what I mean."

It was clear that Julia did not share Edith's reservations, or, if she did, she was anxious to overcome them. "Will we be able to meet them?" she asked.

Edith said that they would. But first, she insisted, she should consult a document that she had—somewhere—to see if there was any further information to be had about the men who came back. She doubted it, but she would try. "And then I shall see about talking to these people," she continued. "There is an old woman from that family. She may remember. Or not—she is very old, Mma, and sometimes these very old people have so many memories that they . . ." She made a circular movement with her right hand, as if stirring a cooking pot. "Sometimes the memories get mixed up."

"You don't have to be all that old to mix things up," remarked Mma Ramotswe. "I know many people who are still young and are very vague about what has happened because they don't pay enough attention and are looking elsewhere, or thinking about other things." She paused. "Now where was I . . . ?"

They all laughed.

"Why not go and take a look about the village," Edith suggested. "Then come back in a couple of hours, and I will have found out whether we can talk to anybody."

"That is a very good idea," said Mma Ramotswe, rising to her feet. She wanted to get Julia to herself, to warn her not to expect too much; to advise her to calm down. There was nothing wrong in having expectations, but hopes had to be kept in check, if disappointment was not inevitably to ensue. And there was something about this whole case, she felt, that had disappointment written all over it. There were so many people in this life who longed to find connections that would make them feel part of a bigger story. Often, they would search and search, snatching at the slightest link, hoping to find relatives or others with whom they might share some scrap

of the past. It was loneliness that lay behind this enthusiasm—
Mma Ramotswe was sure of that. Not that such loneliness was
anything to be ashamed of—all you had to do, she thought, was to
look up at the sky at night, at the great fields of stars, to realise just
how small we were, and how lonely too.

They walked down the hill again, she and Julia, and wandered
off towards the small cluster of shops near the old hospital. There
were patients from the hospital standing in the shade of the trees
near the gate, some of them wearing the faded pink garments that
the hospital gave to those who were receiving long-term treatment
for tuberculosis. One of them greeted Mma Ramotswe, and they
stopped to talk, exchanging views on the things that one shared with
strangers when one met them under trees, and the cicadas were
busy in the background, and you were in a place, a village, that you
had grown up in and still felt would always be home.

They found a small shop that served food. There were rickety
chairs on the shop's verandah and they sat in these, each eating a fat
cake and nursing a mug of steaming tea.

"You're happy here," said Julia. "I can see that."

Mma Ramotswe smiled at her. "This is my place, you see. That
is why I'm happy." And then, as she licked a few crumbs off her
fingers, she asked, "And you, Mma? Are you happy?"

Julia hesitated. "Now? Here?"

"No. Not just here."

There was a long silence, and Mma Ramotswe was about to
change the subject when Julia replied, "As happy as I think I can be,
Mma. After what happened to me."

"Your husband?"

She moved her head slightly, in almost undetectable agreement.

Mma Ramotswe sighed. "How many women are there in the
world who would give the same answer?" she said. "Most of us have

one chance in this life to find a man who will be a good husband to us—one chance, Mma. Oh yes, some of us get another chance—I am one of those, you know—but there are many of our sisters who cannot try again. And they fall in love with a man who makes them unhappy because he is selfish or unkind, or because he cannot stay with one woman and he goes off with this woman and that woman and so on. Oh, Mma, there is so much of that, and we are the ones who carry the sorrow of it all in our hearts."

Julia stared at her. "Oh, Mma Ramotswe," she began. "How can . . ." She stopped, and the unfinished question hung in the air between them.

Yet Mma Ramotswe knew what it was, even though Julia had not had the heart, or the words, to complete it.

"You forgive him," she said. "That is the only way, Mma. You forgive."

Julia looked away. Mma Ramotswe could see that she had closed her eyes and that her face was set. That was what anger looked like—she had seen it so many times. It made its mark on the face of those who felt anger within themselves. It made its mark in the features of the wronged, the harmed, the hurt. Anger was made of stone.

She felt she had to say something more. "I am not just saying this," she continued. "I have had to do it myself. I married a very bad man, Mma—that is the only way of talking about the man I married, Note Mokoti. He was a bad man. But, oh, Mma, I thought he was the most exciting man I had ever set eyes upon. He played the trumpet, you see. He played the trumpet so beautifully. And I could think of nothing but Note—all the time, all the time.

"My father, my late daddy—he could tell that Note was not the right man for me—or for any woman, really. But he realised that my heart was set on him, and so he just waited without saying anything, and when I came back to him—because there is only one thing to do with such men, Mma, and that is to leave them—when I came back home he never said, 'I told you so.' He just put his arms about me and let me cry. That is all. I went back to my daddy and I cried, Mma. All the tears, all the tears that had been waiting to be shed, now they came, like a river. Enough tears to swell the Limpopo River itself. And I cried and cried, because that is all we can do about men like that—we cry.

"But that was not the end of it. He came back, Note did, and he tried to get money from me because he needed it. I gave him some and then I did what I knew I had to do, which was something far more difficult than handing out money. I told him that I forgave him, and Mma, you should have seen his face. He stood there and he struggled to understand what I had said. He was not used to it and he did not know what to say, and so he left, and that was the last I saw of him.

"When I said that I forgave him—that was the strangest moment, Mma. A weight lifted off me. I had put down a big burden—like one of those great sacks of maize that you see those strong men at the railway sidings lifting onto the freight trucks. I had been carrying one of those, you see, and now it was off my shoulders. And it seemed to me that I was like one of those leaves that weigh nothing, that are blown about in the wind. I had no weight, Mma, because it had all gone when I forgave Note."

She stopped. She had said enough. She did not expect, or want, Julia to reply. It was time for them to go back up the hill, where Edith would be waiting for them with whatever it was that she had found.

"Do not expect too much," Mma Ramotswe said to Julia, as she took her empty mug to return to the shopkeeper.

"I am not expecting anything," muttered Julia.

I would like to believe you, thought Mma Ramotswe, but she could not. It was not a deliberate untruth—it was more like one of those things you muttered to yourself when you were hoping against hope that something would happen, although you knew, in your heart, that it might not.

CHAPTER TEN

FAST WOMEN

CHARLIE COULD BARELY contain himself. When Mma Makutsi arrived at the office early that afternoon—she had been out to lunch with an old friend at the President Hotel—she found him sitting in Mma Ramotswe's chair, his feet up on the desk, reading an out-of-date copy of the *Botswana Daily News.* Her look of disapproval had an immediate effect, and he took his feet off the desk and sat up straight, discarding the newspaper.

"You should not sit at Mma Ramotswe's desk when she is not here," Mma Makutsi reproached him. "What if everybody went and sat in other people's chairs when they were out of the office? It would be chaos."

"Mma Ramotswe is not here," Charlie defended himself. "I would not try to sit on her chair while she is sitting on it, Mma."

"The fact that she is not here is not the point," said Mma Makutsi. "It's a question of respect, Charlie. We don't use other people's things when their back is turned. We just don't."

Charlie rose from the chair, as nonchalantly as he could manage. "Mma Ramotswe wouldn't mind," he said. "She is not one of these fussy people. She is not like that."

Mma Makutsi glared at him. "Are you suggesting that I'm fussy, Charlie? Is that what you think?"

He made a placatory gesture. "I'm not thinking anything, Mma. Or at least I am not thinking of that sort of thing. I am thinking of the information that I have to give you. I have some very important news about somebody you do not like at all. Very important."

This had the desired effect. "About somebody I do not like? What is this news, Charlie?"

Mma Makutsi sat down and Charlie began to tell her about his assignment the previous evening and about the visit that he and Mr. J.L.B. Matekoni had made to the Maponde house. She listened intently, and when he reached the denouement—the discovery of the identity of the owner of the Cool Singles Evening Club—she drew in her breath sharply. "Violet Sephotho? Her? That woman?"

"Yes," said Charlie. "Violet Sephotho is behind this club. She is the boss. And she is carrying on with that teacher, Mma. He is helping her."

Mma Makutsi sat back in her chair, astonishment written across her face. "Should we be surprised, Charlie? I don't think so. Nothing should surprise us when it comes to Violet Sephotho. There is nothing that is beneath her—nothing at all."

"She is a very bad woman," said Charlie.

"Oh, she most certainly is," said Mma Makutsi. "And you want to hear something, Charlie? I have known that from the word go—from the beginning. Ever since she and I were in the same year at the Botswana Secretarial College—ever since the very first day of our course—I have known what sort of woman Violet is. I could tell, Charlie—oh yes, I could tell by the way she walked into the lecture room that first day. Her hips, oh my goodness. And her arms. Everything. It was as if she was walking on jelly. The principal came to speak to us, to tell us about the traditions of the college and what it stood for, and what did Violet do while he was speaking? I shall never forget, Rra. She painted her nails. She painted her nails while the principal of the Botswana Secretarial College was addressing the student body. Can you believe it? I could not. I sat there and thought, How can anyone be so disrespectful? That is what I thought, Charlie. And then it got worse—far worse. She flirted with the poor man who taught us accounts. He was a very small man with big ears, and she laughed at him behind his back, but when he was looking, she puckered up her lips—like this—as if she was about to blow him a kiss, and that poor man, who lived with a very large woman with whom he had sixteen children, they said—I think that is an exaggeration, maybe—but she flirted with him, and he became all flustered and forgot whether he was talking about the credit or debit column. I remember thinking: if God is planning to strike anybody down with lightning, then this woman must be at the top of his list. She was that bad, Rra. I am not making any of this up."

Mma Makutsi hesitated. "There is another thing, Charlie, that I have not told anybody about before. But now I will tell you, because you are a married man now and will know about these things. I do not like to speak about these private matters, but I can tell you about what Violet Sephotho said one morning. I have never been so shocked in my life. Never."

"I do not mind hearing about it," said Charlie. "I have heard of plenty of bad things, Mma, and will not be surprised."

Mma Makutsi lowered her voice. "She came into class one morning, late, as usual—she was often late, and she never apologised. She just walked in as if she owned the place. Anyway, she came in and she sat in the chair in front of mine so I could hear everything she said to her friend in the next seat. That friend was almost as bad as Violet, but not quite. There was not much between them, though. She came in and sat down and said to this other woman, 'I had hardly any sleep last night. That is why I am late.' Then she sniggered. A very low snigger, Charlie. Very low. Those were her words, Charlie. She is shameless, that woman."

Charlie looked doubtful. "Some people do not sleep well, Mma Makutsi. They lie awake."

Mma Makutsi gave a derisive snort. "And why is that, Charlie?"

"Because they are worried about things?"

Mma Makutsi shook her head. "You are very naïve, Charlie. You don't say what Violet said and then snigger. That means only one thing: she was with some man." She paused. "But we do not need to go into any of that. We must think about the problem in hand."

"Yes," said Charlie. "That is what I want to talk about. I am in charge of this case, you see. Mma Ramotswe said it is my investigation." He looked away. It was a hard admission to make, but he was at a loss as to what to do next. It had been easy enough to find out what he had found out, but now that he had the information, it was by no means obvious what he should do with it. "But I am not sure what to do now, Mma Makutsi. What's the next step in all this?"

The disapproval that Mma Makutsi had shown earlier was now replaced with undisguised concern. "We must talk about this, Charlie," she said. "We must take stock of where we are. That is what you do, you see, when you are not sure what to do next. You identify what you want to achieve, and then you work out how you can go about it, given what you already know. It's all there in Clovis Andersen's book. You will have read it, I think."

Charlie inclined his head. "Yes, you're right, Mma. What do we know? We know who is behind the club. Now, what do we want to achieve? We want to stop that person from doing what she has been doing—in other words . . ."

Mma Makutsi took over, her voice shrill with indignation: "In other words, we need to stop that famous husband-stealer from causing emotional havoc on an industrial scale. Yes, on an industrial scale, Charlie."

Charlie agreed that this is what they had to do. But that, he thought, was the easy part. How they were to put a stop to Violet Sephotho's activities was a different matter altogether. And no amount of defining or reframing the issue took them any closer to a solution to that.

Mma Makutsi had an idea. "What is in the minds of the men who go to this so-called Cool Singles Evening Club? That's the question we should be asking, Rra."

Charlie did not hesitate to answer. In his mind it was obvious. "Women," he replied. "These men are interested in meeting women."

"But what sort of women?" pressed Mma Makutsi.

Charlie was embarrassed. He looked away. "Fast women," he muttered. "The sort of women you don't meet in church."

Mma Makutsi could not suppress a smile. "Oh, Charlie," she said, "you sound so old-fashioned."

He looked at her reproachfully. Was she expecting him to spell it out? "Ladies who . . ." He trailed off. Mma Makutsi was already shaking her head.

"Ladies who think these men are single," she said, with the air of one explaining a very simple matter. "But there is another thing in the minds of these men, I can tell you. They are one hundred per cent certain not to want their wives to know what they're up to."

"I suppose they don't," said Charlie. "Wives do not like that sort of thing, Mma—or most of them don't. They like their husbands to come home after work. They don't like them to go to clubs like that—and meet women."

"Exactly," said Mma Makutsi. "Now if news of the club got out and there was lots of talk, men like that would be worried. If they thought there was a chance their wives would learn that they were going to such a club, then what would they do, do you think? Men don't like trouble. Not as a general rule."

"They wouldn't go there then," said Charlie.

"And if nobody went to the club," Mma Makutsi continued, "then there would be no club. The Cool Singles Non-Existent Evening Club, I'd say." She paused, a look of pleasure coming over her face. "So much for Violet Sephotho. No men—no club. Business failure, first class. All over and finished." She paused again, clearly relishing the thought. "And that's what happens to you if you get barely fifty per cent in the final examinations of the Botswana Secretarial College. Failure."

Charlie was impressed, but it was still not clear, he thought, how they would ensure that people knew what was going on. He asked about that, and Mma Makutsi did not take long to come up with the answer.

"The newspapers," she said. "We tell the papers."

He considered this. "But will they believe us? There are always lots of stories floating around. They can't publish everything they hear."

Mma Makutsi, it seemed, was ready for this. "We give them facts, Charlie. Facts. You go to them as an employee of the club—which is what you are now. They know all about whistle-blowers—that's what you'll be, you see. You tell them what's really going on, and then we give them an actual example. You tell them about that man who misled that young woman—Mma Ikobeng's daughter. We even know who he is—remember? Or we can find out, because somebody knew that and passed it on."

"But she might not like her name getting into the papers, Mma."

Mma Makutsi thought this a good point. "We say that she wishes to remain anonymous. They respect that sort of thing."

Charlie was still not convinced. He had agreed to go undercover to the club—that was complicated enough—but now he was being asked to go and talk to a journalist, and that was taking matters further. What if the journalist started quizzing him? Such people were known for their nosiness—their suspiciousness—and he was not sure that he wanted to expose himself to that sort of thing.

Mma Makutsi, though, had no doubts. "This is a very good first case for you, Charlie." She fixed him with a challenging stare. "I wouldn't have thought that you were ready for something quite as difficult as this, you know, but now . . . Well, now I think you are definitely capable of doing this."

"Definitely, Mma?"

"That's what I said, Charlie. Definitely."

"Ninety-seven per cent?" he asked.

She frowned. "What's that got to do with it, Charlie?"

Charlie did not answer. Something else had occurred to him, and now he wondered whether he should not discuss the matter with Mma Ramotswe. She was, after all, the boss, even if Mma Makutsi acted as if she had as much authority as Mma Ramotswe. So now he ventured, "Shouldn't we wait until we've discussed it with Mma Ramotswe, Mma?"

Mma Makutsi was brisk. "No need, Charlie. This is your case, remember, and what's the point of having your own case if you go running to Mma Ramotswe whenever a decision has to be taken?"

Charlie bit his lip. "I don't go running to her," he muttered. Yet he knew that Mma Makutsi was probably right. You had to do things of your own accord, sooner or later, just as student pilots had to fly solo at some stage. There was no point in putting things off, he thought, and so he nodded his agreement and listened while Mma Makutsi gave him the name of a journalist whom she had once met and who, she claimed, would be just the person to approach.

"He likes to investigate scandals and such things," she said. "He is known for just this sort of story."

Charlie swallowed hard and noted down the name of the journalist and his telephone number. "He's called Tommy Pilani," Mma Makutsi said. "And he's a very smart man."

Charlie closed his notebook: he would get in touch the following day, he thought.

"Call him now," Mma Makutsi advised. "Never put things off, Charlie. What has to be done, has to be done, and it won't go away if you put it off."

Charlie took a deep breath, and reached for the telephone on Mma Ramotswe's desk. "I will speak to him," he said.

"Good," said Mma Makutsi. "You are being very decisive, Charlie. That is very good."

AND NOW Tommy Pilani's door was being pointed out to him in the offices of the *Botswana Daily News*. He made his way down the corridor and knocked lightly—hoping, even at this late stage, that the journalist might not be in. He could go back to the office, then, and say that he had at least tried to make contact, and he could put this off until he had spoken to Mma Ramotswe, who might even volunteer to accompany him. But Tommy Pilani was there, and called out for him to come in.

Tommy Pilani was a man somewhere in his early thirties, well dressed, and with a casual confidence about him. He had a shrewd, intelligent face, and there was a look in his eye that betrayed the scepticism of his profession. This was a man who had seen everything—even before it happened.

"So, you're Charlie," the journalist said. "You're the person who phoned."

Charlie nodded. "I'm from the . . ."

"From the No. 1 Ladies' Detective Agency?"

"Yes."

Tommy Pilani laughed. Who was this gawky young man with the ill-fitting jacket? "I thought that place was staffed by ladies. Mma What's-her-face and that woman with the big glasses. What are you doing working for them, Rra?"

"Yes, they are ladies, Rra, but I'm their apprentice. I'm learning the job."

Tommy looked thoughtful. "I suppose that's the way to do it. It's the same with journalism—you have to learn on the job. Oh, you can go to college and whatnot, but the real lessons are learned right here, in the newspaper office. You learn by your mistakes."

He invited Charlie to sit down. "You've got a story for me, you said."

"Yes," said Charlie. "There is a story."

Tommy reached for a notebook. "Have you spoken to anybody else about it?"

Charlie said that he had not.

"Because we don't like it when other people have the story too," Tommy explained. "There's nothing worse than spending time—and money too—on something and then discovering that another paper publishes it the day before you've been planning to break it. That's bad."

Charlie repeated his assurances that he had spoken to nobody outside the agency. "The only people who know about this are my colleagues," he said. "Mma Makutsi and Mr. J.L.B. Matekoni."

"The mechanic guy?"

"Yes. His wife is the manager of the agency. She is the chief detective."

Tommy invited Charlie to begin. At the end, when Charlie had finished, he closed his notebook and tucked his pencil into a pocket. "Interesting," he said. He looked up at the ceiling, seemingly lost in thought. "This Violet Sephotho—have you come across her before?"

"I know about her," said Charlie. "Mma Makutsi has known her for a long time."

"Some lady," said Tommy. "She's had a finger in many pies in the past. If there's anything fishy going on, they say that Violet Sephotho is bound to be involved in it somewhere."

"That's what Mma Makutsi says," said Charlie. "She has known her for many years."

"But you say that she has somebody else working with her? Who exactly is that?"

"He's a teacher," replied Charlie.

Tommy looked up. He frowned. "A teacher?"

"Yes, a deputy principal."

Tommy reopened his notebook. "His name? Do you know his name?"

Charlie hesitated. He was not sure that this had anything to do with Mr. Modise. He was simply a helper—a poor man caught in the headlights of the scheming Violet Sephotho. This story was not about him—or his unfortunate infatuation with Violet.

"He's not important in this," said Charlie. "He is just somebody who helps."

"But you say that he's a deputy principal. Are you sure about that?"

"Yes. He was deputy principal when I was at school. We all liked him."

"And his name?"

Charlie felt trapped. "Modise," he said. "It is Mr. Modise."

Tommy made a note in his book. Then he stood up. "Well," he said. "I needn't take up more of your time."

Charlie asked whether the story of the existence of the club was of interest. Tommy shrugged. "Maybe," he said. "I'll see what my editor says." He grinned as he continued, "The problem is that it's not against the law for married men to go off and meet women in bars. At least, not yet. So we'll have to see."

It was clear that the interview was now at an end. Charlie said goodbye and left the room; he did not feel that the interview had been a conspicuous success. Tommy Pilani had been polite enough, but Charlie sensed that he was not all that interested in what he had been told. He had made a few notes, of course, but there was no sign that he was at all fired up with enthusiasm to investigate the Cool Singles Evening Club. If nothing came of this, thought Charlie, then he would definitely have to seek Mma Ramotswe's guidance as to how to proceed.

He went outside, into the warmth of the late afternoon. The sun beat down remorselessly, even as the shadows thrown by the trees and the buildings lengthened. In the cloudless sky above, a few circling birds, eagles or vultures—they were too high for Charlie to identify—circled lazily on thermal currents, watching over the town and its precincts. He felt hot in the jacket he had donned for the interview. He took it off, slung it over his shoulder, and began to trudge back along the roadside towards the place where he knew he could pick up a minibus to take him back to the Tlokweng Road. He felt humiliated: here he was, well into his twenties, still having to travel by cheap public transport, even on business, when all around him were people with their air-conditioned cars. And what was the point of this work he was doing? Did it make any difference to anybody's life? He used to think that it did, but now he was not so sure. And did it offer him any chance of promotion, security, and a comfortable salary? He would have liked to answer those questions in a positive way, but he could not. I'm just a failure, he said to himself. In due course I'll be a thirty-year-old failure, and then a forty-year-old failure. All the way to retirement, in regular increments, when I'll become a retired failure. That is what lies ahead, he thought. Charlie Failure: that's my name. Charlie Failure.

CHAPTER ELEVEN

DRESS DISTRESS

SINCE MMA RAMOTSWE WAS in Mochudi and Charlie was off at his interview with Tommy Pilani, Mma Makutsi decided to close the office and attend to one or two tasks that had been awaiting her attention for some days now. There was a parcel to take to the post office, there was one of Phuti's suits to pick up from the dry cleaners, and there was a dress to be collected from Mma Mogatusi's shop. This was the red dress that she was intending to give to Mma Ramotswe as her birthday present, and that had been specially ordered from a supplier over the border. She had expected to hear from Mma Mogatusi that the dress had arrived, but this had not happened. She thought, though, that it would have been delivered by now, as Mma Mogatusi had assured her that she would not need to wait for more than three or four days. That assistant of hers was the trouble, Mma Makutsi told herself: she looked like the sort who would forget to tell customers when garments were waiting for collection. She had a lazy face, that young woman—you could always tell.

Mma Mogatusi was serving another customer when Mma Makutsi entered the shop. Her assistant was also busy, in her case show-ing two teenage girls a range of glittery tops. There was a certain amount of giggling, and Mma Makutsi decided that that would not be a quick transaction. She would wait for Mma Mogatusi; there was plenty to do in a shop like this, with its large stock of shoes and outfits for all occasions.

Eventually Mma Mogatusi finished with her customer and was able to come over to speak to Mma Makutsi.

"Mma Makutsi," she said, reaching out to take her hand. "I have been thinking about you."

Mma Makutsi made a polite enquiry after the other woman's health.

Mma Mogatusi cleared her throat. She seemed uncomfortable, and Mma Makutsi wondered whether she had come at an awkward time. "You will have come about that dress," said the shopkeeper.

"I thought it might be ready, Mma," said Mma Makutsi. "It was for Mma Ramotswe's birthday, you see, and that was a few days ago now."

Mma Mogatusi looked away. "Ah yes," she said. "Mma Ramotswe."

"Yes, it is for her. It is a present."

Mma Mogatusi shifted her weight from foot to foot. It was an annoying gesture, and Mma Makutsi found herself irritated by it.

"Has it arrived?" she asked. "You said that it would not be long."

Mma Mogatusi said that it had indeed arrived. "It is here in the shop," she said.

"Good," said Mma Makutsi. "Please will you wrap it for me? It is nice to have presents wrapped properly."

There was a short pause before the answer came. "Oh yes, that is quite true. But I'm afraid that this dress . . ."

Mma Makutsi waited. After a minute or so, during which Mma Mogatusi offered no further information, she said, "Is there something wrong with the dress, Mma? Did they send the wrong colour? Is that the problem?"

Mma Mogatusi shook her head. "That happens more often than you might imagine, Mma. Not long ago I ordered a green dress, and they sent a blue one. You cannot confuse green with blue."

Mma Makutsi agreed. "They are quite different colours, I think."

"You are right about that, Mma Makutsi. Quite different. They tried to suggest that it was all my fault, but I had a document to prove that I had ordered green. It is always an idea, Mma, to get documentary evidence, if at all possible. Always print out an order, and then keep it in the appropriate file. If you do that, you will always be able to prove that it is the other person who is wrong—not you."

"Yes, yes, Mma Mogatusi," said Mma Makutsi, a note of irritation creeping into her voice. Who was this shopkeeper to talk about filing—to one who had achieved still unequalled distinction in the subject at the Botswana Secretarial College? But she contained herself, and went on to ask, "What about this particular dress, though? Let us talk about that dress, if you don't mind, Mma."

Mma Mogatusi closed her eyes, as one might do if faced with an unpalatable reality. "I think there is something wrong, Mma. Yes, there is something wrong." She opened her eyes and looked directly, and unflinchingly, at Mma Makutsi. "The dress in question is . . . is non-functional."

Mma Makutsi frowned. Why could people not use simple language? "Non-functional? What does that mean, Mma?"

"It means that it is damaged."

Mma Makutsi's response was brisk and to the point. "If it is damaged, then send it back. That is the simple answer to this sort of thing." That was the policy of Phuti's business, the Double Comfort Furniture Store, and it always worked, Mma Makutsi reminded herself. Everybody knew where they stood if a simple policy of only accepting merchantable quality was applied. "I can tell Mma Ramotswe that she will have to wait a bit longer for her birthday present."

"It did not arrive damaged," said Mma Mogatusi. "It was damaged in the shop."

"That is not my problem," said Mma Makutsi. "If it has been damaged by a member of your staff—or by some other customer—then I'm afraid that is nothing to do with us. As I said, we can wait while a new one is sent by your supplier."

Mma Mogatusi's discomfort was becoming increasingly evident. "There is another party involved," she said.

"Another party?" snapped Mma Makutsi. "Who is this party?"

Now Mma Mogatusi sounded quite miserable. "It is Mma Ramotswe."

This was almost too much for Mma Makutsi. "Mma Mogatusi," she began, "of course Mma Ramotswe is involved. She is the person for whom this dress was intended right from the start. This dress is not for me, nor for any other party. This dress is for Mma Ramotswe, and if it is non-functional, as you put it, then it must be replaced with another dress, or we can wash our hands of the entire affair." She paused. That possibility was becoming increasingly attractive. "In fact, that might be the best thing to do, I think."

Mma Mogatusi now had no alternative but to spell out what had happened. She told Mma Makutsi of the unfortunate incident in which the dress had been ruined, and explained how it was that the issue had so far been left unresolved. In her view, the dress had been ordered by Mma Makutsi and, much as she, Mma Mogatusi, might regret it, it was she who should bear the cost.

At least the situation was now clear—not that this resolved the issues of principle. In Mma Makutsi's view, the damage to the dress was neither her fault nor Mma Ramotswe's. It was possible, though, that it was Mma Mogatusi's fault for failing to see that the dress was obviously too small for Mma Ramotswe— anybody should have been able to see that—and if that was the case, then she, surely, should shoulder the cost. One glance, though, at the now clearly agitated shopkeeper, made it clear that this was unlikely to be well received. That left a further, as yet unexplored possibility.

"Perhaps this is an act of God," Mma Makutsi suggested. "Perhaps that is the best way of looking at what happened."

Mma Mogatusi drew in her breath. Was sacrilege now being piled upon obduracy? "What has God got to do with it, Mma? Why are you bringing him into it?"

Mma Makutsi explained. An act of God was no fault of anybody's, she said; it was simply one of these things that happened, like lightning, or a flood.

"And such things are not the fault of anybody?" asked Mma Mogatusi.

"That is so," said Mma Makutsi. "If you are struck by lightning, nobody will say it's your fault. They will say, how unfortunate; poor person—poor *late* person, probably."

This was enough for Mma Mogatusi. "Then the damage to this dress is not my fault," she said, with an air of satisfaction. "So, I should not have to pay for it."

It was, she thought, a vindication of her original position, and she did not take kindly to Mma Makutsi's immediate riposte that if your house was struck by lightning, while it might not be your fault you still had to pay for the damage to the roof.

And so the discussion might have continued—in the way

of so many of these discussions—for several hours, had it not been for Mma Makutsi's sudden decision that she had to get to the dry cleaners before they closed for the day. That led to her immediate withdrawal, even in the face of Mma Mogatusi's injured reproaches and an intense glare from her assistant, who had been half following the dispute while she attended to the still unsatisfied teenagers.

"This is a very bad thing," came Mma Mogatusi's final observation. "No good will come of this affair, Mma—I'm telling you."

"I shall discuss it with Mma Ramotswe," announced Mma Makutsi as she left. "She is very good at sorting these things out."

It was easy to say that, of course—and Mma Ramotswe was indeed good at resolving even the most awkward issues. But that did not serve to make the situation any less embarrassing, and so Mma Makutsi decided to put the matter out of her mind for the time being. That sometimes worked with these tricky issues— although not always.

IN MOCHUDI, Mma Ramotswe spent an hour and a half sitting with Julia under a frangipani tree while Edith went down into the village. For the most part they sat in silence, not feeling the need to say very much; and what was there to say, anyway, because they were both thinking of Edith's errand, and whether it would lead to anything. Every now and then, though, Mma Ramotswe would make some remark, and Julia would answer, or simply nod her agreement. There would be rain soon, Mma Ramotswe hoped; yes, said Julia, somebody else had said that rain in the next few days was certain—or at least as certain as anything to do with the weather could be. Had Julia noticed how quickly time went by these days, while it dragged so painfully when one was a child? Yes, she had noticed that, and she had read somewhere that it was because we laid down so many memories as a child and that had the effect of altering time. Did Julia like cooking? She did, but she found it hard to get the time to spend on it—frozen food was so, well, *convenient;* and Mma Ramotswe agreed, though she said that she did not like to cook things from the freezer, as that somehow seemed unnatural. And so the languid minutes passed, until at length Mma Ramotswe heard footsteps, the crunching of large grains of sand on rock, and they were joined by Edith, whose brow was covered with beads of perspiration from the heat and the climb up the hill.

Julia looked up in anticipation. "Have you—?"

She did not finish the question. "I have found the lady I was looking for," said Edith. "She is still in the house I remembered her living in."

"And will she see us?" asked Mma Ramotswe.

"She will. She is very old, and it is not always easy to hear what she is saying. But she will see us."

"When, Mma?" asked Julia.

"Now," replied Edith. "People like her have nowhere to go. One day is very much like any other."

"Right now?" pressed Julia.

"She is expecting us," said Edith.

They made their way down to Mma Ramotswe's van. The windows had been left open, because of the heat, but it was still oppressively warm inside, especially where the sun had beaten down through the windows onto the seats, which were uncomfortably hot to the touch.

"Once we are moving, it will get cooler," said Mma Ramotswe.

Julia seemed indifferent to the heat and to being squashed between Edith and Mma Ramotswe in the cab of the van. Glancing at her from behind the wheel, Mma Ramotswe saw the excitement written on her visitor's face. This worried her. She understood what finding family—even a connection such as this, not a blood one, but what might be called a longed-for connection of the heart— might mean, but it seemed to her that the chances of disappoint- ment were looming large. There was no certainty that, just because the people whom Edith knew shared Khumo's family name, they would be relatives. And even if they were related, the relationship could be a distant one. People spoke of third and fourth cousins— those to whom their link was founded upon the sharing of a third or fourth great-grandparent. That meant very little in real terms. There would be no shared memories and probably no shared character- istics. One would look in vain for familiar features of the sort that one saw occurring between generations. Such relatives really were strangers, to all intents and purposes.

It did not take them long to reach the isolated homestead on the edge of the village. It was not much of a building—two circular rondavels, pasted with decaying brown outside plaster, and a small square block of uneven brick. The yard surrounding the buildings was bounded by a low, mud-plastered wall, a *lelapa,* encircling the world of the family within. As was customary, they called out a greeting before entering this simple sanctum. From one of the rondavels, a man in dishevelled khaki trousers and shirt appeared, looked in their direction, and beckoned. They fol- lowed the man into the brick-built house, which was dark inside, lit only by a couple of small, high windows. It took a moment or two for Mma Ramotswe's eyes to accustom themselves to the gloom, but, when they did, she took in the simple table, covered with a stained oiled cloth, the metal folding chairs of the sort that were to be found in older church halls, and a small elec- tric cooker. On a blanket-covered sofa at the end of the room, an elderly woman sat, propped up with cushions. There was a smell of staleness in the air, a smell of rancid food, a smell of poverty.

Edith introduced the woman. "This is Mma Sepole," she said.

Sepole. The effect of the name on Julia was immediate. She moved forward and took the old woman's hand. "Hello, Mma. Hello Mma Sepole."

Mma Sepole spoke only Setswana, and Mma Ramotswe now acted as interpreter. "She says that she is happy that you have come to see her. She says that she has been waiting for this day. She says that now it has come, she is very happy."

Julia began to speak, but emotion prevented her from saying more than a few words. And Mma Sepole had not finished. "She says," Mma Ramotswe continued, "that she has heard the story from Mma Edith. She says that the man who was your grandfather was the cousin of her uncle, by a different mother. I am not sure what she means by that, but that is what she says. She says that she had heard from her uncle that he had gone off when there was a war and that everybody had thought he was late. She says that many people became late in that war."

Now the man spoke. As he did so, Mma Ramotswe turned to him and saw that his eyes were clouded. He spoke in English, half turning to Julia as he did so.

"I am very happy that you have come to us," he said. "We are very poor here. I cannot work because my eyes do not let me see very much. I was a driver. I drove cattle trucks down to Lobatse. I did that for many years. Now I cannot see the road. It is worse at night. It is as if a small light, a small one, is a big sun."

There was silence.

Then the man continued, "Would you like water?"

Edith signalled that they should accept the water, which they drank from tin cups. Then Julia said, "I would like to tell you the story of Khumo."

The old woman waited for this to be translated. She listened attentively as Mma Ramotswe relayed what Julia said, and she nodded in agreement at random points. Then she asked, "Why are you here, Mma?"

Julia looked puzzled as Mma Ramotswe told her what Mma Sepole had said.

"I think she is confused, Mma."

"My eyes are very bad," interjected the man. "I can see light, though. I cannot read—not even road signs." He paused. "They say they can fix these things."

Julia glanced at Mma Ramotswe. She did not need to say anything. Mma Ramotswe understood.

Now Mma Ramotswe asked the man a question. "You are not from Mochudi, are you? Not originally. I was wondering where your village was, Rra."

The man stared at her with his unseeing eyes. "It is that side," he said, pointing to the north. "We have not been there for a long time."

"But did your mother here ever meet this man they call Khumo? He was from Mochudi, you see, and I think your people are—"

He did not let her finish. There was a note of resentment in his voice now. "They are the same people, Mma. Some from here—some not from here. They are the same. You heard what she said."

Mma Ramotswe was silent.

Now Julia asked, "Could they tell me anything more about other relatives?"

The man had understood. He said something to his mother—something they did not catch—and then he replied, "They are late. The others are all late. We are a small family now. We are not many." He fingered the hem of his khaki shirt. "My eyesight is bad now. If I could go to the doctor in Gaborone. There is a special doctor there, I think."

Julia cleared her throat. "I can help you, Rra," she said.

He reached out to take her hand. Mma Ramotswe noticed that he saw where it was—he did not fumble.

"The Lord has sent you to us," he said.

CHAPTER TWELVE

UNINTENDED CONSEQUENCES

TWO DAYS LATER, Mma Ramotswe drove out to see her friend, Mma Potokwane, and had a worrying and entirely unwelcome surprise. She had parked in her usual place, under a sheltering acacia tree, and had mounted the steps to Mma Potokwane's office, when she heard, drifting through the window, the sound of the matron's voice.

"Yes, I have seen it," said Mma Potokwane. "Somebody has given me a copy."

There was a brief pause, as the person on the other end of the line spoke. Then Mma Potokwane continued, "It is very sad. It is always sad when the innocent suffer. Always."

There followed a brief exchange, only half of which Mma Ramotswe heard, and then the telephone call came to an end.

"It's me, Mma," said Mma Ramotswe, pushing at Mma Potokwane's half-open door.

Mma Potokwane looked up from her desk. "Oh, Mma Ramotswe," she said. "This is not very good news at all." She gestured to the copy of the *Botswana Daily News* laid out before her. "You've seen it, Mma?"

Mma Ramotswe had not seen it. She read the newspaper conscientiously—she had to be well informed in her job—but she had not seen the latest issue. She was silent as Mma Potokwane handed her the newspaper, folded to expose a double-page internal spread. The headline, set in large type, leaped out at her with heart-sinking clarity.

"Deputy Principal's Secret Life"

She looked across the desk at Mma Potokwane, who lowered her eyes in shame.

"Oh, Mma Potokwane . . ."

Mma Potokwane moved her head slowly from side to side—an acknowledgment of human weakness. "Yes, Mma," she said. "It is all there—the whole story." She paused. "I have just been on the telephone to somebody who knows the wife of this man. There is always a wife somewhere—and family—who suffer. I have heard that she knew nothing about what was going on."

Mma Ramotswe looked down at the report.

"Read it out," said Mma Potokwane. "I have already read it, but I would like to hear it again. The first time, I might have been a bit too shocked to take it in properly."

Mma Ramotswe began. "How do we expect the occupants of senior positions in our school system to spend their spare time? In reading? In making sure that they are up to date with all the most recent educational theories? In studying for additional qualifica-tions? All of these are worthy pursuits. But what we do not expect is that they should be earning a bit of extra money running night-clubs—and disreputable nightclubs at that! So I was astonished as anybody when I investigated information passed on to me from a reliable source and found that a much-respected local deputy prin-cipal was playing an active part in the running of a club called the Cool Singles Evening Club. What sort of example does that set? I asked myself. The answer, of course: not a very good one."

Mma Ramotswe put down the paper. "Oh, Mma, this is not good at all."

"No," said Mma Potokwane. "And if you read on, you will see that the principal of the school has announced his suspension. The paper says that the most likely result will be his dismissal, with loss of pension rights."

Mma Ramotswe read the rest of the report silently. When she had finished, she let out a low groan. "I also know his wife, Mma. She is the lady who does a lot of work for the winter blanket appeal."

Mma Potokwane made a clicking sound. Mma Ramotswe recognised it as the sound she made whenever her disapproval of something ran deep. "It's one thing to bring attention to that club," she said. "It's another thing to bring disgrace to a wife. And the pension is half hers, of course—if he loses that, then so does she."

"That is very true, Mma." Mma Ramotswe was staring fixedly at the floor. "This is my fault, I think. I sent Charlie round there—and now this has happened."

Now she explained to Mma Potokwane that although she had seen neither Charlie nor Mma Makutsi that day, Mr. J.L.B. Matekoni had passed on to her the previous night what he had learned from Charlie. He had then told her about their visit to the Modises' neighbours and about what they had learned there of the relationship between Violet and the deputy principal.

"I think that what has happened is that Charlie has told all this to this journalist," she said. "He must be the source mentioned in the report." She paused. It occurred to her that Charlie might have been advised in the case by Mma Makutsi, as she was not sure that it would have occurred to him to approach the newspaper himself. Now she continued, "The whole thing is very messy, Mma. But I fear that it is all my fault. I put Charlie on to this because I felt that he needed to get a bit more experience. I did not think that this would happen. It is all my fault, Mma Potokwane."

Her friend was quick to object. "No, Mma. It is *my* fault. I brought you into this. I took you to see Mma Ikobeng. I encouraged the whole thing, even if I didn't know that Modise was mixed up in it."

"Perhaps we are both a bit to blame," said Mma Ramotswe. "I am not sure whether there is much point in crying over spilt milk, though—and there is definitely some spilt milk here, Mma."

They looked at one another, and slowly Mma Potokwane began to smile. "We are just two interfering ladies," she said. "We have poked our noses into something that really was none of our business, and this is the result. What can interfering ladies expect, Mma Ramotswe? They can expect exactly this sort of thing to happen."

Mma Ramotswe managed a smile—just. What Mma Potokwane said was true enough, she thought, but she nonetheless was not sure that she completely regretted her involvement—even with this unexpected, and rather serious result. It would have been easy enough to have fobbed Mma Ikobeng off with some excuse for not getting involved—something about how although it was utterly reprehensible that an organisation like the Cool Singles Evening Club should be able to facilitate male bad behaviour with impunity, nonetheless it was just one of these things that had to be borne with resignation. The world was an imperfect place, and there were always people who were prepared to exploit weakness. In an ideal world, they would be exposed and shamed, but in the world in which we lived they might get away with it. You could not make *everyone* good, she might have said to Mma Ikobeng. It was most unfortunate that her daughter had been treated badly, but she would simply have to write the whole thing off to experience and be more careful next time she went out to meet men in bars.

She could have said that, but even as she thought of it,

Mma Ramotswe realised that she could never have said anything like that with conviction. She was not one to let injustice or bad behaviour flourish under her nose—she was not one to stand by. And now that she had followed her instincts to help, and everything had gone so badly wrong—at least for Mma Modise—she could hardly disengage.

"I shall have to speak to Charlie," she said. "I shall have to find out what this is all about."

"And then?" asked Mma Potokwane.

"And then I shall see if there is anything we can do to help poor Mma Modise."

Mma Potokwane nodded. "And him? And Modise himself? What about that foolish man?"

"That is something I simply can't understand," answered Mma Ramotswe. "Why should a deputy principal get mixed up in something like this? He must earn a perfectly adequate salary—a good salary, in fact . . ."

She stopped speaking. The reason was staring her in the face: the deputy principal was doing this because of his involvement with Violet Sephotho. She had drawn him into the whole thing and, being a man in love, he had thrown caution to the winds. She suggested this now to Mma Potokwane, who listened, thought for a few moments, and then agreed.

"I think that is probably what happened," said the matron. "Men do peculiar things, don't they? You have heard of the male menopause, I take it?"

Mma Ramotswe had. Modise's age had been given in the newspaper article. He was forty-five—and that, she understood, was a very dangerous age for a man. That was well known, of course.

"Biology, Mma. Biology has a lot to answer for," observed Mma Potokwane. She paused. "Now, Mma Ramotswe, can I give you a cup of tea—and some cake? I believe I have some fresh fruit cake in the cupboard."

For the first time in years—if not ever—Mma Ramotswe declined Mma Potokwane's offer of cake. She was not sure why she did so; perhaps it was to do with heart: one had to have one's heart in the eating of fruit cake, and the mood of her visit had been changed with this disturbing news. "I'll have a quick cup of tea, Mma," she said. "But then I think I should get back straightaway. I need to talk to Charlie—and possibly also to Mma Makutsi. She may know more than I do about all this."

"Then let me wrap up a slice of cake for you, Mma," said Mma Potokwane. "Then you can eat it when you get to the office."

Mma Ramotswe thanked her. It was hard to miss the chance of a slice of Mma Potokwane's fruit cake, even in trying circumstances such as these. However, she felt that she had to point out that it would be invidious to eat a slice of fruit cake in the office with others there to watch her. They would hardly be indifferent: Mr. J.L.B. Matekoni, who often joined them for tea, experienced a delight in Mma Potokwane's cakes that was as profound as it was frequently expressed, and it was almost certainly shared by Charlie; and as for Mma Makutsi, although she sometimes claimed not to have a sweet tooth, the enthusiasm with which she had gobbled up the last fruit cake that Mma Potokwane had brought to the office of the No. 1 Ladies' Detective Agency had been noticeable. No, she could not indulge privately; it would be more polite, she felt, to decline—at least on this occasion.

But Mma Potokwane would have none of that. If the old Botswana code of morality, to which she knew she and Mma Ramotswe both adhered, meant anything, then it dictated that food was to be shared. And so, brushing aside Mma Ramotswe's protestations that she should not go to any trouble, she cut five generous slices and wrapped them up in the *Botswana Daily News,* using the very pages that related Modise's misfortune. That did not escape Mma Ramotswe's notice, and she allowed herself a wry smile. "It might be some comfort to that poor misguided man," she said, "to know that he kept our cake fresh."

"Hah," said Mma Potokwane. "He is having our cake, but we are eating it."

That, thought Mma Ramotswe, was a very clever thing to say. Mma Potokwane was an extremely intelligent woman—as well as an excellent baker of fruit cake. The two went together, she thought—or might do. Possibly.

WHEN MMA RAMOTSWE REACHED the office on her return from her truncated visit to Mma Potokwane, she found Mma Makutsi was busy with a long and complicated letter to a client who was questioning a bill: "If anything," she exploded, "we *under*charged that man. But then there are some very ungrateful people walking around, Mma. There are many of them out there." She waved a hand in the direction of the nearby shopping centre, as if that, for some inexplicable reason, drew the ranks of the ungrateful in large numbers.

"That may be so," said Mma Ramotswe as she settled herself at her desk. "There are many people who do not know how to say thank you. That is undoubtedly true, Mma, but I think that we—"

Mma Makutsi did not let her finish. "You do people a favour, Mma," she continued, "and what do you get? I'll tell you what you get. Sometimes they say thank you—*sometimes* . . . And at other times, you know what they feel? I'll tell you, Mma. They say nothing because they resent the people who want to help them."

"Possibly, Mma Makutsi, possibly. But I think that we—"

Mma Makutsi had the bit between her teeth. Her spectacles flashed momentarily in reflected sunlight. "Let me give you an example. Phuti has a man working for him in the furniture store. He has been working there for six years, and he has been a good worker. He is a very funny-looking man, Mma Ramotswe. I don't like to criticise the appearance of other people, but there are some cases where it's very difficult not to say something about the way a person looks. You can't pretend that something doesn't exist—even if there are many people who say we should pretend not to notice these things. So you meet somebody who has two noses, say. I'm not saying that such a thing is possible, but I think sometimes it might happen. I have heard that there are people up in Cameroon who have two noses. Have you heard that, Mma?"

Mma Ramotswe stared at her colleague. There was no point in trying to steer the conversation back to where she wanted it to be. Once Mma Makutsi was launched, the best strategy was to let her say what it was that she wanted to say, and then slip in one's own contribution when she had finished giving voice to whatever it was she wanted off her chest. So now she simply said, "I have not heard of such people, Mma."

"Well, I have," said Mma Makutsi. "I have heard of them, but I have not seen them. There are big forests up there. These people live in the forests. They are very shy. They do not like to go into town."

Mma Ramotswe thought about this for a few moments. She thought of these strange, timid people, living among the forest shadows, keeping away from people who might point at them and jeer. People were like that: they did not realise, perhaps, how cruel they could be.

"I'm not surprised they do not go into town," said Mma Ramotswe. "Would you, Mma Makutsi? In their position?"

Mma Makutsi gave the matter some thought. "There is a differ-ence between what I think I should do, and what I'd actually do. I might know that it would be better to face people and say, 'So, I've got two noses—what's wrong with that?' Or you might even say, 'I'm proud of my two noses.' You might say that."

Mma Ramotswe nodded. "It is sometimes better to be honest about your failings. To speak about them."

"Though it's not necessarily a failing, Mma," warned Mma Maku-tsi. "Being different is not necessarily a failing."

"I never said it was, Mma. And now I think—"

"You shouldn't apologise for the way you look," said Mma Makutsi. "You've never pretended not to be traditionally built, Mma. I admire you for that—I really do. So you may need a stronger chair. So you may take up more space. What business is that of anybody else's? That's what I ask myself."

Mma Ramotswe pursed her lips. It was all very well for Mma Makutsi to draw attention to her appearance, but what about her own? She might not be traditionally built, but she had a very prominent rear end—not that Mma Ramotswe would ever say anything about it, but she had seen Mr. J.L.B. Matekoni gazing at it from time to time, and she had understood why. And as for these people with their alleged extra nose, that was a highly unlikely story—a ridiculous one of the sort that schoolchildren told one another. Nobody could have two noses—it just did not happen. Where would the extra nose go? And how would it be connected to the airways? There was no point in even thinking about that: these people did not exist, whether in the forests of Cameroon or any-where. If they did, there would surely have been pictures of them in the papers. That was exactly the sort of thing that newspapers liked to report on. *People found in Cameroon with two noses.* That sort of thing. There had been no such report—and there never would be.

"This man who works for Phuti," Mma Ramotswe prompted. "You said that he looked different. Why was that, Mma?"

Mma Makutsi took a moment to return to the story she had started to tell. "Yes, that man. Yes. He has very prominent teeth, Mma. They grow out of his mouth like a rabbit's teeth. Have you seen those teeth rabbits have, Mma Ramotswe? They have these big front teeth. It looks all right on a rabbit, but when you get it in a person, the effect is not so good. And his teeth were like that. I often said to Phuti, 'That man looks as if he's going to bite you, Phuti. You must be careful.' And he always laughed, because he is a very kind man and he would never think anybody was going to bite him."

"But this man," she went on, "this man with the teeth, he had a herd of ten cattle, you see. Not very many. And some animal came and bit four of them. They didn't know what it was. A hyena, maybe. You know what those creatures are like, Mma. They are very nasty. I would not like to be bitten by a hyena. A jackal—well, that would be a little nip, because they are smaller creatures, but a hyena has these very big jaws and you would not want to be bitten by such a creature."

"What happened to his cattle, Mma?"

"The wounds were very bad," Mma Makutsi replied. "The cattle could hardly walk, and there were many flies. You know how flies are attracted to wounds in cattle. Big clouds of them, and the poor cattle couldn't do anything about it because the wounds were on their legs and they couldn't brush the flies away with their tails. So the cattle became late—all four of them that had been bitten."

Mma Ramotswe grimaced. To lose almost half one's herd was a tragedy that every Motswana would instinctively recognise as being almost too much to bear.

"Phuti was very sad when he heard this story," Mma Makutsi continued. "He called him into his office and asked him whether

it was true. And he said—this man with the teeth like a rabbit's—
he said that it was true and that he and his family were very sad. He
said that his wife had cried all night after she had heard about it.
'We love our cattle,' he said. That is what he said, Mma. And who
would argue with that? We all love our cattle. We all do."

It was true. And it went to the heart of who their people were,
thought Mma Ramotswe. Botswana would not be Botswana without that feeling for cattle.

Mma Makutsi continued with her story. "So Phuti said to him
that he would buy him two cows and that when these cows had their
calves, his herd would be back to the same size. The man seemed
very grateful, and he thanked Phuti then and there. Phuti arranged
for them to be bought and to be taken to that man's cattle post. But
then do you know what happened, Mma? One of the cows turned
out not to be carrying a calf after all. And do you know what this
man did? He came to Phuti and complained. Yes, he complained.
He said that the cow was not suitable for breeding, and what was
Phuti going to do about it?"

Mma Ramotswe drew in her breath. "That is very bad behaviour, Mma. Very bad."

Mma Makutsi nodded. "I said to Phuti: you go and tell him
that he's lucky to have any sort of cow and that he does not deserve
to have a present like the one Phuti gave him. People are strange,
aren't they, Mma?"

Mma Ramotswe said that they were indeed strange, and took
the opportunity to move the discussion on. "Strange, Mma? Yes,
they are very strange. You take this business with Mr. Modise. I
believe that Charlie discovered—"

Mma Makutsi interrupted her. "He discussed that with me,
Mma Ramotswe. He was not sure what to do about what he had
found out. I gave him some advice."

"To speak to the newspaper, Mma?"

Mma Makutsi sat back in her chair. She had been pleased with her intervention. "That is exactly what I recommended, yes. And he went to see Tommy Pilani. You may know that man, Mma? This is the sort of thing that he writes about."

Mma Ramotswe was silent. It was clear that Mma Makutsi had not seen the article in that day's paper. She would have to tell her about it, and she did not relish the censure that would be implicit in whatever she said. She did not want to upbraid Mma Makutsi, as that never helped, and, anyway, the advice she had given Charlie might have worked out well . . . except that it had not, and we judge advice, in retrospect, by its consequences—intended or otherwise.

Mma Ramotswe cleared her throat. "Where is Charlie now, Mma?" she asked.

Mma Makutsi explained that he had gone to fetch the post from the post-box and that he would be back in a few minutes. As she said this, they heard his voice outside, shouting something unintelligible to Mr. J.L.B. Matekoni in the garage. Then the door opened, and Charlie sauntered in.

"Lots of letters," he began, cascading envelopes onto Mma Makutsi's desk. "Some of them look like bills, I'm afraid. Money in, money out—" He broke off. He had just seen Mma Ramotswe.

Mma Ramotswe told Charlie to sit down. He did so, his expression revealing that he sensed that something was amiss.

"You spoke to Tommy Pilani?" asked Mma Ramotswe.

Charlie nodded. He glanced at Mma Makutsi, as if for reassurance. "He was interested—but not very much. I think he has many things to write."

Mma Ramotswe made a gesture of acceptance. "We are all busy. Those newspaper people have to get their paper out. They finish writing one thing, and then it is time for the next edition. They can never rest." She paused. "And you told him about Mr. Modise being involved?"

Charlie shrugged. "I mentioned that. It was not the main subject of our conversation, though."

"It was the thing that interested him," said Mma Ramotswe quietly.

Charlie bit his lip. He half turned to look at Mma Makutsi. "Mma Makutsi suggested that I should go to see him, Mma. I was just doing what she told me to do."

Mma Ramotswe held up a hand. "I'm not blaming anybody for anything," she said. "But since neither of you has seen today's paper, I should tell you that there's an article in it all about Mr. Modise and how he should not be working in such a place when he is a deputy principal. That is what they have published—they don't seem to mind about the club itself. There's not much about that."

Mma Makutsi's spectacles flashed. "That woman," she hissed. "Will there be no end to the trouble she causes?"

"Not for the Modise family," Mma Ramotswe replied. "He has been suspended by the school principal. He is facing dismissal."

Mma Makutsi looked down at her hands, folded on the desk in front of her. "He should not get involved with women like that," she said quietly.

"And it seems that if Mr. Modise is dismissed," Mma Ramotswe continued, "then he will lose his pension. His family will be ruined." She paused, watching the effect of the disclosure. Both Charlie and Mma Makutsi looked dismayed, but there was no way round this: they had to know.

Charlie shifted in his seat. His discomfort was obvious, and Mma Ramotswe felt a surge of sympathy for the young man. She had put him in charge of this case, and if anybody was to be held responsible for the consequences, it should be her. Now she sought to comfort him. "It's all right, Charlie," she said. "Nobody can tell how these things will develop. I'm the one who is responsible for this."

Charlie gave a low moan. "He was my teacher, Mma. He was so kind to me. Oh, Mma, this is bad, bad, bad . . ."

"Listen to me, Charlie," said Mma Ramotswe. "You must not blame yourself. You must not. You have done your best here and you weren't to know."

Mma Makutsi had been following this exchange in silence. Now she intervened. "No," she said, "it is *my* fault. I suggested that Charlie go to speak to the newspaper. I should have known. I am the one to blame."

Mma Ramotswe said that it was good of Mma Makutsi to say that, but the advice that she gave Charlie had been perfectly reasonable, and she should not reproach herself for giving it. "Maybe we should stop talking about blame," she said, "and talk, rather, about what we can do to limit the damage."

They looked at each other. Then Mma Makutsi spoke. "I think I should make tea," she said.

Mma Ramotswe felt that this was a very good idea. Tea was so often the solution, although in this particular case, with its potentially devastating consequences, it might be that even tea might not help very much to avert disaster. Still, it would create the conditions in which some solution might emerge—and there had to be a solution, she thought. Somewhere. The agency had been in business for some years now, and during that time she had faced numerous delicate issues. At times it had seemed to her that there could be no good outcome to a difficult problem, but time and time again, one had presented itself. This thought, though reassuring to an extent, should not blind one to the fact that sooner or later one of her cases would end in tears—for everybody involved. That would happen—the question now was whether this was that occasion.

"Tea is a very good idea," said Mma Ramotswe. "Then we can discuss what, if anything, can be done."

Charlie gave another groan. "Mr. Modise is a really good man," he said. "He was the best teacher we had. We all liked him. He does not deserve this."

"We do not always deserve the things that happen to us in life, Charlie," said Mma Ramotswe. "But I hear what you say about that man. We must do what we can."

Charlie shook his head. "I am so sad, Mma. I have never done anything this bad in my whole life. Never."

Mma Makutsi looked interested. "Are you sure, Charlie?"

Mma Ramotswe threw her a glance. There were times when she thought Mma Makutsi showed considerably less understanding than one might expect of one who got ninety-seven per cent in the final examinations of the Botswana Secretarial College.

CHAPTER THIRTEEN

THINKING OF SHOES,
AND THE WAYS OF SHOES

WHEN SHE ARRIVED HOME that evening, Mma Ramotswe saw that Mr. J.L.B. Matekoni was already there, his truck parked in its accustomed place, leaving just enough room for his wife's van to nose in under the shade of the house's generous eaves. She went inside and heard the sound of the shower and of the particularly tuneless singing that Mr. J.L.B. Matekoni, normally a quiet man, felt he could engage in while under this temporary deluge. She had always been amused by this, and had asked him why the shower produced this sudden musicality. He had seemed surprised, and not a little embarrassed, by the question. "Do you hear me, Mma? I did not think anybody could hear."

"It is because of the sound of the water," she said. "You think that what people will hear is just the water. But they hear the singing, too, Rra. Not that anybody would object. You are a very good singer, you know, and would be even better if you were in tune. You could give a big concert, maybe. They could put a shower up on the stage and—"

"You are making fun of me, Mma," he said. "We cannot all be famous singers. I am just a mechanic, you see . . ."

"And the best one in the country," she said quickly. "Mechanics are more useful than singers, you know. If I were up in the north somewhere, up near Maun, and I was on one of those dirt roads and my van stopped, and there were lions not far away, who would I rather have with me? A singer or a mechanic?"

He had taken the opportunity to speak to her firmly about her van. "But why would your van stop, Mma? It is because it is too old to be taken up north—and on those dangerous roads that are made of soft white sand. What vehicle would not find those sort of conditions very upsetting? I have been saying that for years. You should get a new van."

"We shall see," she said. "I am not planning to go up north at the moment, and there are not many lions on the roads around Gaborone. So I think my van is still safe, Rra."

But now, standing outside the shower, she called out to her husband. The sound of the water stopped, and the singing died away.

"I am back now, Rra," she called out. "I shall make tea for us and we can have it out on the verandah. We can look round the garden before it gets dark."

She went into the kitchen to switch on the kettle. Then she slipped out of her office shoes, and into a pair of ancient and comfortable sandals. It was important for your feet to feel *at home,* she thought. There were so many shoes these days that were designed by people who seemed to forget what shoes were *for.* These shoe people spent all their time thinking up new colours and shapes, went to any amount of trouble to make shoes noticeable, whereas what they should be asking themselves was this: are these shoes going to do the job for which shoes are intended? Are they going to fit comfortably around all sorts of unsuitable feet—feet that are too wide, like small frying pans; or too bony, like pieces of corrugated cardboard; or in any other way not really fit for purpose? If shoes were fashionable, then there was a very good chance—a certainty perhaps—that they would not be all that comfortable and would, in many cases, be downright painful to wear. That was why you saw women slip out of their shoes—discreetly, of course—when they were at a formal occasion and they thought nobody could see. Mma Ramotswe had been to one such event—a charity tea morning at the President Hotel—and had happened to glance under a table around which some well-known and highly fashionable Gaborone ladies were seated. And what she saw astonished her—a floor littered with shoes that had been temporarily abandoned by their wearers. And at the end of that occasion there had been an embarrassing moment when one of the ladies had slipped into the wrong shoes and had started to walk away from the table without noticing her error. The awkwardness of the situation had been compounded by the fact that the lady who had inadvertently purloined the other lady's shoes was a person of extremely traditional build. The shoes she had taken were not constructed to cope with such loads and the heel of one of them had snapped, causing the traditionally built lady to list to one side. That was the sort of situation from which there was no obvious tactful escape, although now it was remembered by those involved with some mirth.

Looking down at her dusty and well-worn sandals, it occurred to her that she was fortunate not to have to worry about things like shoes. Mma Ramotswe, like all of us, wanted to look her best for her friends. She liked a bright and cheerful dress as much as anybody; at times she liked to wear a hat, and was not averse to decorating it with a flower or a colourful piece of cloth; she had always had a soft spot for blouses in a particular shade of blue—her *sky blouses*, as she called them; she liked, if at all possible, to be reasonably well dressed. But when it came to shoes, she was quite different to Mma Makutsi, who had a fairly large collection of fashionable shoes in a surprisingly wide range of shades. There were blue shoes and green shoes; there were shoes that were one colour on the outside, and another colour inside; there were shoes with bows, and shoes without bows; there were shoes with buttons stitched onto them so that they looked like eyes—Mma Ramotswe had always felt uncomfortable when confronted with those shoes, which she thought were looking at her with a certain intrusiveness, if not actual insolence: there was no reason why anybody should take insolence from shoes—shoes, she felt, should know their place.

Of course there was something distinctly odd about Mma Makutsi's shoes—or, rather, was it that there was something odd about Mma Makutsi herself? This was the fact that Mma Makutsi had once revealed, in a moment of candour, that her shoes occasionally spoke to her. Mma Ramotswe had been wide-eyed and had wondered whether she should perhaps suggest that her colleague should consult a doctor. But that was a difficult thing to say to anybody, and had she said it to Mma Makutsi it would undoubtedly have led to a prolonged huff. So she had listened to the story of how the Makutsi shoes occasionally made some comment or other, or, as in one famous case, warned her of the presence on the bedroom floor of a cobra that had slithered into the house. For the most part, though, the comments addressed to Mma Makutsi by her shoes were banal, although frequently impertinent. They had on one occasion, she said, told her to spend more time brushing her teeth, and on another had complained quite peevishly about not being polished before being worn to the supermarket.

"They are very fussy," said Mma Makutsi. "At least, some of the time. Most of the time, though, they are silent and do not interfere."

Mma Ramotswe knew that hearing voices was a bad sign, and that in some cases it led to a spell in the psychiatric hospital down at Lobatse. Yet Mma Makutsi was in other respects completely normal, and not, it seemed, in need of psychiatric help. The imagination was an odd thing, Mma Ramotswe concluded—as was eyesight. Sometimes we saw things that were not there, simply because light and shade played a trick on our eyes. Sometimes we misheard, because many things sound like other things, and it is only too easy to get them mixed up if one is not paying attention. So if Mma Makutsi thought she heard her shoes talking to her, that was not necessarily a sign of something going seriously wrong, but could be a minor mistake of the sort that we make all the time in almost all the spheres of our lives.

And then, to her surprise, Mma Ramotswe had on two separate occasions heard a small, distant voice that seemed to come from somewhere down below; and when she looked in the direction from which she imagined she heard the sound emanating, she found herself staring at Mma Makutsi's feet. That had disturbed her, but not for long. There were more worrying things on this earth than shoes that appeared to make the occasional remark.

Now, standing in the kitchen, she looked down at her sandals and thought that if they were ever to speak—which they never would, of course—they would use very plain and old-fashioned Setswana, of the sort spoken in remote regions, and possibly even a bit difficult to understand. Nor would they have much to say, she thought, because they never left her house and yard, and would know nothing of the outside world. She smiled at the thought. It was too easy to lapse into daydreaming, once you started, and flights of fancy were the result. That might be all right for people who did not have much to do, who did not have many decisions to make, but it was not a road down which the owner of a successful—well, slightly successful—detective agency would want to travel.

She made tea and poured two mugs. Mr. J.L.B. Matekoni normally drank ordinary black tea, but had recently developed a taste for red bush tea, which made life a bit simpler. In an ideal world, husbands would follow their wives' tastes in all things, which would solve the problem of those fussy men who wouldn't eat pumpkin, who turned their nose up at dairy products, or who insisted on having grilled tomatoes with every meal, as the husband of one of her friends did. He was a very fussy man indeed, who had a thermometer to check the temperature of his bathwater before he stepped into it, and would only use a particular sort of soap. It was not easy being married to him, Mma Ramotswe imagined, and when she heard her friend sighing, as she did quite often, Mma Ramotswe knew what lay behind those sighs.

She made her way out onto the verandah, her favourite spot at this time of day, when the sun sank slowly over the line of the horizon, that green line of distant acacia trees, and when small flocks of chattering birds darted across the sky, back to the trees that were to be their home for the night. She thought of this as a time of winding down, when the concerns of the workplace were put aside, and families came together to perform the domestic tasks that would put the day to bed. She often sat there with the children in the evening, before they went off to bed. They would tell her of the events of their day, of the issues that had arisen at school, of the passions and problems of their world—so small to outsiders, but so big to a child. And she would tell them of how she had spent her day, of how Mma Makutsi had said something amusing, or of how Fanwell had told a funny story he had heard from one of his friends; or they would just sit and think about things in general, not needing to say anything to one another.

She sat down and waited for Mr. J.L.B. Matekoni to join her. When he did, she caught the smell of the soap he had used. It was hers, a present from a client who ran a beauty products shop. It was floral, and feminine, but she knew that he liked it too. Perhaps that was because men, even uncomplicated, mechanically minded men like Mr. J.L.B. Matekoni, yearned at times for comfort and softness, and all the things to which they otherwise affected indifference. Men were wearing perfume now, she realised, although they called it something different. What would her late father have said, she wondered, and smiled at the thought of how puzzled he would be by the modern world. It was good, though, that men were changing, because she felt that the moulds into which they had been forced in the past had not made their lives any easier. As long as they remained men, though; because she liked men and it would be very dull, she thought, if all differences between men and women were eradicated. And women, too, she believed, should not abandon the concerns that they traditionally had just because they wanted to compete with men for things that men had traditionally, and unfairly, kept for themselves. Women should still be thoughtful of others; women should still give comfort to those who were bruised and battered by life; women should still feel maternal and wish to nurture and protect the young. Of course they should; and there was no reason why they should not do all that while at the same time doing the jobs that men did. Women should do the things they had always done—but men should do them too. That was something that still had to be worked at: getting men to shoulder their responsibilities in the home—to help with the cooking and the washing-up and looking after children. The days when it was only women who did those things were over, although there were some men who did not seem to have heard that yet.

She handed Mr. J.L.B. Matekoni his mug of tea. "Nice soap," she said.

He gave her a sideways glance. "I hope you don't mind, Mma Ramotswe. I have always liked the smell of that soap."

"I don't mind at all, Rra," she assured him. "I think that many men these days like the smell of flowers."

He took a sip of his tea. "Is that what it is?" he asked.

"It is called lily of the valley," she said. "That is the name of the soap. It smells of lilies, you see."

Mr. J.L.B. Matekoni looked thoughtful. "It is very good at getting oil and grease off the skin," he said. "That is the most important thing, in my view." And it was, he thought, especially if you were a mechanic, which he was, of course.

Mma Ramotswe smiled. She had seen an advertisement for the soap in question, and it had said nothing about oil and grease. She looked at him over the rim of his mug. He was such a good man, who had never once wavered in his goodness. If only, if only . . . if only he could be somehow multiplied, and the world populated by more Mr. J.L.B. Matekonis, rather than by . . . and here she thought of several men whose faces were often in the newspapers and who were his very opposite in every way. *It is sometimes the wrong cattle who get all the grass,* her late father was fond of observing. She thought of that from time to time, and reflected on how fortunate she had been to have had a father who was right—not only about cattle, but about so much else.

And now Mr. J.L.B. Matekoni asked after her day. Had she been busy? Had anything noteworthy happened?

She told him, quoting, in so far as she could remember it, what the article in the *Botswana Daily News* had said. He listened in silence, although he winced when she mentioned what the principal had said about Mr. Modise's loss of his pension.

When she finished, he looked at her and very slowly shook his head. "This is all because of her," he said. "When I heard that he was having an affair with Violet Sephotho, I knew that this was going to end in disaster, Mma. I knew it."

She agreed that it was difficult to imagine any other outcome.

"When men fall in love with women like that," he observed, "they stop thinking. They'll do anything that such ladies tell them to do. That has happened so many times, Mma."

They lapsed into a silence that lasted several minutes. Then Mr. J.L.B. Matekoni said, "Are you going to be able to do anything to help him? It would be good, I think, if you were able to do something. We've got him into this mess, I think. It was us, wasn't it, Mma Ramotswe?"

She did not accept that. "No, Mr. J.L.B. Matekoni," she protested. "We did *not* get Modise into this mess. He got himself into it. He got involved with that woman—we didn't introduce him to her. He agreed to go and help with that ridiculous club—we had nothing to do with that."

"And yet, had Charlie not gone to the papers," Mr. J.L.B. Matekoni pointed out, "then they wouldn't have spoken to the principal and told him all about what Modise was up to. And if that hadn't happened, he would not have been suspended."

"I know what you mean, Rra," she said. "But there is a difference between doing something that makes something else happen, and being to blame for it. They are different things, I think."

He thought about this. He was not sure if he could see that distinction, but he saw no point in taking it further. The real question, Mr. J.L.B. Matekoni thought, was whether anything could be done to save the deputy principal from ruin. He asked whether Mma Ramotswe might speak to him and get him to see the error of his ways. If he abandoned Violet Sephotho and went to the principal a chastened and apologetic man, might there be a chance that the enquiry into his conduct would be abandoned? Mma Ramotswe considered this, and thought it unlikely. And anyway, she was not sure that Modise would give up Violet. If he was as deeply in her thrall as they suspected, then she was not sure that he would be prepared to renounce her.

"And what about the principal, Mma?" he asked. "Could you not speak to him?"

She gazed out into the garden. A bat swooped crazily in an erratic dash. Somewhere an engine whined, and then faded, the sound swallowed by the sky. You could speak to anyone, of course; you could always make an appeal. Sometimes it worked, and your words touched another's heart in such a way as to bring about a softening, but that did not always happen. The principal was a manager as much as he was a teacher, and he had to make hard management decisions. He had rules to follow.

Then Mr. J.L.B. Matekoni said, "I know that man, by the way."

She turned to look at him. "The principal? You know him?"

"Yes. His mother had an old truck. She had a big vegetable garden halfway down the Lobatse Road. She used it to bring the produce into town. She is a very senior lady, now, and I'm not sure that she's a very good driver. She crashed it into a telephone pole one day. She was lucky not to be hurt. The truck was a write-off."

"Poor woman," said Mma Ramotswe. "Sometimes those poles are in the wrong place, I think. It is easy to hit them."

Mr. J.L.B. Matekoni looked doubtful. "Not really," he said. "It is usually people who hit poles, not poles who hit people. But it made no difference, anyway. I couldn't do anything about her truck."

"So, what happened, Rra?"

"He—the principal—his name is Mr. Kebadile—he came to see me to ask whether I could find a second-hand truck for her. I said that perhaps it would be best if she stopped driving, but he just said, 'You do not know my mother, Rra. She has not stopped doing anything—ever. She will only stop driving when her heart stops beating.'"

Mma Ramotswe sighed. It was important to know when to stop, she thought.

Mr. J.L.B. Matekoni was of the same mind. "I know," he said. "But you know how some old people can be, Mma. They will not be told."

"And there are some young people like that, too," observed Mma Ramotswe.

He nodded, and continued, "I managed to locate another truck, but it was in very bad condition. I spent a weekend fixing it, though, and it ran quite well after that. I put in new rings. And it needed new brakes—you have to be very careful about brakes, Mma— if you want to be able to stop, that is. But I got it at a very good price, and I sold it to them at cost, because I think that a school principal is somebody one should help, if at all possible."

"That was kind of you, Rra." It was typical of him, she thought. She knew of numerous cases in which he had helped people in their car difficulties. This was just another such case.

"He was very pleased," Mr. J.L.B. Matekoni went on. "I remember him smiling and smiling—I thought his face would crack. He was very happy for his mother."

Mma Ramotswe looked thoughtful. "He thanked you, I suppose, Rra?"

"Of course. He was very polite. And I knew how pleased he was because he told me he wanted to do something for me."

She waited for a few moments. Then she asked, "And did he?"

Mr. J.L.B. Matekoni shook his head. "No, there was nothing I needed—not at the time. So he said that if ever—"

Mma Ramotswe cut him short. "He said that if ever he could help you, Rra? Is that what he said?"

"Something like that."

Mma Ramotswe put down her mug of tea. She almost clapped

her hands together in triumph, but controlled herself. She would have to persuade Mr. J.L.B. Matekoni, and he could be reticent. This would have to be played carefully, she decided.

"I think we should go and look at the beans," she said. "I think that some of them will be ready soon."

They rose to their feet.

"I feel very sad for that man, Modise," said Mr. J.L.B. Matekoni as they made their way round the side of the house towards Mma Ramotswe's vegetable garden. "To work all those years and then lose everything because of . . ."

"Because of a lack of self-control," Mma Ramotswe supplied. "Yes. It is a great pity, Rra. But I have had an idea, you know. I'll tell you about it very soon."

They had reached the beans. She bent down to examine one of the pods. An insect had nibbled at the fibrous green sheath, exposing the bean within. She looked at the pod next to it. The same thing had happened. She was not sure what to do. It seemed that this was what life consisted of: a constant struggle to keep the encroachments of nature at bay: drought, voracious pests, torrential rains, termites, insects for which she had no name . . . And when it came to human affairs, there was a similar battle: at every turn, you were confronted by human imperfection—by bad behaviour, by carelessness, by men who went off and did foolish things that brought sorrow and shame to their families; by women who knowingly encouraged men to do those very things and then stood by while others suffered the consequences . . . Why could we not do something about it? Why could we not say: "That's enough—we've had enough of all that. Now all of us are going to have to be just like people were in Botswana in the past—good and kind and well behaved, and worthy of this lovely country." Oh, that would be a fine day, it would; and it would be an end to unkindness and cruelty and tears, and people would bless the day that the world became like Botswana as it had been under the wise rule of the late Seretse Khama, who was so loved by his people. Oh, that would be a fine day, she thought.

She stood up and took her husband's arm. "Let me tell you what I think we should do, Mr. J.L.B. Matekoni. But before I explain, can you tell me that you will say yes."

It was a bold beginning, and she almost laughed at herself. But he inclined his head and gave his response. "I always trust you in these things, Mma Ramotswe—you know that."

"Good," she said. "Then let me tell you."

CHAPTER FOURTEEN

A RIGHTEOUS MAN

I T WAS THE LARGEST DELEGATION in the history of the No. 1
Ladies' Detective Agency. There had been occasions in the past
when Mma Ramotswe had gone on a mission accompanied by
Mma Makutsi and Charlie, travelling together in the tiny white
van, with Charlie relegated to the least comfortable seat, elbows
intruding on Mma Makutsi's space, and rebuffed by her. But now
there were five of them—Mma Ramotswe, Mma Makutsi, Charlie,
Mr. J.L.B. Matekoni, and Mma Potokwane—all travelling in convoy,
in the van and in the green truck on which *Tlokweng Road Speedy
Motors* was emblazoned. Their destination was the school at which
Mr. Modise had, until very recently, been deputy principal, and
from which he was now excluded, pending the results of the enquiry
set up by his immediate superior, Mr. Kebadile. Not that there was
any doubt in anybody's mind about the outcome of that enquiry:
the principal had made it clear in his comments in the *Botswana
Daily News* how he felt about members off his staff engaging in
professionally inappropriate activities. The rules, he had said, were
quite clear: no member of staff was to undertake any other employ-

ment while on the school payroll, and that prohibition applied with extra force if the extra-curricular employment was of such a nature as to bring the school, or the Botswana government's Ministry of Education into disrepute. This was an open-and-shut case, and the eventual result should surprise nobody.

Mma Ramotswe had toyed with the idea of getting Mr. J.L.B. Matekoni to visit the principal unaccompanied, but had decided against this. Mr. Kebadile had a reputation as a stern disciplinarian, and was generally forceful in his dealings with others. She could imagine that Mr. J.L.B. Matekoni, being a mild man in every respect, might quickly be intimidated into silence by the principal's righteous wrath. She imagined the exchange:

"You have come to ask me to reverse my decision, Rra? You are asking me to *condone* a member of my staff being involved in the running of something called the Cool Singles Evening Club? Is that what you are asking me to do, Rra? In all seriousness?"

"Well, Rra, I am just raising the possibility. You see, he has been led astray by—"

"By Violet Sephotho, Rra? Is that what you were about to say?"

"I was—"

"So, if a man—any man—does something shocking it will be all right, as long as some *Jezebel* . . . yes, some *Jezebel Sephotho* has prevailed upon him to do it? Do you think that somebody in my position can run a big, important school on that basis? Is that what you think, Rra?"

And so it might continue for a few minutes more, until a chastened and now silent Mr. J.L.B. Matekoni would leave the principal's office like some abashed schoolboy who has just been given a dressing-down and sent on his way. No, it would not do to send Mr. J.L.B. Matekoni by himself; rather there should be as large a presence as possible of people hoping for a more lenient approach.

If there were four or five voices raised for Mr. Modise, then the principal might pay some attention, rather than dig in on the position he had already decided upon. In particular, she felt that Mma Potokwane would add strength to their request—the matron was known for her persuasive powers, and for her determination, too. It would be a brave person who resisted Mma Potokwane in full advocacy mode, and even a school principal, with all the authority that such an office invested in those who occupied it, would find it difficult to resist Mma Potokwane.

They parked the van and truck in the school parking place, and then made their way towards a porch over which a sign proclaimed, *Main Entrance and All Enquiries.* Underneath this message was the school crest and motto: *To Study Is to Know the World.*

Mma Ramotswe glanced upwards. "You were at this school, Charlie," she said. "Do you remember the school motto?"

Charlie frowned. He had not seen the sign above the door. "Something about not running in the corridors, I think. Something like that."

Mma Makutsi gave him a scathing look. "That is not a motto, Charlie," she said. "That is a school rule. There are many of those." She laughed. "Can you imagine the school crest on the students' blazers and the embroidered message: *Always wash your hands before eating.* Or, *Hand your homework in on time.* Or something like that. Hah!"

Mr. J.L.B. Matekoni came to his rescue. "I see it is up there," he said. "To study is to know the world. You see. That is what it says."

Charlie muttered something about having so much to remember. "And I have not been at this school for a long time, you know."

"It does not matter," said Mma Potokwane. "We are here now and we must start thinking about what we are going to say to the principal."

They went inside, where they were met by the principal's secretary. He had been told of their phone call, she said, and he was expecting them. "He is very busy today," she warned, "so he has no more than half an hour for you, I'm afraid. There are many things that you have to do if you are principal of a school like this. Every day, every single day, there are things that are going wrong."

Mma Potokwane said that she fully understood. It was the same with running an orphanage, she said. You never knew what was going to go wrong, but it always did.

The secretary led them to a door marked *Principal: do not enter without permission.* Charlie looked at it anxiously—he clearly felt unhappy, and so did Mr. J.L.B. Matekoni, who was looking about him nervously, holding his best hat in front of him, his fingers tight about the rim.

"You are not still at school," whispered Mma Potokwane, with a smile. "The principal cannot punish you for running in the corridors. You mustn't worry."

Mr. J.L.B. Matekoni grinned weakly. "I must admit I am a bit nervous," he said. "This is an important man we're going to see, Mma Potokwane."

Mma Ramotswe sought to reassure him. "He is a public servant, Rra," she said. "He is paid out of our taxes. He works for us. It's not as if we're going to see the President or the Chief Justice, or whatever."

Mma Potokwane knocked on the door. From within there came an invitation to enter.

The principal stood up as they went into the office. A tall man, dressed in a dark suit, he was silhouetted against the light from the window behind him. On the desk before him, a small pile of files was stacked beside a jar from which a selection of pens and pencils protruded. On the wall to his right were two framed photographs of the sort found in all government offices: the President and the Minister of Education. Below these, in a more discreet frame, was a diploma from the University of Botswana and a certificate of some sort, complete with red rosette seal.

The secretary announced them. "This is Mma Ramotswe and her colleagues," she said. "They telephoned yesterday."

The principal spread his hands in a gesture of welcome. "And Mr. Matekoni, I see. It is good to see you too, Rra. This is a very big pleasure."

Further introductions were made. To Mma Makutsi he said, "Your husband, Mma, is in my Rotary Club. Please give him my best regards."

And to Mma Potokwane he said, "I have seen your picture in the papers many times, Mma—with the children. We have had some of them in the school, I think, and they have always done well."

"We encourage them to work hard," said Mma Potokwane. "And, by and large, they respond."

"That is very true," said the principal. "Children need to be stretched. Give them a challenge, and as often as not they'll surprise you with what they manage to achieve." He paused. "But now, please sit down—I think we have just enough chairs—and tell me to what I owe the pleasure of this visit."

Mma Ramotswe spoke first. "It is good of you to see us," she said. "I know how busy you must be, Rra." She noticed that as she spoke, Mma Makutsi's eye was on the pile of files. Filing was her passion, of course, and here was a challenge.

The principal seemed pleased with Mma Ramotswe's comment. "Thank you, Mma," he said. "There is always something to do, I find." He paused. "Earlier this morning, I was on the telephone to the minister—the Minister of Education, that is. I speak to him regularly." He spoke with such pride—as might one who

could pick up the phone and reach Heaven itself, directly, without
going through the operator.

Mma Ramotswe inclined her head. "I can imagine that, Rra."

"Yes," he said. "And the Permanent Secretary too. She is a very
charming lady, Mma—one of the very best people in the civil service, in my opinion. Indeed, there are some people who say that she
might be going into Parliament soon. They say that she's tipped for
office—for *very* high office, if you see what I mean, Mma."

Mma Ramotswe did her best to look impressed. What must it be
like, she asked herself, to be a *permanent* anything? Mma Makutsi,
no doubt, would like to be a permanent detective . . .

"I know her very well," continued the principal.

"I'm sure you do, Rra."

The principal hesitated. "It is always useful," he continued, "to
be able to pick this thing up"—he gestured towards the telephone
on his desk—"and speak to the people who make the decisions."

"It must make a big difference, Rra," said Mma Ramotswe.

"Especially if they know who you are," added the principal.
"There is nothing wrong in using your connections if they mean
that you can get things done."

"That will be a big help," agreed Mma Ramotswe.

"Most of the time," mused the principal, "I do not have to spell
out to these people who I am." He lowered his voice. "I do not need
to say which family my family is connected to. People seem to know
that."

Mma Ramotswe thought hard. Who *was* this self-opinionated
man? Then it came back to her. He was related to a former president—
there had been something about it in the newspaper.

"Of course—your family is so well known, Rra," she said. "You
would not have to tell anybody."

"True," said the principal. "But I never make a big thing of it."

"Of course not."

"Modesty is definitely the best policy," the principal concluded.

Mma Ramotswe noticed Mma Potokwane's lip trembling. Now the matron joined in, "We have come about Mr. Modise," she said. "We would like to speak about him, Rra."

The effect of this was immediate. The principal's genial manner suddenly changed. "That is a very unfortunate case," he said icily. "But I assure you—the very firmest action is being taken to deal with it. It will be resolved in a matter of days—please don't doubt that. That man will be severely punished."

This was too much for Mma Makutsi. "But I thought you were still in the middle of an enquiry. Now you are talking about punishment."

The principal hesitated, but only for a few moments. "I am not prejudging the matter," he said. "But I do not think there is any doubt regarding that man's guilt. And you mustn't worry—I know that the public is rightly concerned about this matter, but he will definitely be punished. He will be dismissed."

Now Mr. J.L.B. Matekoni joined in. "I think you misunderstand us, Rra. We are here to ask you not to punish Mr. Modise too harshly. We are not condoning what he did, but we think that this is a case of a good man who has made one bad mistake. He does not deserve to lose his pension."

Charlie was emboldened to speak. "He was my teacher, Rra. All of us admired him a lot. He was good to many, many people—and I am one of them."

The principal frowned. "Do I take it that you want me to be *less* strict in this case?"

Mma Potokwane leaned forward. "It would be the right thing to do, Rra. There is a lot of sympathy for this poor man. He has only temporarily lost his head."

"A woman," said Mr. J.L.B. Matekoni. "His head was turned by a woman—and then he lost it."

The principal was staring straight ahead—the picture of a man determined to do his duty and not to waver. Now he sat back in his seat. "I am not an unreasonable man," he said. "But what you are asking is impossible. There are procedures, as you know, and I am following them to the letter. This is not an occasion for softness. We cannot have senior people being written about in the press in these terms. We cannot have our senior teachers making a laughing stock of the school. No, there is nothing that can be done—I am very sorry, but that is my final word. Final. Final."

Mr. J.L.B. Matekoni bit his lip. "I am sorry that you cannot help us," he said. "Some time ago, I was able to help you, Rra, with your mother's truck."

There was a short silence. The principal frowned, and then shook his head. "I don't remember that, Rra. It must have been a long time ago."

"Not all that long," said Mr. J.L.B. Matekoni.

But the principal was not to be moved. He stared out of the window, as if impatient for the meeting to be over.

Mma Ramotswe glanced at Mma Potokwane, who shrugged her shoulders.

"Will you not at least reconsider?" she asked the principal.

He shook his head. "It is not possible," he said. "I am very sorry." He looked at his watch. "And now, I'm afraid, I really must get on with my work—there is so much to do."

To underline the finality of his words, he stood up—and they, too, rose to their feet.

"It is very sad for his wife, you know," said Mma Ramotswe, as she brushed at the creases in her dress.

"Without doubt," said the principal. "But he should have thought about that, shouldn't he? I do not make the rules, Mma."

"No," said Mma Ramotswe, under her breath. "The rules are always made by somebody else—always."

They began to move towards the door. Mma Makutsi, however, lingered, and as the others began to file out into the corridor, she went up to the principal, leaned forward, and began to engage him in whispered conversation. The principal listened. He seemed to freeze. Then he recoiled, as if he had been shocked by something that Mma Makutsi had said. But what could that be? Mma Ramotswe asked herself.

Now the principal did something unexpected. He shook a finger at Mma Makutsi, as if he were admonishing a child. She responded by shaking a finger back at him. Then she turned away unceremoniously and joined her friends.

"What happened there?" whispered Mma Ramotswe.

"Oh, nothing," replied Mma Makutsi. "I was just saying good-bye."

Mma Ramotswe could see that she did not wish to add to that unlikely explanation, and so she let the matter drop. That was sometimes the best thing to do with Mma Makutsi—to let things drop.

THE THREE WOMEN—Mma Ramotswe, Mma Makutsi, and Mma Potokwane—travelled back from the school together, leaving Charlie to return to the garage with Mr. J.L.B. Matekoni in the Tlokweng Road Speedy Motors truck. Their route home took them past the café in the shopping centre where Mma Ramotswe liked to have tea after doing her weekly supermarket shop. She considered it a treat to drop into the café, something to be looked forward to each week and not overdone, but now, after this uncomfortable and unproductive meeting with the principal, she felt that they all needed to spend some time together reviewing what had happened and discussing where they now were in their plan to help Mr. Modise. And that, unfortunately, was nowhere very much.

"That man," sighed Mma Potokwane, as she settled into her chair in the café. "Have you ever met a more self-important, puffed-up . . ." Words seemed to fail her, and she sighed again.

"Never," said Mma Makutsi. "He was so pleased with himself. All that talk about government ministers and being able to pick up the telephone and speak to anybody he chose. Hah! If he phoned the No. 1 Ladies' Detective Agency and asked to speak to Mma Ramotswe it would give me pleasure—a lot of pleasure—to say to him that she is too busy to take calls from strangers. That's what I would say, Mma Potokwane. And then I would ring off. No argument. Just ring off. That would show him."

It was one of Mma Makutsi's favourite phrases: *that would show him,* and she used it to put a finishing touch when somebody who needed to be put in his place was appropriately put down. *That would show him.*

Mma Ramotswe was inclined to agree with both of them. She had found the principal extremely irritating, although she had used all the tact at her disposal to ensure that he might at least consider their request. Her effort had proved futile, but even in the face of his obduracy, she had continued to be polite throughout their encounter. And even now, her natural sympathy made her search for reasons why he should have behaved as he did.

"He is a proud man," she said. "And proud people are often insecure, I think."

Mma Makutsi frowned. "I don't think it's insecurity, Mma Ramotswe—it's pride we're talking about. Sheer conceit. He thinks he's very important—that's all there is to it."

Mma Ramotswe sipped at her tea. They had not given her red bush tea, as she had requested, but ordinary Five Roses. She did not mind that too much, although she wished that they would *remember*. The waitress who had served them, and who often served her on her weekly visits, was not known for her good memory. Mma Ramotswe had once suggested to her that she write down the orders, but her advice had been summarily rebuffed. "No need to write," said the waitress, tapping her head as she spoke. "It all goes in there."

Now Mma Ramotswe addressed Mma Makutsi. "There is always a reason why people are the way they are, Mma." She spoke mildly—it did not do to disagree too starkly with Mma Makutsi, especially when something had happened to annoy her.

"Yes, of course there is," Mma Makutsi retorted. "He is the way he is because he is filled with pride. That's his trouble, Mma. We had somebody like that at the Botswana Secretarial College. He was the bursar. He was very pleased with himself—like one of those roosters you see in people's yards—and he would walk around the college in exactly that way, checking that there was no waste. He had only a small book-keeping qualification, you know—basic membership of the Institute of Book-keepers, or something like that. And yet he behaved as if he was the biggest accountant in the country." She paused. "Actually, he was very small. He was shorter even than the shortest lady in our class. And . . ." She remembered something. "You know what I've just remembered? There was an occasion when Violet Sephotho actually patted him on the head as he walked past. I don't know why she did it, but she reached out and patted him on the head. He stopped in his tracks and glared at her. And she just laughed and said, 'Good morning, Mr. Superman.'"

Mma Potokwane shook her head. "That was very unkind, Mma. He did not deserve that."

Mma Ramotswe gave Mma Makutsi a reproachful look.

"I didn't think it was funny," Mma Makutsi said hurriedly.

"No," said Mma Ramotswe. "And to get back to the principal, I think that man is making up for something, something that he feels he lacks. You don't go on like that if you are secure in yourself."

"That is probably true," said Mma Potokwane. "He wants the world to think highly of him, I imagine, and it does not. It is always like that." She turned to Mma Ramotswe. "You said he is lacking something, Mma. I think you are probably right. And you know what explains almost any bad behaviour you care to mention? It's a lack of love, you know. That's what I've found time and time again with the poor children who come to us. Sometimes they come to us very damaged. Sometimes they won't even speak because of what has happened to them. They sit in the corner or lie on their beds and refuse to join in the games. They wet the bed, every night, every night. Sometimes they are ready to cry over the smallest things. And I say to the housemothers, 'There is only one thing that will make these children better, and that thing is love. That is the answer. Love.' And, do you know, it almost always works. The children suddenly discover that there are people who are ready to love them, and everything changes. Love is like rain after a long drought. The land is ready for it, and green shoots come up here, there, all over the place, and with love it is the same: silence is replaced by words; scowls by smiles; unhappiness by joy. It happens—it really does."

For a few moments nobody spoke. Mma Potokwane was right, and both Mma Ramotswe and Mma Makutsi were aware of it. Eventually it was Mma Makutsi who broke the silence. She said, "I think that is true, Mma Potokwane. Perhaps I was being too harsh."

"No, Mma," said Mma Ramotswe. "You were only saying what we were thinking. Maybe you said it a bit more forcefully, that is all."

"I was very cross with him," muttered Mma Makutsi.

Mma Ramotswe gave her a searching look. "You had a word with him just before we left, Mma. What did you say to him? Because I don't think he liked it very much."

Mma Makutsi hesitated. She looked a bit ashamed, thought Mma Ramotswe.

"Oh, nothing much," said Mma Makutsi. "Nothing important."

They finished their tea. Nobody had any ideas as to what they might do to retrieve the situation and it seemed to each of them that the fate of the unfortunate Mr. Modise was now more or less sealed. Mma Ramotswe felt that this was just one more thing to add to the list of misfortunes that seemed to be an inevitable part of life. It was hard, but you had to accept them, because if there were things about which you could do nothing, then nothing was what you had to do.

Mma Makutsi returned to the office, but Mma Ramotswe decided that she would stay to chat with Mma Potokwane, who seemed to be in no hurry to get back to the Orphan Farm. She did not come into town all that often—such were the constant demands of her job—so when she did, she liked to make the most of her time away. Sensing this, Mma Ramotswe suggested that they order a further pot of tea—red bush this time, if the waitress remembered—and they sat, in comfortable companionship, exchanging snippets of news of the sort that interested old friends, if nobody else, until Mma Ramotswe mentioned the recent awkwardness over the dress that Mma Makutsi had ordered as her birthday present. She had done nothing about this for the last few days, and she felt that at any moment Mma Makutsi might get back in touch with the shop and the whole embarrassing issue would resurface.

Mma Potokwane listened with amusement. "I'm sorry to smile, Mma," she said, excusing her ill-concealed grin. "But these misunderstandings are so funny."

"Not if you're caught up in them," said Mma Ramotswe.

Mma Potokwane put on a serious expression. "I do not believe," she said, "that there is any damage to material—any damage at all—that can't be put right if you have a skilful enough needleworker. And we have such a person, Mma—we have just such a lady."

Mma Ramotswe waited.

"Mma Ikobeng," said Mma Potokwane. "She is a miracle worker when it comes to mending things. There is no other word for what she can do, Mma. She works miracles."

Mma Ramotswe reached out to take Mma Potokwane's hand. "You are the miracle worker, Mma Potokwane. You have worked . . . oh, I don't know how many miracles in your life." She was thinking of the children—of what Mma Potokwane had done to transform so many young lives. That was the sort of miracle that really counted for something.

Mma Potokwane waved a dismissive hand. "Nonsense, Mma." Then she added, "It is very kind of you to say that, though."

They sat in silence for a few moments. Then Mma Potokwane proposed that they finish their tea and go straight to the dress shop, which was just round the corner. "A stitch in time," she said, "saves nine."

"Or even more," said Mma Ramotswe. She was not sure of the relevance of what Mma Potokwane had just said, but it was a familiar expression, and such sayings, she thought, tended to be true, which was why they were sayings in the first place.

Mma Potokwane was pleased that Mma Ramotswe agreed with her. They usually saw eye to eye on most subjects, which was reassuring to both of them. If somebody you respect agrees with you, then that suggests that what you say is likely to be right. So now she said, simply, "Indeed, Mma. Indeed," and stood up to leave the café.

CHAPTER FIFTEEN

AN EXTRA-LOW-GRADE MAN

THE FOLLOWING DAY Mma Makutsi did not come into the office until well after ten, by which time Mma Ramotswe had had two tea breaks—one by herself, and one with Charlie and Fanwell, both of whom were working in the garage that morning and both of whom were covered from head to toe with spots of engine oil. A line connected to an oil pump had burst, and they had been in the line of fire, although Mr. J.L.B. Matekoni had narrowly avoided being spattered. Mma Ramotswe helped them clean up, and then made them each a cup of strong tea. It had not been anybody's fault, Charlie told her, and getting covered in engine oil was an occupational risk that every mechanic had to accept. "You cannot be a mechanic and be fussy about these things," he said. "It is the same with doctors, I think. If you don't like the sight of blood, don't be a doctor. If you don't like the sight of engine oil, don't be a mechanic. It stands to reason, I think."

When Mma Makutsi arrived, it was immediately obvious to Mma Ramotswe that something was amiss. There was a certain expression that Mma Makutsi had that meant that either something serious had happened, or was about to happen.

"I have made tea," Mma Ramotswe said. "I think there is still some in the pot—and it shouldn't be too cold."

Mma Makutsi helped herself and then sat down at her desk with a sigh. "There are more problems, Mma. One problem comes, and then another one knocks at the door. Soon there is a long line of problems, each of them saying, 'Deal with me first because I am a big, number one problem.'"

Mma Ramotswe made a gesture of acceptance. There were always problems—had there ever been a time, anywhere, where there were no problems? She did not think so. Problems made up the natural background to human affairs, she thought, and it was best to accept that. The only issue, really, was whether the problems in question were ones to which a solution might be found, or ones that were destined to remain stubbornly problematic. If you could not resolve something, there was no point in lamenting it because all that happened was that you ended up wasting your time worrying. And there were plenty of other things with which you might occupy yourself, including watering your beans in the garden; or walking out in the garden first thing in the morning and watching the sun float up, a great red ball over the line of the horizon; or drinking tea with Mma Potokwane. These were all alternatives to worrying about problems that could not be solved.

"Mma Julia," said Mma Makutsi. And then she added, "Oh, Mma, there is something very bad happening."

Mma Ramotswe took a deep breath. She knew, even before Mma Makutsi spoke, what the issue would be: the cousin, the man with the cloudy eyes; his all-too-evident neediness; the mention of the eye operation. It was completely predictable.

But even if she was right about that part of it, there was something more.

"You told me about those people you found in Mochudi," said Mma Makutsi.

Mma Ramotswe had given Mma Makutsi an account of the Mochudi visit. She had not expressed any misgivings about the distant relative they had found for Julia—after all, she had no firm grounds for any concern. And yet her every instinct had provoked the ringing of an alarm bell, and now she suspected that intuition was about to be confirmed.

Mma Makutsi took off her large round spectacles and began to polish them. This was a sign that what was to follow was weighty. "There is somebody who works in Phuti's store," she began, "who comes from Mochudi."

Mma Ramotswe stared down at her desk. She wondered what it would be: a criminal conviction? A record of importuning the vulnerable? There were so many traps into which those who were looking for something might fall.

"This woman," Mma Makutsi continued, "spoke to Phuti about something she had heard from her aunt up there in the village. This aunt . . ." There were always aunts, thought Mma Ramotswe. There were strategically placed aunts through the country—in every village, in every town—watching what was going on. They made up a network of listening posts, ready to report on what was happening, by means of what people sometimes called the bush telegraph—for that, surely, was what it was.

"The aunt," Mma Makutsi went on, "lives close by to a man who likes to drink. He is not one of those people who drinks all the time, but he likes to go to a bar that they call the Big Jazz Bar, and this lady, the aunt of the woman who works for Phuti, has a brother who also likes that bar—although he does not like some of the people who go there—including this man who likes to drink a lot."

Mma Ramotswe listened to this patiently. Mma Makutsi liked to give the full context of any story she told.

"He—that is, the brother of the aunt of the woman who works in Phuti's store, that person—does not like that man; that is, the man who goes to the Big Jazz Bar and drinks too much. He—that is the other man, the brother of the aunt I already mentioned—does not like him, because he is always boasting. And he, not the brother but the other man, was saying in this bar—he had had too much to drink, apparently—that he was going to get money from some American lady who had turned up and who thought she might be related to somebody he had never heard of but who was a distant relative of some sort. He said that this relative had gone off to a war a long time ago and not come back. He said he didn't care about that, but the important thing was that he was going to get money from this woman. He said, 'Don't tell me that money doesn't grow on trees—it does! Plenty of it. Big time.' Those were his exact words, Mma. That was what I was told."

Mma Ramotswe looked away. It was more or less as she feared.

"I met that man," she said. "I didn't like him, I'm afraid."

Mma Makutsi pursed her lips. "I am not surprised, Mma. Apparently, he moved in with a lady from Francistown who lost all her property. Nobody knew what happened. All her cattle disappeared. She had gone down to see relatives in Mafikeng, and when she came back the cattle were gone. And so was the man. He also took her car. He took everything, more or less."

Mma Ramotswe gasped. "Oh, Mma, this is very bad."

"Yes," said Mma Makutsi. "You must warn Mma Julia."

"Of course."

She had agreed without hesitation, but now she realised that this was not a meeting to which she could look forward. She had seen Julia's delight on her meeting with the Sepole family; now she would have to tell her that they were probably not family at all, and, moreover, their intentions towards her were dishonest. Did she have to do it? Was it really any of her business? The answer to both of these questions was yes, although she would dearly have loved it to be no.

Mma Makutsi shook her heard disapprovingly. "There are so many extra-low-grade people about, Mma. Why is this, I ask myself?"

Mma Ramotswe had no idea how to answer this. She was familiar with the rather odd terms Mma Makutsi used for people of whom she disapproved. She had talked in the past of *rubbish people* and *no-good people,* and now here was this category of *extra-low-grade people.* (People who were ninety-seven per cent bad?) It was a bit extreme, perhaps, and these terms did not sit well with Mma Ramotswe's charitable view of others. Surely nobody was completely *rubbish* or *no good;* there were always at least some good points in most people, even if at times they might be hard to discern. But she knew what Mma Makutsi meant: there were plenty of people who were indifferent to the feelings and interests of others, who behaved with nastiness and selfishness, who simply did not care about the effect of their actions and thought, when they thought at all, only of themselves. Those people existed, and were often conspicuously successful in their lives—or at least in the material sense. They even got into high office, sometimes even the highest of all offices, and, while they were there, continued to lie and cheat in the way they had always lied and cheated. Or they simply operated at a lower level, causing minor damage here and there, treading on others who were at the same level as they were, content with the small pickings they came across in everyday business.

And what Mma Makutsi had said was undoubtedly true: there seemed to be rather a lot of these people around. Why was this? Because people were being brought up without a sense of what was right or wrong? Because we were forgetting that we were brothers and sisters to one another? Because greed and lying had been promoted as things of which you need not be ashamed? Because people were encouraged to want more and more? Any one of these reasons was possible—or possibly all of them, thought Mma Ramotswe, and decided yes, probably all.

But she was not one to be defeated. It would be the undeserving, Mma Makutsi's low-grade types, who would be defeated. They always were—eventually. Then she thought: *almost* always, as we should be careful, she felt, not to assert as true that which we wanted to be true but that we knew was not always so.

AT LEAST she had her work to keep her busy and save her from thinking of the awkward tasks that lay ahead. She had been in correspondence with the local tax office, and needed to provide them with more information before the end of the month. They had been perfectly polite in the phrasing of their request, but it had been clear to Mma Ramotswe that they had their suspicions about her last return. These queries were not the usual ones concerning the concealment of profit or the claiming of unjustified expenses: in her case, she had claimed so few expenses that they had become suspicious. If people claimed too few expenses, it might be that they were trying to prevent any unwanted attention being paid to more important matters.

Mma Ramotswe had read the enquiry letter with growing dismay. "These people think that our accounts are not telling the whole truth," she complained to Mma Makutsi.

Mma Makutsi's response had been robust. "They are very suspicious people, Mma," she said. "They do not believe anybody—about anything. That is how they are trained to behave." She laughed. "If they asked you the time and you told them it was ten o'clock, they wouldn't believe you—even over something like that. They would think that it was really nine forty-five, but you were trying to mislead them. That is what they are like, Mma."

"Well, that is just ridiculous," said Mma Ramotswe. "We have to trust people. You can be careful, yes, but there still has to be some trust."

Mma Makutsi agreed with that. Trust, she said, was important, but the problem was that with so many liars about, it was becoming more and more difficult to trust anybody.

With so many liars about . . . You had to be careful, Mma Ramotswe felt, not to become distrustful of everybody—there were people, she knew, who went through life believing that everybody they came across was intent on taking advantage of them. That simply was not true, Mma Ramotswe felt, and such people must find it difficult to develop or keep any friendships at all. You had to trust people because without trust, friendship was impossible. Similarly, in doing business with others you simply had to trust them or you would never get anywhere.

And yet, here was the tax department showing distrust when she had gone out of her way, as she always had, to be scrupulously honest in the reporting of her business affairs. And if she had not claimed enough by way of expenses, then surely they should be grateful for that, as it meant more tax was payable to them than they would have got had she inflated the costs of running the agency.

She had discussed the issue of expenses with Mma Makutsi, to see if there were any that she had missed and that she could add to her return.

"What about tea, Mma Makutsi?" she had asked. "Do you think I could claim the cost of buying tea? After all, we do drink a fair amount of tea in the office."

Mma Makutsi looked thoughtful. "I suppose it might be a business expense," she said at last. "Tea, after all, is an essential, I think. We need tea to work."

Mma Ramotswe agreed, but then it occurred to her that the same could be said about a whole lot of other things. We needed food to work and yet, as far as she knew, the government of Botswana did not allow you to claim food as a business expense. What was the distinction between tea and food, then? Perhaps tea was different because it was served to clients, and could be claimed as a running expense on those grounds. And then there was clothing. Could she claim the dresses that she wore to work as a business expense? You needed clothes to be in business—you could hardly interview clients in the nude, although sometimes, in the very hot weather, that might perhaps be a bit more comfortable . . . Yet the clients, surely, would find it embarrassing, and might feel overdressed if they had normal clothes on and you were sitting there with not a stitch on.

And transport? She had claimed a certain amount for fuel, but perhaps she had been too honest in that claim and had deliberately not included the fuel cost of driving out to see Mma Potokwane. Those, she had decided, were personal trips and therefore non-claimable. And yet, how many times had she and Mma Potokwane spent long hours discussing some of her cases—over tea and fruit cake (non-claimable)? She had claimed no other expenses for the tiny white van, on the grounds that it had long since depreciated down to nothing, and there were no servicing costs. Mr. J.L.B. Matekoni carried out regular services on the van and, of course, charged nothing for that—what was the point of having a mechanic husband if he charged for such things? So there were no expenses that could be added in that respect.

Mma Makutsi, though, had some ideas. "I think we could have a carpet in the office," she suggested. "That could be put down as an expense."

Mma Ramotswe was surprised. "A carpet, Mma? But why should we need a carpet?"

Mma Makutsi shrugged. "There are many businesses that have carpets these days, Mma. Carpets inspire confidence—and you can take your shoes off, if you have a carpet."

Mma Makutsi became animated. "Speaking of shoes, Mma Ramotswe. I think that shoes might be a legitimate expense."

"Work boots, yes," said Mma Ramotswe. "But ordinary shoes, Mma? I don't think so."

Mma Makutsi was not to be fobbed off so easily. "I'm not talking about ordinary shoes, Mma—I'm thinking of the sort of shoes that I wear. These are professional shoes."

Mma Ramotswe waited.

"Some of my shoes are intended for a particular sort of investigation," Mma Makutsi continued. "They are working tools."

Mma Ramotswe looked doubtful. "I'm not so sure of that, Mma. I do not think the tax people would be sympathetic to that. After all, we all need shoes—and our shoes need to be suitable for what we do. We couldn't have the whole country claiming its shoes against tax."

Mma Makutsi sighed. "If you want to increase the number of expenses you can claim, Mma, you will have to be prepared to think more adventurously. No wonder the tax people are suspicious. They will never have met somebody who is so unwilling to claim expenses."

"Well," said Mma Ramotswe, "carpets must be a legitimate expense—along with chairs and filing cabinets."

"And paint," added Mma Makutsi. "We could paint the office and get new desks."

Mma Ramotswe frowned. She did not see anything wrong with her existing desk—nor was there anything manifestly wrong with Mma Makutsi's.

"And a bell," said Mma Makutsi. "At the moment, people have to knock. If we had a bell at the door, they could ring that and then we could admit them. It would look more professional, I think."

Mma Ramotswe pointed out that the office was a small one—a single room—and that when somebody knocked on the door, they never had any difficulty hearing it. In those circumstances, it was difficult to see what difference a bell would make—unless, of course, it would be better at waking them up if they both happened to be asleep at their desks.

Mma Makutsi bristled. "I was just thinking of an example, Mma. I was not saying that we definitely needed a bell. You are quite right: we can hear people knocking, but I was just thinking of the need to keep pace with technology—that was all." She gave Mma Ramotswe a reproving look before continuing, "Most modern people, Mma, have a bell. I am not saying that *everyone* should have one, however—I am not saying that."

Mma Ramotswe was conciliatory. "Certainly, a bell would be a deductible expense from the tax point of view, Mma. You were quite right to raise it. Perhaps we could think of other items, too, that could help to give us more expenses. Perhaps a burglar alarm would be a good idea—and a safe, too, for that matter. We do not have a safe at present, Mma, and I am not sure how secure it is keeping money in the old teapot. Burglars are very clever these days, Mma. They see a teapot and they think, That would be a good place for people to hide money. They would think that, Mma, because they imagine that we think they are stupid. But they aren't, Mma."

"Oh, I know that, Mma," said Mma Makutsi. "In fact, I wouldn't be surprised if you could study burglary at some colleges these days. They are studying many ridiculous things now."

Mma Ramotswe smiled. That would not be at the Botswana Secretarial College, of course.

"I know you are not serious, Mma Makutsi," she said. "But it would be quite a thing, wouldn't it, if they did allow that. Naturally, the people who enrolled in the course would all cheat in the final examinations. That would be very much expected."

Mma Makutsi raised a finger. "Oh, Mma, did I ever tell you

about how I saw Violet Sephotho cheating? It wasn't in the final examinations at the college—it was only a term exam, but you shouldn't cheat in those either. It was a shorthand test, which was always very difficult—and almost impossible for a lazy person like Violet. You can bluff your way or guess the answer in many other subjects, but when it comes to shorthand, then you either know something or you don't. And she usually didn't—because she was spending too much time painting her nails or flirting with men, or gossiping with those idle friends of hers."

Mma Ramotswe listened. She had heard most of Mma Makutsi's stories of the iniquities of Violet Sephotho's days at the Botswana Secretarial College, but this one was new.

"She had written down a whole lot of the most common shorthand symbols on a large handkerchief, and she took this out, pretending to blow her nose. But I saw what was happening. I should have reported her there and then, but I'm afraid that I didn't do anything. It is often the case that we don't do the things we should do, Mma, because we don't want to stand out from the crowd—especially when we're young, Mma. It is different later on. I would not hesitate to report Violet these days. I would be the first one in the long line of people waiting to report her, Mma. I would be there." She turned the delicious thought over in her mind. "The police would have to put up barriers to control the crowds coming to report Violet for various things, I think. There would be signs saying, 'Please line up here to report Violet Sephotho.' That is what they would have to do, Mma."

But now Mma Ramotswe had to cope with the rather more mundane issue of the tax return, and that meant she had to comb through months of invoices and bank statements. It was not a task she relished, but at least it prevented her from brooding on what to do about Julia. Not that there were many options in that regard:

Julia would simply have to be told, and she would then have to deal with her disappointment as best she could. It saddened Mma Ramotswe, though, that somebody should come to her beloved Botswana and then be taken advantage of by some unscrupulous n'er-do-well, some—what had Mma Makutsi called him?—some *extra-low-grade* man.

She worked hard on the accounts and the tax return. Mma Ramotswe had never had a head for figures but it passed the time rather quickly, and when she eventually looked at her watch, she discovered it was half past twelve. The document she had been preparing for the tax office was now complete, and she sat back with a feeling of satisfaction.

"Finished, Mma?" asked Mma Makutsi from the other side of the room.

"I think so," said Mma Ramotswe. "I am very glad that I am not an accountant—having to do that sort of work all day. My head is swimming a bit, Mma."

Mma Makutsi rose to her feet to stretch her legs. "I think that we should get out of the office, Mma. We have had a busy morning, with one thing and another." She paused. "Would you like to go out for lunch, Mma. As my guest?"

It did not take Mma Ramotswe long to accept. "I would like that very much, Mma," she said. She, too, wanted to get out of the office. She wanted to have lunch—an unhurried one—in which they would talk about anything and everything, except work, and when she could remove her shoes under the table and give her toes a taste of fresh air and freedom. Her toes, for the most part, were uncomplaining—unlike the toes of some—but she knew that they appreciated freedom.

"And after we have had lunch I have a special surprise for you," added Mma Makutsi.

SINCE IT WAS MMA MAKUTSI'S TREAT, it was she who chose the restaurant for their lunch. Much to Mma Ramotswe's delight, this was the peri-peri restaurant where she had enjoyed her birthday dinner with Mr. J.L.B. Matekoni. It was a generous choice, as there were many much cheaper establishments that Mma Makutsi might equally have selected, and Mma Ramotswe was quick to express her appreciation.

"I love peri-peri," she said. "This is a very big treat, Mma Makutsi. But won't you let me pay my share? This is not an inexpensive restaurant."

Mma Makutsi hesitated. "I was going to treat you, Mma Ramotswe," she said. "But now that you offer . . ."

Mma Ramotswe tried to hide her disappointment. Really! Mma Makutsi should have been able to distinguish between the token offer—the sort of offer which is not meant to be taken seriously—and a genuine attempt to relieve the host of half of the bill.

"Thank you, Mma Ramotswe," Mma Makutsi now said. "It is very kind of you to offer."

They were in Mma Makutsi's car, halfway to the restaurant, when this conversation took place. Now Mma Ramotswe remembered something.

"Actually, Mma," she said apologetically, "I haven't brought any money with me. You had said . . ."

Mma Makutsi made a reassuring gesture. "Don't worry, Mma Ramotswe," she said. "I shall pay . . ."

"You're very kind, Mma," said Mma Ramotswe.

"And then you can pay me back later on," continued Mma Makutsi.

Mma Ramotswe bit her lip. She would not let this minor setback interfere with the pleasure of going out for lunch. So she said, as graciously as she could, "That will be fine, Mma. But make sure you remind me."

"I won't forget," Mma Makutsi assured her.

THE RESTAURANT WAS NOT CROWDED and they were quickly given a table in the small outside dining area, under a pergola of carefully cultivated vine. Shade netting had been stretched out over the pergola supports, providing a canopy to protect customers from the sun. In one corner of the dining area, a caged bird, colourful in its plumage, rehearsed its small repertoire of song, while a small, slightly discouraged-looking fountain dribbled in the other corner.

"This is a very exclusive place," commented Mma Makutsi, looking around as they sat down at their table. "There's no riff-raff here."

Mma Ramotswe smiled. *Riff-raff, extra-low-grade people*— Mma Makutsi could sometimes be a touch disapproving, not to say forbidding. "Riff-raff people have to eat," she said. "They have a right to be in restaurants. We all have to eat, Mma."

"Oh, I know that, Mma," said Mma Makutsi. "I am just saying that I do not like it when they start shouting."

"And who exactly are these riff-raff people, Mma?" asked Mma Ramotswe.

"People who have made a lot of money and who are determined to show it off," explained Mma Makutsi. "Those are the people I call riff-raff."

"I see." Mma Ramotswe had misjudged Mma Makutsi. This was not snobbery—a vice for which she had no time—it was a distaste for vulgar display. And that, in a country where there were people who had difficulty making ends meet, was perfectly understandable.

"Anyway, they are not here," said Mma Makutsi. "The people here are, I think, ordinary respectable people . . ." She broke off. She was staring at a table at the far side of the dining area. A man and a woman were sitting there, perusing the menu prior to placing their order.

"Mma Ramotswe, those people at that table over there. See them, Mma? Is that who I think it is?"

Mma Ramotswe glanced in the direction indicated by Mma Makutsi. She did not want to make her interest too obvious—a detective should never do that, she reminded herself. *Always be discreet in your observation,* Clovis Andersen wrote. *Try to give the impression that you aren't looking.* Now, following that advice, Mma Ramotswe found herself staring at the back of the man's head—he was facing away from her—but turned now and then to look at the fountain when it gave a spurt or a gurgle.

"Mr. Modise," whispered Mma Makutsi. "That's him. And that's his wife with him. I definitely recognise her."

Mma Ramotswe frowned. "Poor woman," she said.

Mma Makutsi stole another glance. "She looks cheerful enough," she said. "And listen, that's him laughing. Yes, he's laughing at something, Mma Ramotswe."

"That man doesn't have much to laugh about at the moment," said Mma Ramotswe.

"Perhaps he doesn't care what happens to him any longer," said Mma Makutsi. "That sometimes happens, you know. People get to the point where they just don't care."

There was another burst of laughter and then, unexpectedly, Mma Modise rose from the table and started walking towards the interior of the restaurant. Halfway across the floor, though, she stopped: she had seen Mma Ramotswe and Mma Makutsi. And now she came over towards their table, a broad smile on her face.

"It is you, then," she said, as she approached their table. "My husband said he thought it was, but I was not sure."

They greeted her politely.

"I am very glad that it is you," began Mma Modise. "My husband and I are celebrating, you see, and the reason we are celebrating has something to do with you, I believe."

Neither Mma Ramotswe nor Mma Makutsi said anything. Neither knew what to think.

"Modise has been un-suspended," said Mma Modise. "As of yesterday. All that nonsense is over."

Mma Ramotswe could not conceal her astonishment. "He is back at work, Mma? Back at the school?"

"Yes," said Mma Modise. "And given a salary increment."

Mma Ramotswe looked at Mma Makutsi. This was a most unexpected development.

Mma Modise leaned forward. "I hear that you were part of a group that went to persuade the principal to relent," she said. "And he did."

"That is very good news," said Mma Ramotswe. She wondered, though, about all the rest, and in particular the affair with Violet Sephotho.

Mma Modise provided the answer to Mma Ramotswe's unspoken question.

"My husband has been a little bit wayward," she said, her voice lowered. "You know how men can be."

Mma Ramotswe made a gesture that suggested she knew all about the waywardness of men; and she did, really—in her job it was inevitable that one would see most of humanity's faults, including that one.

"He has come to his senses now," she said. "And I have forgiven him." She paused. "He is only a man, Mma Ramotswe. What can one do but forgive him?"

"It is very good of you," said Mma Ramotswe. "Forgiveness is important."

"Very," said Mma Modise. "And I think it was probably that woman's fault, anyway. She has a long record of tempting men, Mma. She is the one who is to blame for that sort of thing happening."

"Although it is important that men should say sorry," interjected Mma Ramotswe. "Men should not be allowed to get away with too much. Nobody should."

"Oh, he is being punished," said Mma Modise. "I have made him agree to take me out to lunch or dinner every week for a whole year. That is his sentence."

Mma Ramotswe laughed. "Well, he will get nice meals out of that, anyway."

Mma Modise shook a finger. "No, Mma. He is not eating, you will see. He has to pay for my lunch—he has none." She gave a sweet smile. "Otherwise, it would not be much of a punishment."

There was nothing to be added to that, and Mma Modise excused herself and went off inside.

"That is a very firm lady," said Mma Makutsi, after she had gone. "Do you think you or I could be like that, Mma?"

Mma Ramotswe thought not. But then, Mr. J.L.B. Matekoni would never be tempted by Violet Sephotho, and nor would Phuti Radiphuti. Not all men were weak, she decided—just some, and when those men were weak, they were often *really* weak.

They ordered their peri-peri chicken, which they both enjoyed greatly. Then, as they were sipping at a cup of tea served with a chocolate éclair, Mma Ramotswe had a thought that required an immediate answer. She remembered that Mma Makutsi had exchanged words with the principal at the end of their meeting. Now she fixed Mma Makutsi with a challenging stare. "Tell me, Mma," she said. "What did you say to the principal when we went to see him? You ended up pointing fingers at one another."

Mma Makutsi licked a spot of cream off a finger. "I suppose what I said had an effect after all," she said casually.

"What was it, Mma? Please tell me."

Mma Makutsi seemed to enjoy herself as she revealed what she had said.

"I told him that before he finally made up his mind, he should remind himself that there were people who knew what *he* had done."

Mma Ramotswe's jaw dropped. "What *he* had done? The principal?"

"Yes."

"And what was that?"

Mma Makutsi shrugged. "Heaven knows. I certainly don't. But I have long suspected that everyone has done *something*, Mma. Just about everyone has a secret tucked away."

"But Mma Makutsi," protested Mma Ramotswe. "You threatened him. You blackmailed him . . ."

Mma Makutsi's reply came in a tone of only slightly offended innocence. This was a serious allegation to make of a colleague, but she would not allow herself to appear riled. Mma Ramotswe could not have meant to offend—it was not in her nature to do so—and so now she replied, quite calmly, "I wouldn't call it that. I never accused him of anything in particular. But as it turned out, I was right, wasn't I? That principal had done something that could land him in trouble if it ever came out. Perhaps he had had an affair. Perhaps even with Violet Sephotho . . ."

Mma Ramotswe laughed. "Well, it worked, Mma. It really worked. And you saved that man—and his marriage, I imagine."

"Possibly," said Mma Makutsi. "But let us not sit here and talk for too long. I have a treat for you, Mma Ramotswe, and it's turning into a very positive day—just the sort of day for a treat, I would say."

IT WAS NOW THREE O'CLOCK in the afternoon. It had been a most satisfactory day. A fair amount of office work had been accomplished in the morning, not without several tea breaks; then there had been a delicious lunch at the peri-peri restaurant, paid for by Mma Makutsi, who had generously said when the bill was presented that Mma Ramotswe need not pay her back her share after all.

"You are very kind, Mma Makutsi," said Mma Ramotswe. "It is always a very pleasant feeling, when you have eaten a good lunch, to know that you don't have to pay for it."

Mma Makutsi looked thoughtful, and for a few moments Mma Ramotswe wondered whether her comment, well intended though it might have been, was perhaps slightly tactless in the circumstances. But then her friend had smiled, and remarked, "That is a very interesting thing to say, Mma. I think you are quite right—even if, I suppose, *somebody* has to pay at the end of the day. Lunch is never free, I believe." She paused. "Does Clovis Andersen say something about that? I think he might, but I cannot remember exactly where he says it."

Mma Ramotswe thought about it. She, too, felt she had heard something about that, somewhere or other, and if you could not remember exactly where some observation about the world came from, then there was always a good chance that it came from the pages of that great and useful work, *The Principles of Private Detection*. That was well known, she now told herself.

Lunch had been followed by the surprise that Mma Makutsi had alluded to, which was not, of course, much of a surprise at all—a visit to the dress shop. There they were met by a smiling Mma Mogatusi, who scurried off into a storeroom to emerge with a neatly wrapped box. She handed this to Mma Makutsi, who passed it on to Mma Ramotswe.

"This present is a bit late, Mma," she said. "But better late than never, I think."

Mma Ramotswe smiled. "Did Clovis Andersen say that, Mma?"

Mma Makutsi was not sure, but it was highly likely, she thought. Clovis Andersen was never at a loss for something to say, and the things that he said were generally true.

Mma Ramotswe saw that there was a card attached to the box. On this was written, in Mma Makutsi's characteristic hand— Bobonong script, as Mma Ramotswe sometimes called it—*To my great friend, who has been so kind to me over the years, with my best wishes for your birthday, of which I hope there are many more, stretching out into the future, from Grace Makutsi, Dip. Sec. (BSC)*

It was a perfect inscription, because it expressed, in a few carefully chosen words, the gratitude that Mma Makutsi felt towards Mma Ramotswe.

She opened the box, and there inside were two red garments, not one: a skirt and a blouse. There had been a split of a quite different sort: the dress had been expertly divided into two. She could tell, just by looking, that each garment would be a comfortable fit.

She looked to Mma Makutsi for an explanation.

"You remember Solomon, Mma?" she asked. "You remember the story?"

Mma Ramotswe did—in the recesses of her memory the tale still lurked. Solomon had suggested that a baby be divided in two in order to find out who the real mother was. So Mma Potokwane had asked Mma Ikobeng to make a skirt and a blouse out of a damaged dress. You could not divide a baby—but you could do that with a dress.

Mma Ramotswe looked at Mma Makutsi. They were both smiling.

"Mma Potokwane is as wise as Solomon, I think," she said.

"She is," said Mma Makutsi.

She held up the blouse. The stitching was faultless. Nobody

would know that this had once been part of something else. Turning to Mma Makutsi, she said, "This is the best present I have received for a long time, Mma. You have been so kind."

"No, you are the kind one, Mma Ramotswe," said Mma Makutsi.

Mma Mogatusi now broke her silence. "You are both kind ladies, I think." Then she went on, "Working in a dress shop, I see all sorts of people, I can tell you. And I have developed the ability to see what is going on inside people." She tapped her chest, where her heart was; correctly, as it happened, although most people get it wrong. "I can tell. And I can see that you are both very kind ladies. It's obvious to me—very obvious."

"You yourself are kind to say that," said Mma Ramotswe. "Is that not true, Mma Makutsi?"

Mma Makutsi nodded. "Yes, it is," she said.

AFTER ALL THAT, it seemed there was not much point in going back to the office, but every point in driving out to Tlokweng, in the cooling hours of the late afternoon, to have tea with Mma Poto-kwane, to thank her for whatever it was that she had done, and to tell her about the remarkable outcome of the Modise affair. That, by any standards, was good news—a foolish man had come to his senses, a marriage had been saved, and mercy, an underrated but so important virtue, had been brought to bear on a potentially painful situation. The fact that mercy had been exercised as a result of a threatening remark made by Mma Makutsi might take the shine off the outcome, but only to a very small extent. Sometimes, thought Mma Ramotswe, one achieved a good result in this life by cutting corners, but the positive result was what really mattered. As long as one did not make a habit of working that way, she told herself—and Mma Makutsi would not do that, she hoped; at least not too often.

Mind you, you never knew with Mma Makutsi, who was unconventional and could come up with surprising things. But it was, on the whole, better to work with such people, Mma Ramotswe told herself: life would be dull indeed if you did not have the companionship of people with strong views, talking shoes, and ninety-seven per cent in their final examinations.

When they arrived at Mma Potokwane's office, they were given a more than usually warm welcome.

"This is turning into a full-scale tea party," the matron enthused. "Mma Julia has telephoned to say that she is coming to see me. We can all have tea together—and there is plenty of cake, too."

Mma Ramotswe's heart sank. She had not spoken to Julia, and she knew that she had to do so. That was the trouble with putting off painful conversations: you met the people you should have spoken to, and you felt guilty because you had not said what you should have said. And then sometimes it was too late, and you never said anything.

Mma Potokwane noticed Mma Ramotswe's reaction. Drawing her aside, while Mma Makutsi exchanged a few remarks with the Orphan Farm secretary, she whispered, "I thought you would be pleased to see that lady. But your expression tells me a different story, Mma."

Mma Ramotswe could not conceal her feelings from her old friend. "I feel very guilty, Mma," she explained. "I have needed to speak to her about something difficult, and I have put it off."

Mma Potokwane frowned. "You must tell me what it is."

So Mma Ramotswe did, and Mma Potokwane listened gravely. At the end of the explanation, she sighed. "That is very bad, Mma Ramotswe. But you are right—you will have to warn her."

Mma Ramotswe nodded. "Will you give us some time together?" she asked. "Privately—so that she is not embarrassed."

Mma Potokwane said that she would do this. "It is never easy," she added, "to have to warn people about not trusting another person."

"It is not," said Mma Ramotswe. "But before she arrives, Mma, we must talk about a certain blouse and a certain skirt."

Mma Potokwane brightened. "Do you like them, Mma?"

"I do," said Mma Ramotswe. "You said that Mma Ikobeng was a miracle worker, but that is a very remarkable miracle, I think."

Mma Potokwane laughed. "All of our ladies have some special talent," she said. "Mma Ikobeng is good with children. She is good at making stew. She is good at changing dresses into blouses and skirts—that sort of thing."

"Some people are good with life," said Mma Ramotswe. And she thought that this was particularly true of Mma Potokwane. But she did not say that, as people who are good with life are often modest, too—which is another good thing to be.

Mma Ramotswe smiled, and she was still smiling when Julia arrived. That made her task all the more difficult, she thought. But then my job is difficult by its nature, she told herself: what I do is never easy, because I am called upon to deal with the problems that people have, and was there ever a problem that was not in some way difficult? She thought there was not.

Mma Potokwane detached Mma Makutsi, and suggested that there was something she wanted to show her in one of the other offices. That gave Mma Ramotswe her opportunity, and she suggested to Julia that they go for a walk to the vegetable garden now that it was cooler. "We can see how their crops are going," she said. "They are very good at growing things here."

"I'd like that," said Julia. "And we might hear the children singing. They always seem to be singing here."

Mma Ramotswe led the way. The children were singing—rather

faintly, but they were singing because it was in them to sing, and this was their place, and their country, and they had their lives ahead of them. That was what Mma Ramotswe thought, as she walked with Julia along the path that led to the vegetable gardens.

She took a deep breath and began, "Mma Julia, I have something to tell you. Those people I took you to see in Mochudi—"

Julia stopped her. "I know, Mma Ramotswe," she said. "I know what you are going to say."

Mma Ramotswe stared at her. "I don't think you do, Mma."

But Julia seemed certain. "They are not good people, I'm afraid. Or, rather, they are not the people I would have liked them to be."

Mma Ramotswe stopped walking, and Julia stopped too.

Julia held her gaze. "All they wanted was money," she said. "He—the man—said it was for treatment for his eyes, but I am not sure that was where it went."

Mma Ramotswe sighed. It was too late; she should have spoken to Julia earlier. This was her fault.

"I gave them something," said Julia. "I'm in a position to do that, and they needed it. So I gave them something—and they seemed pleased enough. But I do not think we shall be seeing one another again."

"No," said Mma Ramotswe. "That would be wise."

Julia took Mma Ramotswe's hand. "You mustn't blame yourself. You found the right people. They are who they say they are—and I was able to tell them the story I wanted to tell them."

Mma Ramotswe wondered whether they had been interested, and now Julia answered her unspoken question. "They didn't really care much," she said. "I told them my story, but they didn't seem all that interested."

"I'm sorry," said Mma Ramotswe.

"But it didn't matter," she said. "I came looking for people, and do you know what? I found a country."

They resumed their walk. "I wish I could have found you a proper family," said Mma Ramotswe. "I would have been pleased with that."

Julia looked at her. "But Mma Ramotswe," she said. "You did."

She turned and pointed back towards a small building from which they could now see Mma Potokwane emerging, along with Mma Makutsi and Mma Ikobeng. "You did find me a family," she said. "You did, Mma."

It took Mma Ramotswe a moment or two to see what she meant. But then she saw it. She saw it perfectly.

They looked at the gardens, and then walked back to Mma Potokwane's office, where the tea was ready. The children had stopped singing, but the birds, it seemed, had taken up a chorus on their behalf, and it was sweet upon the ear. Above them was the sky of that beloved country, a sky upon which we all might gaze, on our portion of it at least, wherever we were; a sky that forgave and sheltered and ultimately made us feel that we were where we should be, among people we felt we should be with.

afrika
afrika afrika
afrika afrika afrika
afrika afrika
afrika

Alexander McCall Smith is the author of the No. 1 Ladies' Detective Agency novels and of a number of other series and stand-alone books. His works have been translated into more than forty languages and have been best sellers throughout the world. He lives in Scotland.